# THE VAMPIRE'S OBSESSION

## MORETTI BLOOD BROTHERS

## BOOK TWELVE

# By Juliette N. Banks

# COPYRIGHT

**Author: Juliette N. Banks**

**Editor: Violet Rae**

**Proofreader: Lunar Rose Editing Services**

**Cover design by: Elizabeth Cartwright, EC Editorial**

## THE DUFORT DYNASTY
*Steamy billionaire romance*
Sinful Duty - **FREE**
Forbidden Touch
Total Possession
Desire Unbound
Dark Surrender
Ruthless Temptation
Naughty Festivities
Wicked Praise
Beautiful Ruin


## BLACK HAWKE SECURITY
The SEAL
The BODYGUARD
The MARINE


## REALM OF THE IMMORTALS
*Steamy paranormal fantasy romance*
The Archangels Battle - **FREE**
The Archangel's Heart
The Archangel's Star

# ABOUT THE AUTHOR

Juliette is an indie romance author who has taken the romance genre by storm with her mafia, billionaire, military and vampire romances.

Juliette has a vast background in consumer marketing and has previously published with Random House. She lives in Auckland, New Zealand, with Tilly, her Mainecoon kitty.

Official Juliette N. Banks website:
www.juliettebanks.com

JULIETTE
N. BANKS

# ALSO BY JULIETTE N. BANKS

## THE MORETTI BLOOD BROTHERS
*Steamy paranormal romance*
The Vampire Prince - **FREE**
The Vampire Protector
The Vampire Spy
The Vampire's Christmas
The Vampire Assassin
The Vampire Awoken
The Vampire Lover
The Vampire Wolf
The Vampire Warrior
The Vampire's Oath
The Vampire's Fate
The Vampire's Obsession
The Vampire's Storm


Related books in the Moretti universe
The Vampire King
The Claimed Wolf - **FREE**
The Alpha Wolf


## THE DARK KINGS OF NYC — NEW
*Steamy dark mafia romance*
The Darkest King - **FREE**
The Ruthless King
The Savage King
The Avenged King

# THE VAMPIRE'S OBSESSION

# CHAPTER ONE

Darnell pulled on his black Moretti jacket and crouched down to tighten the shoestrings of his Nikes. As he stood, he rearranged the waistband of his black sweatpants and watched the three females walk across the training room floor.

His lips stretched into a private smile.

God, she was pretty.

Amber Evans.

"You're heading toward stalker status," Tristan said, tossing a ball at him.

Darnell caught it with an *oomph*.

Around him, his team was packing up and heading out after finishing their training session. As the newest SLCs—senior lieutenant commanders—for the Moretti royal army, he and Tristan were doubling down on their team training.

They had to.

A small group of humans had developed a serum that could render vampires unconscious for a short period. Something that had never been possible before.

They weren't immortals, but they were far more powerful than the other intelligent species on the planet.

In fact, until now, most substances on earth had very little effect on them due to their fast metabolism. Alcohol had to be consumed rapidly at high doses to feel the drunken high that humans enjoyed.

It was possible.

But it didn't last long.

Ditto drugs.

But if he was honest, the vampire drug of choice was sex.

They were highly erotic creatures and viewed the act quite differently than prudish humans.

In his opinion.

That being said, when vampires mated, they committed for life. Generally. Not everyone bought into the fated mate's thing, and he was one of them.

"Nothing wrong with enjoying the luscious curves of a beautiful female," Darnell said, dribbling the ball across the floor. With a glance, he tossed the ball through the nearby hoop.

Score!

"Unless she's about to take out a restraining order against you." Tristan caught the ball, laughing, and threw it back to him.

This time, Darnell tucked it under his arm. He stared across the enormous training room as Amber laughed at something Madison said and then pushed open one of the main double doors. Before she disappeared, Amber glanced over her shoulder at him.

He smirked.

Her cheeks flushed pink a split second before the doors shut behind her, but it was enough. She might have refused all his advances, but Darnell was confident the little five-foot-nothing red-headed beauty with the tightest ass he'd ever seen wanted a piece of him. And she could bite off as much of his dark-skinned body as she wanted.

Maybe he was getting a little obsessed.

But damn, her sexy pulse ticked fast when he was near, and Darnell wasn't buying her cool-as-a-cucumber act one little bit.

Amber worked as a server at Max Bar in the castle, and he might've been going there a lot more than usual to get a glimpse of the sexy little firecracker.

It was a highlight at the end of his shift, winding her up while she pretended she wasn't affected by him.

She was.

Her blush was an almost permanent feature on her creamy skin.

If Amber would only give in to him, he'd drag her out the back of the bar, lift one of her sexy thighs over his hip, and slide his fingers under her panties.

Then, her cool act would be over.

He knew she was hot and wet for him, and her resistance seemed like a waste of time when they could be having so much fun.

Yet, she continued to act as if she were immune to his charm. Some would say he had none.

Like Ben.

But fuck Ben.

Darnell would keep that thought to himself because, yeah, the guy was a former assassin. Ben was also one of his fellow SLCs, along with Kurt, Lance, Tom, Marcus, Tristan, and Alex.

At the head of the food chain was the king, of course, then the prince, Brayden Moretti, who was also their captain. Then there was the guy walking toward him right now.

"Meeting in five. Get moving," Craig, their commander, grunted. He didn't stop. He kept walking, directing everyone in the training room.

Loudly.

"You know, I'd put money on that little barmaid wanting my cock," Darnell said, adjusting himself through his sweats. "Some females love the chase."

"Is it so hard to believe a female doesn't want you?" Tristan laughed, slapping him on the shoulder as they walked toward the exit.

He spotted Marcus to their left, driving his team hard on the pushups. Kurt was standing beside him, shaking his head.

"No," he answered. "Casey and Charlotte didn't."

"Totally different. Char and Case are our friends." Tristan shrugged.

"Amber wants me. Wait and see," Darnell said confidently.

He might act the fool, but he never failed at life. In any area. It wasn't in his DNA. His parents had brought him up to believe he could be anything, have anything, and achieve anything.

And he had.

Failure didn't happen. Nor was it encouraged.

Darnell worked hard, believed in himself, and ensured he made his parents proud.

Or rather, met their expectations.

The only time Darnell had failed was during the Vampire Games. Alex was the true contender for first place, and Darnell had been faced with the acceptance that he wasn't going to win.

Darnell hadn't shared the stress he was under during that time with anyone. Or the phone calls from his father.

"I know you can do this, Darnell," his father had said. "Give it your best tomorrow."

He'd been giving it his best every fucking day, but there was no way he would say that to his dad.

"I'll never let you experience what I did in life, Darnell," Joseph Miller had told him over and over. "My father lost his reputable bookkeeping company after gambling it away. Your uncle and I were forced to work from a young age. I served tables and worked behind the bar. Instead of being grateful, Dad drank heavily and told us how useless we were."

Darnell's father had often told him about the shame he felt working in low-income jobs when he dreamed of becoming a chef. He scribbled in his notebook, dreaming up recipes during his breaks or days off. One day, his father found it and told him he was a loser and would never amount to anything more than a no-hoper pouring beer.

A year later, he met Darnell's mom, Grace.

A vampire.

Who was also a lawyer. Despite his lack of self-worth, Joseph cooked her a meal one night—before learning she was a vampire—and shared his dreams with her. Fast forward ten years, they had mated and together created a chain of Michelin Star restaurants around the United States.

"Your grandfather never lived to see my success, and it grates at me every day that I never got to prove to that asshole I was better than some server pouring drinks," his father constantly grumbled.

When Darnell arrived in their lives, his father declared their son would never be treated as a lower-class citizen and would always have the best.

They lived in the best neighborhood. He went to the best schools, and his parents even advised him on the friends he kept. He was encouraged not to spend time with anyone lacking drive and motivation.

When it was apparent he had less of a business brain and was more physically motivated, there was a sit-down family meeting. His parents asked whether he'd be interested in joining the royal army.

*Fuck, yes*, was the answer.

But if he'd said no and wanted to, say, be a personal trainer, would his father have been as happy with the outcome of the meeting? Fortunately, he'd been accepted into the Moretti army immediately and worked his way up the ranks.

And thankfully, when the prince had announced Alex as the winner of the Games—awarding him the coveted SLC role—he'd also surprised everyone by promoting Tristan and Darnell.

The three of them had joined the king's senior team after being sworn in soon after.

It was a strategic move by the prince, who knew he needed a larger team to deal with the changing times and growing threat to the race.

And one Darnell was grateful for.

His parents had done a lot for him and loved him from the moment he took his first breath. He wanted to make his dad proud and never make him experience that shame again.

If being the best he could be every day was the price he had to pay, it was hardly a tough one.

"How's your team coming along?" he asked Tristan, changing the topic as they stepped into the hallway and made their way to the SLC operations room.

They'd both managed teams of warriors before but were now leading former peers. It was an adjustment for some of them.

Darnell knew Tristan was having a challenge with some of his guys.

"Some teething issues," Tristan said. "Might need to move a few people around."

"I get why you'd want to, but out in the field, those same warriors will be fighting beside you. If they don't respect you in here, they won't out there," Darnell said.

"Yeah, fuck. I'll speak to Bray or Craig. See what they recommend." Tristan twisted his cap. "Fucks me off. We don't have time for this shit."

He wasn't wrong, but that wasn't how leadership worked.

Especially for vampires. They were predators. They smelled weakness ten miles away and went for the jugular.

Of the two of them, Darnell had been ready to step into the senior role. Tristan was a powerful vampire, yes, but tended to be one of the boys. Which was fine in the bar, but when you put on your Moretti cap and stood in front of your men, they had to know who was boss.

Darnell was confident Tris would work it out.

Brayden wouldn't let him fail. But no one could do it for him.

They turned the corner and—*Whoomph.*

Darnell's face broke into a big smile as he caught the sexy tornado and lifted her off the floor.

"Sorry. Shit!" she cried.

"I told you I was a sure thing, baby. No need to throw yourself at me," Darnell purred as wide green eyes surrounded by wild red hair stared back at him.

Furiously.

"Not your baby. For the hundredth time." Amber tugged at his hold on her upper arms. "Put me down."

"Jesus, I'm out of here," Tristan laughed, leaving them to it with a wave over his head.

"Don't leave me!" she cried.

Darnell let out a deep growl in the back of his throat as Amber's body pressed against his.

She was like fire during a snowstorm.

"I'm warning you," she said, placing her hands on his shoulders and digging her nails into him.

"God, that feels good. Harder." He winked.

"Darnell, put me down. My shift starts in ten minutes. I left my key in the yoga room. And I still need to shower."

*Lord.* Visions of her naked standing under the flowing water had him hardening.

Amber narrowed her eyes, confirming she could feel him. *Oh, dear. How sad.*

He lowered her to the floor. Slowly. Via the hardness of his body. Every inch of it.

"Was that necessary?" Amber groaned.

"Very fucking necessary," Darnell purred, then leaned down to her stupidly short height of five-foot-nothing and tucked a finger under her chin. "Wear that short black skirt tonight. I love imagining what I'll find underneath."

Nothing.

That's what he imagined.

Just a smooth-shaven pussy that he could slide into.

"You mean my big control panties? The kind that clings in thick nude fabric up to my waist and down mid-thigh?"

"What?"

She smiled.

"What the fuck are control panties?" Darnell held up a hand. "Do not answer that. I get the feeling I won't like it, and you'll destroy my fantasy."

"Exactly. A fantasy," Amber said, placing her hands on her hips. "I told you. I'm not interested. So just…don't."

*Liar.*

His eyes roamed her face as absolute desire and determination overwhelmed him. The chemistry was as thick as molasses between them.

"You're so fucking pretty," he rasped, and that's when he saw it. The flicker of desire as her guard dropped for a split second.

*That's it, baby. Let me in.*

She swallowed, and the walls of ice returned.

"I don't give up easily," Darnell warned.

"Neither do I."

A small smile hit his lips as he straightened and stepped away. Amber seemed to take a second to compose herself, her eyes roaming his body, before walking around him and continuing on her way.

*It's all yours, Amber. One night. Just say the word.*

She would.

Eventually.

Because he never failed.

DARNELL SLID INTO a chair between Kurt and Tristan and kicked out his legs, crossing his ankles.

"Heard you were harassing Amber again." Kurt smirked.

"Define harassing." He shrugged.

"Trying to get your dick inside her when she's said no." Kurt laughed.

"I know what no sounds like. Trust me, she wants me." Darnell smirked, but when Kurt went quiet, he turned to face him directly. "Fuck off, man. I would never cross that line if a chick really meant no."

He wouldn't.

The tension between him and Amber was palpable. Darnell loved pursuing her just as much as it was driving him insane. To say he was getting carpal tunnel in his right hand was an understatement.

But he wouldn't touch her if she seriously said no.

"Good. Don't." Kurt nodded once. "Madison and Amber are becoming good friends. Yoga friends or what the fuck ever."

"She likes the chase," Darnell said.

"Who does?" Ben joined them, sitting his ass on the edge of the table.

"Amber," Tristan replied.

"Yeah, nah. She's not interested in you." Ben shook his head as if it was a fact.

Darnell laughed. "How would you know?"

"First, I know females. Second, she told Madison, who told Anna," Ben replied.

*Jesus.*

Darnell rolled his eyes. "This isn't the Housewives of Moretti Castle."

Tristan choked on his soda and wiped his mouth.

"Trust me." Kurt nodded slowly. "It is."

"Doesn't change anything. She's just not into you, dude." Ben kicked Darnell's sneaker.

He leaped up, and the two of them tumbled onto the floor as Ben broke into laughter.

Asshole.

"Warriors," Brayden's voice boomed as he and Vincent pushed through the doors and strode into the room. Ari and Craig followed.

Darnell climbed to his feet, nudging Ben in the shoulder. The two shared a grin before dropping into their chairs.

Then, a small figure caught his attention out of the corner of his eye. Darnell did a double-take when he saw Brianna. Mostly because she wasn't tucked under Craig's arm.

The commander headed toward his desk at the front of the room and glared at his mate as she followed the king.

"Jesus," Kurt mumbled, rubbing his forehead. Craig shot him a look.

Kurt held up his hands.

"See? Get the fuck over here, Bri," Craig growled.

Brianna ignored him, placed her laptop on the table, and stubbornly crossed her arms. "I'm working. Boundaries, Craig."

*Oh, boy.*

Brayden ran a hand over his mouth and, fucking hell, Darnell used every muscle in his face to not smile himself.

The big vampire commander dropped into his chair and, after a slow look around the room threatening every single one of them to dare say something, he turned his attention back to his mate.

"Well, now that's over with," Vincent rolled his eyes, "let's get the fuck started."

Tom and Brianna got busy connecting her laptop while Brayden rolled up his sleeves. It looked like they were getting straight down to business today.

"Ari's team will join us in a minute," Brayden began as Oliver, Jason, Elijah, and Logan pushed through the doors.

"Apologies, we were finishing a call with the team in Seattle," said Oliver, the head assassin from Ari Moretti's organization, The Institute.

"Right on time." Brayden crossed his arms. "Now that everyone is here, we have an announcement to make. As you know, Lance and Tom have been managing the recruitment of new warriors from around the globe to increase our numbers. Over the past few weeks, we've made some progress."

"There were a few we couldn't accept," Marcus said. He was the head trainer for the royal army, and Brayden had tasked him with having the final say. "But a lot we could. It's been an enormous job for all of you. Thanks for all the hard work and extra hours."

Brayden then nodded to the commander.

Craig unfolded his arms. "We've landed on two hundred and eighty new bodies. We'll need every single one of them in the coming days, weeks, and months. Which is why I had Kurt speak to Callan and the wolves."

The hybrid wolves?

Darnell twisted his head to find Kurt nodding.

"Callan and Mack are returning to the castle and joining the army," Brayden continued.

*Holy shit.*

"Noah will stay on and lead the pack in Greenwood and keep them all safe and thriving," Kurt said, referring to the dozen-odd wolf-vampire hybrids.

"That's a big deal," Tristan said what everyone was thinking.

Scientists had captured Callan and altered his DNA before he escaped. Before he understood what had happened to him, he had infected a dozen other vampires, and they had all now shifted into their wolves.

As far as he knew, anyway.

Darnell had only recently been briefed on this entire situation when he'd become a SLC. It was kept confidential from everyone except those sitting in this room. Oliver and the other assassins were the most recent to find out.

Kurt acted as the primary wolf contact, and he figured it was because of his vested interest—his mate, Madison, was a hybrid wolf.

"Neither of them are trained warriors," Lance said.

"Callan is an alpha and a strong vampire," Brayden said. "Don't underestimate him. He's proven to be a keen leader. And keep an eye on Mack. He's a big vampire. And a wolf."

Darnell took in everyone's point of view. The prince had a point. From what he knew so far, they had only begun to understand their abilities.

"They have full control of their wolves after spending a year in Greenwood. I'm confident we can contain their secret when they join us," Vincent said. "We need them here."

"We'll do whatever we can to support their training," Marcus said, shooting a look at Kurt. "Let me know when they arrive."

"Will do," Kurt replied.

Darnell was looking forward to meeting them. While he saw Madison nearly every day, he never thought of her as a wolf. She didn't display any behaviors that gave her away, so the king was right. No one would be the wiser.

"Sage is happy and looking forward to studying them while they're in the castle. We can no longer risk her traveling to Greenwood. I won't risk it," Ari Moretti said about his mate, who was a scientist.

As he understood it, she was predominantly working on an antidote to the dreaded serum originally created by BioZen and now in the hands of Nikolay Mikhailov. He was the Bratva Pakhan, or mob boss, and their arch-enemy.

Nikolay was planning to mass-produce the serum and sell it to humanity after announcing that vampires existed. You didn't need to be an economist to work out how rich he'd be once that kind of fear and pandemonium broke out.

Nor the danger it would pose to the vampire race.

It would be a multi-species war.

With only ten million vampires to eight billion humans, it was anyone's guess how it would play out.

Darnell had gone over and over it in his head.

They were vastly more powerful than humans. Faster, stronger, and nearly immortal. Therein lay the issue. They weren't immortal. They could die by simple exposure to sunlight. Or if their heart was damaged.

Or head removed.

The latter not as common now that swords were a thing of the past.

The serum might knock them unconscious for small amounts of time, but they soon metabolized that shit through their systems. Then what?

Humans didn't have the ability to hold them.

Not without Tungsten, and it was a rare and expensive steel.

So, an antidote was one of the king's priorities, and Sage had been given a lot of resources to do her research. Studying the wolves was part of it.

Did their new DNA hold some answers?

Darnell had no clue. He wasn't a scientist. He was a warrior. But he fucking hoped they got some answers soon. Nikolay Mikhailov was a sociopath. He didn't care who he hurt or what he had to do to gain power. Hell, the guy had killed his father to take over the Russian mob.

Letting him gain that much power on the planet?

No fucking way.

Nikolay had partnered with a number of different mafias in the United States to form what they were calling the mega-mafia. Their intel said it was for the purposes of producing and distributing the serum.

Jesus.

Darnell couldn't think of a more dangerous time for their race. Fortunately, he'd never been shot with one of the serum darts, but a few of the SLCs had, and they were not fans of the experience.

Charlotte, Marcus' mate, had been kidnapped by Nikolay, but the team got her back before she was loaded onto a jet and… yeah, it wasn't worth thinking about what could have happened.

They needed to be stopped.

"The government has created chaos in the mega-mafia plans," Vincent shared. "But only their distribution channels. We haven't found their production facilities yet."

"Fuckers," Craig muttered.

"What he said," someone else agreed.

"Nikolay is a dangerous human," Ari said. "We need to take him very seriously. He called the king a few weeks ago and threatened to capture vampires. It appears he has followed through on that promise."

Fuck.

Darnell's brows lifted as the warriors around him cursed and grunted out *asshole* and *over my dead body*.

"That's right. We think he might have succeeded," Vincent said. "Reports of missing vampires are coming through on VampNet. Could be unrelated, but there are six in the New York area alone."

Louder curses sounded throughout the room.

"It's an assumption at this point." Brayden held up his hand to silence everyone. "You know as well as I do that vamps can turn to ash. The race is required to report them, so are they missing people or natural deaths? The number is above average for the time period, so it's been flagged by our team."

"Correct," the king said. "Especially considering Nikolay's threat. What we don't know is if he has the means to contain a vampire after he's captured one of us."

Tungsten.

Darnell was right. The only material strong enough on the planet to hold a vampire, and he doubted a bunch of Tungsten cells were available for the mafia to use willy-nilly.

"If he has all of Xander Tomassi's data, they'll know this," Ari said, lifting a shoulder. "I wouldn't put it past the Russian to coerce that out of BioZen. It's what I would do if I were him."

"Same." Darnell lifted his foot onto his knee. "Classic mafia move, too."

Craig nodded slowly in agreement.

"Even if they don't have Tungsten, they could keep injecting them with that shit." Marcus cursed as Kurt exaggerated a shiver. The two of them had been injected with it and knew how bad it was.

Darnell hoped like hell he never did.

Being rendered powerless and unconscious was not something any vampire wanted to experience, least of all a vampire warrior who relied on the ability to use their body and power to protect others.

But Ari was right. Xander might be dead—may he rest in hell—but as the man responsible for capturing Callan and starting all this with his experiments on vampires, his data would be unbelievably valuable in the hands of their enemy.

There was also the minor detail of the super soldiers that BioZen had created.

Nikolay now had them in his army.

They were another type of hybrid. Half human, half vampire. Not as powerful as a full-blooded vampire, but an unknown subspecies. Darnell had a bad feeling every time he thought about them.

Marcus and Charlotte had met one of them. Even fought it. Both said the hybrid had appeared unstable and dangerous.

He doubted those creatures had the same support as their wolves. The mafia would simply be using them as soldiers. As weapons.

The poor fuckers.

But first, they needed to care for their own. If these civilian vampires were missing and being held in any way or form, they needed to find them.

"Do we need to go to NYC?" Darnell growled. "To find these missing vamps?"

"A team is being deployed as we speak," Craig said, nodding at Oliver. "Oli and the team will be in the air within an hour and report back to us as soon as they find or hear anything."

"You guys do way more work than I thought," Brianna said, sounding impressed.

The room fell silent, and Darnell glanced at the king. His fingers were at his temple.

Craig cringed. "Babe."

"What?" she asked as if her comment was totally normal. "I'm impressed."

"Brianna," Vincent said slowly, "the Moretti royal army has existed for over a thousand years."

"Good point. You have systems and stuff." She nodded.

Darnell stifled his laugh. But hell, she was funny.

And brave.

"Systems and stuff," Vincent murmured, repeating her words. He seemed to catch himself and pulled in a long breath heavily laced with patience. "Okay… Anyway, Ari, I believe you were right. Nikolay hasn't announced our existence yet, so it's likely he's saving that shock value until he has a product to sell. Something marketable."

As in the serum.

The Russian mob boss thought he was going to take over the fucking world with a product humans would pay good money for—once they discovered vampires were real—to defend themselves.

He might be right. And he might succeed.

Except for one small point.

They'd lived among humans for over fifteen hundred years. Peacefully.

If they had their way, they'd keep doing that.

It didn't look like it would be possible for much longer.

Still, never say never.

"So, we cut him off at the knees," Brayden said.

"I have made the decision that we will announce our race to the human beings," the king shared. "The first step is updating our people. My team has been working on a video that shares the process and answers questions they may have. It will prepare them in advance, and we hope to give them some confidence for the days ahead."

*Holy hell.*

"We will release it on VampNet globally after briefing key support people to manage any panic," the king added.

Oh, there was going to be panic, all right.

A huge amount.

His mind went to his mom and dad and how they would react. They were pretty pragmatic but had all grown up with the strong dictate that they must keep their vampire nature hidden.

Now, that was all changing.

"That's going to be a huge job," Darnell said, glancing around to see if anyone else was surprised by the news.

"It is, but we've worked on this for a long time," Brianna said. "Let me show you what we've prepared."

*So this is really fucking happening.*

Shit.

A few buttons were pushed, and the lights dimmed.

Movie time.

# CHAPTER TWO

Amber stepped out of the shower and tossed the wet towel onto her bed. She pulled out her hair tie and let her red, curly frizz do what it would. There was no controlling it, not on a typical day and certainly not today when she'd almost run out of time.

Thanks to that stupidly sexy, big, dark vampire, Darnell.

Why wouldn't he leave her alone?

The last thing she needed was someone like him messing up her life. She'd found a place that was starting to feel like home. For the first time since…

I miss you, Mom. And… Papa.

She missed him as well. Her emotions were overshadowed by anger and resentment. Still.

And fair enough after what she'd had to endure since they died.

Like all vampires, Amber was aware of the dominance of the mating bond, but it still hurt when her father chose to end his life and leave her all alone after his mate, her mother, had died.

She'd been a little girl. How could he have done that to her? Hadn't he loved her too?

Amber had asked this question a million times since that horrible day. She could logicalize it until she was blue in the face, but abandonment was abandonment.

Sure, mates couldn't live without one another, but she had needed her parents, and life had nearly broken her.

Nearly.

Amber wasn't sure she wasn't broken, to be honest. Most days, she was piecing herself back together and trying to find a place where she fit in this big world.

Somewhere safe.

She was twenty-three now and beginning to wonder if perhaps some people were destined to be alone. Had her childhood damaged her irrevocably?

Or did she simply need to find the right people to trust?

Yeah, she'd read all the self-help *of everything.* It all came back to her choosing to open up and trust.

Good one.

Written by people who'd had a loving mother and father all their lives, most likely.

Well, not everyone had that.

Not everyone had the inner workings that led to self-worth and healthy relationships. Or the confidence to go after them.

In theory, she'd had a good start. A happy, loving home until the day the phone rang to say her mom had died. Witnesses told police two men had held her at gunpoint after carjacking her at a set of lights.

Her mom wasn't a strong vampire like the Moretti warriors, but she was stronger than humans.

Faster than a bullet? No.

The witnesses explained one of the men had tried to– Amber pushed back the bile which always rose when she recalled this time in her life–sexually abuse her mom. But she, and this was a direct quote, *"fought very well."*

Unfortunately, it had been her undoing.

The other bad guy shot her six times, and then the men leaped into the car and drove off, leaving her mom bleeding on the ground as the sun rose.

Unbeknownst to everyone around her, she was a vampire.

Amber suspected a bullet had struck her mom's heart. Otherwise, she would've healed quickly and teleported away. Instead, while the ambulance and police were called and people stood around waiting, the sun had risen and turned her to ash.

Taking her mom from her life and starting a chain of events that couldn't be undone.

Still, no one cared about that. They cared about a woman vanishing in plain sight. It had been a breaking news piece as they tried to work out the phenomenon, calling it a freak of nature.

Her father hadn't cared either. He'd been selfishly focused on losing his mate. At twelve, Amber hadn't known enough about what could come next. She'd desperately needed someone to tell her she would be okay.

That's not what happened.

A few weeks later, heavy with grief, her father got up off the sofa, crossed the room, and kissed Amber on the forehead, saying, "I'm sorry my little darling. Please forgive me." Then he unlocked the front door as she screamed, "No, Papa!"

A moment she would never forget.

Amber had dropped to the floor behind the sofa as the sun tore through the room, bawling her eyes out, knowing at that moment her father's ashes were being scattered into the wind.

He'd given no care to the impact on her emotionally or that she'd been exposed to the sunlight—fortunately, not directly.

It had set several hours later, and during that time, Amber remained in that spot, frozen with anguish and grief as she cried herself dry.

When the sun set, she crawled across the room, closed the door, and leaned against it, completely drained. It must have taken another hour for her to reach the kitchen and get a blood pouch to replenish. Then, more tears had come.

Finally, the realization set in that she was alone in the world.

Both her parents were gone.

She grieved for her mom while hating her father for his decision.

Amber had assumed forgiveness would come eventually, and it had as she'd matured. Or was it acceptance?

To be honest, she'd been in a state of survival her entire life. She hadn't had time to focus on whether she forgave her father. She resented him.

She also missed him.

How different would her life be if her mom hadn't been driving along that road that night?

Much.

But the real question was whether she could create a family of her own one day. Find her people. A place she could rest her soul and be loved and wanted.

Somewhere she felt safe.

It seemed like a pipe dream. Until now.

Maybe.

Coming to Moretti Castle to work for the royal family had been a random decision on her part. She'd needed a job after her last boss thought her body belonged to him. Amber then found the position at Max Bar listed on VampNet and applied.

Surprised that she had been successful, she moved from NYC to Maine the next day and hadn't regretted it.

In fact, she loved it here.

She'd made friends with Madison, Anna, and the others in their social circle.

Unfortunately, that included Darnell.

Darnell, who made no secret about what he wanted from her. Worse, he knew she was just as attracted to him. Sure, she could shag him and enjoy some incredible sex. She didn't doubt that for a second. The vampire got her heart racing with just a wink.

His stupid arrogance made her laugh, but there was no way in hell she was letting him know that.

Sex muddied the waters.

For the first time in her horrible damn life, she felt she might belong here. Sleeping with one of their friends would only cause issues.

And there were a ton of gorgeous men in the castle, so it was unlikely she'd be using her black dildo every day.

Amber was waiting to find one she was as attracted to as Darnell.

It would happen.

Right?

Maybe if he stopped coming to Max Bar every fucking day after his shift in his stupid tight black Moretti T-shirts. Didn't they make them with sleeves that fit? She was tempted to take to them with a pair of scissors and be all like, *fixed it.* But she knew he liked his bulging biceps and… God, so did she.

Plus, his chest. Lord, he had those thick pecs that were clearly visible through the cotton. Ugh, and you just wanted to press yourself against them.

And thighs. Oh, that man had thighs like lampposts, and Amber wanted to wrap herself around them. If proportions were a real thing, then…

Yeah, he'd be big.

Thick.

Long.

"Fuck," she cursed and spun around, looking for her jeans. With minutes left before she had to be on shift and a long trek to the other side of the castle, Amber was starting to panic.

She did not want to lose this job.

Then she saw it. Her short black skirt.

"Damn you, Darnell," Amber grumbled, pulling it on. Then she did something she wasn't sure she would regret.

She slipped off her panties.

She'd been in a constant state of arousal after Darnell had purposely slid her down his body and over his erection. If he wanted to play games with her, she was going to make it painful for him.

"Black Stallion, we have a date when I get home," Amber said to her bedside drawer.

It was better this way.

She wanted to make it work here. Sleeping with Madison and Anna's friend was not smart.

*Think big picture, Amber. Not about that one sweet orgasm he could give you.*

But damn, it was becoming harder.

# CHAPTER THREE

"Feedback?" Vincent asked as the video ended.

"Scares the living hell out of me, honestly," Tom said, rubbing the top of his head and saying what they all felt.

Darnell watched everyone kind of nod around him, and he wondered if they actually had a say.

No.

They didn't.

He wasn't sure this was the right thing to do.

It would freak out their entire race, and who knew how they'd react? Sure, Brianna and her team had covered a lot of points, but...

It was going to shock everyone.

Then, there were the rebel fractions still under control after Stefano Russo and his brothers had lost their lives. But not gone.

How would they react?

It was Stefano who had told Xander Tomassi about vampires and caused so many issues. What if other rebels decided to side with humans? They knew it was power they were after. For centuries, they had been against the idea of a monarch, and Vincent Moretti and his father had allowed them to have a quiet voice despite not being a democracy.

It was fair of them. But the consequences of that in more modern times were much greater.

Darnell would follow what his king wanted, but that didn't mean he didn't have thoughts of his own.

"Not what I want to hear, but I get it. This is a huge moment for our race, and it'll take some time for people to wrap their heads around it," Vincent said. "But I'd like to take a moment to acknowledge Brianna and her team. They've done an excellent job."

"Thanks, V." She grinned.

This time, a few of them did snort.

"V?" Craig's brows lifted. "The fuck?"

Brianna grinned and crossed the room, sliding onto Craig's lap, and apparently, everything was forgiven.

Unless you were the king.

Vincent was glaring at her with lowered brows.

"You give them a fucking inch, I swear." Vincent shook his head, talking to no one in particular.

Darnell shot Tristan a smirk.

"Any other feedback?" Brayden asked, cutting the tension.

Darnell leaned back in his chair. "You haven't mentioned the serum. I get that you don't want to terrify people, but surely being fully informed is better."

Bray took a few steps as the king sat on the edge of a table. He watched the two Moretti brothers share a glance, and then Ari joined in the eye tennis.

He knew it was a sensitive subject, but someone had to ask.

"This has been a tough decision. Between all of us, we have many centuries of war strategy behind us. None more than Ari," Brayden said. "He's studied and been involved with many armies, including the Roman army in his early years."

Jesus, they all knew he was the ancient vampire, but some days, it got put in perspective and blew your mind.

Ari nodded. "Correct. I served Odavacer, the first king of Rome, in the later part of the fifth century."

*Fucking hell.*

They were all old compared to humans, but Ari Moretti was over fifteen hundred years old. He was the remaining original vampire: his brother was Gio, their first king, and his deceased twin brother.

How they became vampires, no one knew.

Ari refused to tell that tale. Darnell wondered if the ancient male remembered.

Or if he would ever tell someone.

Unlike humans, none of them believed in a God. Or an afterlife. Or even a higher being.

Being semi-immortal made you look at things differently. Yes, they could die, and they did. But only from exposure to the sun, destruction of the heart, or decapitation. Otherwise, they just kept living.

Fifteen hundred years and counting.

But *like* humans, they were prone to wondering how they came into existence. Had they suddenly shown up on the planet?

Darnell believed vampires were like Superman. Dropped on the planet from outer space, and one day, they would meet their origins. Science didn't seem to point to them existing and evolving naturally like other creatures on Earth. They knew that because humans would know of them.

Wouldn't they?

Darnell wasn't sure he liked the idea of being called an alien when they were revealed publicly.

Earth was his home. Just as it was any other living being.

All of these things would be discussed in the media when they went public.

He could see the headlines on CNN and BBC now: *Where did the vampires come from?*

Brianna's presentation had covered this and advised them to prepare for a range of reactions, from the physical to the emotional and psychological.

Humans were nothing if not predictable.

One thing they couldn't do, however, was identify a vampire from looking at him on the street. Which would cause a level of panic for those who immediately labeled them the enemy.

They were the unknown and more powerful.

It went without saying they would be treated as the enemy.

This was why Vincent, POTUS, and all the other UN leaders had been putting a framework in place to slowly reveal their species. With communications being what they were in this day and age, Darnell wasn't sure it could be contained.

One TikTok and the rest was history.

Still, none of that mattered now. Nikolay had taken away that choice.

Unless they could stop him.

"We're working hard on an antidote," Brayden said.

"Yet," Vincent said.

"Until we do, our strategy, which Vincent and Bri just shared, is to inform and prepare everyone. Then pivot as this unfolds," the prince added. "Telling them about the serum will only induce mass fear, which won't help anyone. It's not in circulation, and if we have our way, it won't be."

Fair enough.

But the serum was the biggest threat to them right now.

Then again, having ten million vampires absolutely freaking out would create chaos and wouldn't help anything.

Craig dropped Brianna to her feet as he stood and walked over to Brayden. "There's a chance we can destroy this mega-mafia operation before it becomes a critical issue. The human governments are effectively fucking up their distribution channels, hence Mikhailov's reaction. We need to figure out where they're planning to produce the serum."

"Let me guess." Kurt laughed. "The government can't touch them, but we can."

"Bingo," Craig said, shooting him with his finger.

Darnell grinned and leaned his elbows on his knees. Now things were getting good.

FOR THE NEXT hour, after the king and Brianna left the warriors to do their thing, Brayden, Craig, and Ari walked through their plans to seek out the mega-mafia production lines. It would take a team effort with their crews around the world, but they had to start somewhere.

They couldn't sit this out and hope it all fell to pieces. They could start piecing things together with the data they already had on many of the gangs.

"I'll get Darren to pull the data we have on known mafia properties," Oliver, the head assassin at The Institute, said.

"Tell him to send it my way while you're in Manhattan," Craig instructed. "When you get back, I'll have you and Ben go over the locations for anything you've seen before."

"The dream team back together again," Ben said.

"Jesus." Craig rolled his eyes as Brayden smirked.

Oli and Ben fist-bumped while Ari leaned his ass against the window ledge and shook his head at the two males.

Ben had been his Head Assassin for a long time before joining the Moretti army, so Ari was familiar with the antics of those two vampires.

"Okay, so let's get to work. Remember, the video will be broadcast to the race in the next few days along with the king's speech," Brayden shared. "I want you all prepared to answer questions, but I know I don't need to remind you all that anything regarding BioZen, this mega-mafia, or the serum is strictly top-level information."

They knew.

But sometimes, you needed to say things out loud. Especially when they were this important.

"Tom and I will be briefing our global ambassadors so each region will have a free calling number and a team ready to provide support," Craig said.

"Million-dollar question," Darnell began, rubbing his jaw. "Will we be relocating the king at any point?"

The room went quiet.

"No," Brayden replied after a slight hesitation. "Not unless it's absolutely necessary. Lucas and Isabella are too little to be moved unnecessarily."

Fuck, he could only imagine how Brayden and Vincent, and hell, Willow, and Kate, felt about having their young so vulnerable right now.

Darnell was even worried about his parents.

"The emergency plan remains if the situation changes," Craig said, shooting Brayden a look. One that hinted there was a slight disagreement on the matter.

Darnell might not be mated, but at a guess, he suspected the prince didn't want to be separated from Willow and Isabella.

But they were royalty, and the stakes were different.

However, good luck to anyone who tried to cross Willow Moretti. She was a force to be reckoned with. He'd seen her with the baby a couple of times, and unless she was staring lovingly at the prince, she was a wild momma bear protecting her little girl.

It had made him wonder if he wanted a family one day.

He did.

The idea of taking his mate home to meet his family and making them proud was exciting. His mom would love to have little Vamplets running around the house.

"Darnell and Tristan, I want you two to stay focused on your teams and solidify your new leadership with them. That will be vital out in the field," Brayden said.

"Got it," Darnell replied.

Kurt's phone beeped, and the guy smiled as he swiped. "The wolves are here."

"Excellent." Brayden grinned. "Let's wrap this up and say hello."

"Then drinks at Max Bar, boys," Kurt announced, leaping to his feet.

Hell, yeah. As it turned out, that was exactly where Darnell was heading.

To see his sexy little firecracker.

# CHAPTER FOUR

Amber pushed the beer tap and slid the tall glass across the bar. "There you go,"

"Two," the male said, holding up two fingers.

"Oh, sorry," she replied, grabbing another glass and pulling the tab to fill it.

She was off her game tonight and blamed Darnell. Plus, that trip down memory lane about her parents hadn't helped.

"Hey, babe," Anna said, sliding onto a bar stool beside the guy waiting for his beer. When he grinned at her, she did a double take, then sighed. "Move along. My mate's an assassin."

Amber coughed as the guy's face dropped. She slid him his beer, and he disappeared.

Anna leaned forward. "Don't tell Ben I said that. He'd kick my ass."

Amber laughed. "Promise. But it was hilarious."

"What are we whispering about?" Madison asked, plonking onto the barstool beside Anna. Casey was right behind her but stood leaning and gazing around the bar.

Amber recognized the behavior in all the warriors—males and females—and suspected it was part of their training to keep an eye on their surroundings. Subconsciously or otherwise.

"Nothing." Anna grinned. "So, what time are they arriving?"

"Who?" Amber asked.

"Oh… ah, friends from Greenwood. Callan and his mate, Virginia, and Mack." Madison replied excitedly, but Amber noted she'd chosen her words carefully for some reason. "They are special to me. Sort of like family."

Family.

Something she didn't have.

"Nice," Amber replied, wiping the bar with her towel, and averting her eyes.

These females had made her extremely welcome since she'd arrived. They'd brought her into the group and invited her to things. Which was a big deal given their mates were SLCs. She opted out of a lot of the couple's stuff but loved hanging out with the girls.

They went to yoga, shopping in town, and they'd hit the local bar in downtown Portland for dinner and drinks once or twice. It always seemed to get ambushed by the males, which was amusing.

But it was a reminder of how alone she was. These amazing vampires had a whole network of people who had their backs, cared about them, and loved them.

Being mated to a protective and powerful Moretti warrior meant you were looked after for life, and she couldn't help wondering how it would feel.

Suffocating? Or comforting?

It wasn't something she needed to worry about.

Hearing Madison say she had this other family of sorts was a reminder that Amber didn't belong. Not yet.

Maybe not ever.

She wouldn't take them for granted.

But it certainly seemed like everyone had a place or a person in this life, while Amber was still trying to find hers.

Maybe she never would. She'd be this other person that people knew. An outsider they sometimes let into their circle.

"What do ya'll want to drink?" Amber asked, planting her hand on her jutting hip.

"Beer," Casey replied.

"Vodka," Madison said, and Anna nodded, indicating the same. "They should be here soon. Kurt said everyone would be meeting here to welcome them back."

"You'll like them," Anna said, wiggling her eyebrows. "Especially Mack."

"True. He is hot," Casey said. "Shit, please tell me Alex isn't behind me."

Madison giggled as Amber slid the drinks over to them.

"No, he's not. And no, thanks. I already spend half my life fending off your friend, Darnell," Amber replied, pouring herself a glass of water and tossing in a slice of lemon.

She lifted the straw to her lips.

"He's persistent." Casey nodded. "The more you fight, the more of a challenge you become. Just ignore him."

Amber raised her brows. "So, what? Sleep with him and get him off my back."

"Literally." Anna giggled.

Madison shrugged. "I mean, he's not horrible."

No, he was not. He was tall, dark, and absolutely fucking gorgeous. She was sure he had ten layers of muscles on him, and there might have been one day she was counting his abs through his tight Moretti T-shirt. Eight.

Jesus.

The problem was that Darnell knew he was hot.

Females, she'd noticed during her time in the castle, all checked out the SLC warriors. The power and celebrity status that came with their roles was one thing, but the fact was, they were all insanely good-looking vampires.

Good looking, enormous, and oozing power and confidence. It was intoxicating.

However, only Darnell and Tristan were single.

Although there were newbies on board now. Some of the newcomers from Ari Moretti's Seattle team had temporarily become honorary SLCs. Amber only knew this from the girls gossiping, but their presence had created quite a stir.

She'd seen Logan a few nights ago when he came into Max Bar, and holy smokes, the man was definitely a ten. He hadn't stayed long, but a lot of the females were left hot and bothered.

Including her.

Darnell had thrown a straw at her when she'd watched him walk out. Stupid male. If only he knew she still thought he was ten times hotter.

Amber liked that it had pissed him off for a second, though.

But it was Darnell she annoyingly dreamed about at night. His hand sliding over her breasts, his lips finally claiming hers, and that gorgeous, broad dark body covering hers…

*Damn him.*

Why couldn't she like one of the other warriors? Someone not in the same inner circle. The last thing she needed was him being an irritating ex wrecking the friendships she was building.

The life she was building.

But she'd seen the size of his hands and—

"Do you like him?" Madison asked.

Amber felt herself blush as she realized she'd zoned out and was wondering what his cock looked like. Could cocks have muscles? She bet he did.

"You do!" Anna exclaimed.

*Oh, crap.*

"No, not like that. Of course, he's hot. I mean, look at the guy," she said figuratively, waving her water in front of her. "But I'm not in the market for a one-night stand."

Casey shrugged. "Make it an hour then."

Madison and Anna burst into giggles.

An hour wouldn't be enough. She had a feeling a man like Darnell would take his sweet time. The sexual energy emitting from his body when he was near sent shivers through her each and every time.

Even now, her nipples were hard, and for God's sake, he wasn't even in the same damn room. Which changed two seconds later as the door opened and those bright, unnaturally blue eyes locked with hers.

And cue the smirk.

"Ugh." Amber dropped her glass into the sink and walked away as Madison and Anna giggled.

Brad, the bar manager, could serve him. She had some boxes out back to unpack.

And a vampire to hide from.


"AMBER, ARE YOU alphabetizing the booze?" Brad asked, staring at the rows of bottles she'd reorganized on the shelf.

Was she?

"Yup. I thought it might help us find everything easier," Amber said, dusting off her hands and placing them on her hips, pleased with her results.

Brad frowned, his eyes drifting to hers. "Not really."

Yeah. Not really.

But the good news was that there were no blue-eyed vampires she was trying not to have sex with in here.

"It's getting busy. Leave the rest for the next shift," Brad said. "Need you out front."

Damn.

"Sure." Amber followed him out to the bar.

Brad was right. Things had picked up in the time she'd been out back. It was pumping. All the tables were full, and the bar was two deep.

The girls had moved to a table near the back with the males. She recognized Ben, Kurt, Tristan, Darnell, and Marcus. Two other males, Callan and Mack, were with them, whom she assumed were their Greenwood friends.

Two more big vampires.

Callan was tall and less broad than the Moretti warriors, but she could tell he was a strong male. Mack was bulkier. And yes, he was good looking.

Very.

Lord, where did they breed these males?

Mack had dark hair, that sexy scruff on his face, and she could tell he was confident and a little cheeky by the way he chatted animatedly with everyone.

Yet there was no sexual tug like she felt when her ebony warrior was near.

Like now, as her eyes drifted to his, and she found herself locked in Darnell's glowering gaze. His familiar smirk was gone, and her heart began to pound as the dark predator within him created a powerful throb of arousal inside her.

Then, with a blink, it vanished, and his lips curled.

Goddamn him.

# CHAPTER FIVE

"So where are you going to run?" Darnell asked Callan and Mack, draining the last of his beer from the bottle and dropping it onto the table.

Had he drunk it faster because Little Miss Amber had finally emerged from behind the bar?

Yes. Yes, he had.

The little firecracker looked flustered after their encounter today, and he wasn't sorry.

Unzipping his black Moretti jacket, he slid it off his shoulders and shoved it under the table. When he glanced up, those green eyes were on him once more.

Or rather, on his arms.

Flex.

*That's right, baby. Strong enough to lift you and hold you in position while I fuck that needy pussy.*

Amber's eyes darted up to his, and he winked. Then laughed out loud as she slammed the glass she was filling on the bar and stormed off.

"Stop messing with her." Madison punched his arm.

"No can do," he replied, ignoring Kurt's sharp glare. "The more she resists, the har—"

"Talk about your cock to my mate, and you won't have one for much longer," Kurt growled.

Darnell held his hands up and stepped back with a laugh.

"Kurt," Madison chastised her mate and was rewarded with a sharp kiss on the mouth.

Which turned her to putty.

*Ridiculous.*

"Thank God, not all of you are mated. It's hard enough living with this guy," Mack grinned, nudging Callan with his elbow.

"Your time will come," Callan said, sipping his beer. "To answer your question, Darnell, we'll shift into our wolves and run on the castle grounds. We're used to sticking to a small space after living in Greenwood. Our wolves don't need too much management as long as we shift every few days."

Callan kept his voice low as knowledge of the hybrids was contained to only the Moretti's and the top-level. Meaning Craig, the SLCs and their mates, and Ari's assassins.

"It's great to have you here," Kurt said, and Madison nodded under his arm.

Callan reached for her hand and squeezed it for a second, and the two of them shared a moment. That his head was still connected to his body and not being used as a basketball by Kurt was less of a surprise now Darnell knew Madison was also a hybrid.

Still, watching Callan get away with it in real life was a whole other thing. Even if he was mated himself.

It appeared Kurt and Callan had a solid relationship of their own. It took a lot to gain the experienced SLC's respect and friendship. Darnell fit in with the team seamlessly, but the relationships were still deepening.

"I know it's important. Noah is a strong second in command, so leaving the pack in his hands was an easy handover while Mack and I are here to help," Callan said.

"Assuming Noah and Ava don't kill each other." Mack rolled his eyes.

Callan snickered silently, nodding.

"You should have brought her with you," Casey said, sipping her drink as Charlotte and Anna agreed.

"It's not a party, ladies," Ben said. "They're here to fight."

"What he said." Marcus nodded at Ben.

Alex reached across the table and scooped up some corn chips. "Pretty sure our females are forming their own army."

"It's called a girl gang," Anna stated.

"Can I join?" Mack asked. "I like girls."

"No," they all chimed.

Darnell laughed, liking the guy already. It was good to have some other singles in the group.

"Stick with me, buddy, and I'll get you into an exclusive club in the community," Tristan said. It wasn't a book club. It was a sex club. "I heard you wolves have insatiable drives."

"You heard right. And yes, hook me up. Otherwise, my wolf will get all angsty," Mack said, shooting a glance toward Amber.

Oh, hell no.

"She's taken," Darnell said darkly.

"Is she?" he asked.

"Yes," he replied firmly. He didn't like the guy that much. And he'd seen Amber checking him out recently. That wasn't fucking happening. Not on his watch.

"Is she?" Madison asked, smirking.

When he ripped his eyes from Mack, he saw all the females watching him.

"Babe," Callan said, spinning on his stool and standing, distracting everyone as a woman with long dark hair walked into his arms. The hybrid's mouth dropped to hers.

Madison leaped up, and then all the girls were hugging the woman.

"This is my mate, Ginny." Callan introduced her to those who didn't already know her. "Virginia."

"Nice to meet you all," Ginny said as Callan lifted her onto the bar stool and stood behind her.

"We're starting a girl gang. Want to join?" Anna asked, giggling.

"Sure. Need a lawyer?" Ginny laughed.

"Definitely," Madison said.

"What will this girl gang do exactly?" Darnell asked, kicking his boot up onto the footrest of the barstool and leaning his forearm on his knee.

"Girl stuff. Like a consultancy for those dealing with males who won't take no for an answer," Anna said.

Tristan and Darnell shared a look. Sounded like trouble to him.

"Like a dating agency? Or an anti-dating agency?" Darnell asked.

The girls glanced at one another and then, as one, turned to him and said, "Both."

"I don't like it," Tristan said.

"We should discuss liability," Ginny said.

"Christ, what did I start?" Alex moaned into his drink as Ben laughed and slapped him on the back.

"They'll be onto something else tomorrow. Drink up," the assassin said.

"I'm already designing logos," Anna said.

*Christ.*

Suddenly, a shiver flushed through his body. Darnell lifted his eyes, and there she was.

Amber wore a tight black, short-sleeved Max Bar shirt and that fucking black skirt. Her red curls were fighting to get loose from her hairband, and Darnell wanted to reach out and help it.

Fuck, she'd look sexy with all that fire lying on his black silk sheets.

But he doubted he'd get home if she said yes to him. It wouldn't take much to clear the bar, tug her skirt up, and find out how aroused she was.

Because she was. He had zero doubt about that.

"What can I get y'all?" Amber asked, avoiding his eyes from across the table.

She cleared the empty bottles as people placed their orders, and when he made no effort to slide his over, she finally looked up.

He stared back.

She raised her brows.

He did the same.

Madison went to grab the bottle, but Kurt stopped her.

Smart male.

He knew what was going on here.

Conversation started up around them, and he wasn't sure which of the warriors had done it on purpose, but he knew they had.

Amber's cheeks pinkened. Not from embarrassment. She was aroused.

*Come here, my little firecracker.*

It'd been weeks since he'd first seen her in the training room in her tight Lycra, showing off her curves. He wondered how many males had enjoyed her body and if her peach had been breached by anyone before.

Because Darnell very much wanted to be the one to show her how fucking much more pleasure was available if she would allow it.

First, he wanted to get his brown hands on that creamy skin. Rub his thumb over her lip and get her to open up to him, then spread her thighs and taste the wetness he knew was waiting for him.

With a lift of her chin, she circled the table and, with her back to him, pressed between him and Kurt to grab his bottle.

Good try, baby, but bad move.

Darnell's hand curved around her hip and slid down her thigh. He stayed in the safe zone but teased her enough that her breath hitched, sending a jolt of arousal straight to his cock.

"Nice skirt," Darnell growled softly into her hair.

As his arm stretched further, he hit her bare silky skin, and the temptation to reach between her thighs and stimulate her almost fucking undid him.

"I wore it for you," she said boldly, turning and forcing his hand back over her hip to her ass.

That's when he realized she wasn't wearing panties.

Holy fucking God.

Scorching eyes found his as he lost his fucking mind, and his mouth parted.

*Baby, you are playing with fire.*

Then, like she had no idea she was in a lion's cave, Amber tiptoed up and placed a hand on his chest. "That's right, big guy. No panties. Hope you enjoy tossing off to that image later because that's as close as you're ever going to get."

*Fucking hell.*

His cock jerked in his pants, and before he could throw her over his broad shoulders and run off into the forest to fuck her goddamn brains out like a wild animal, Amber dropped back down on her feet and spun away, leaving him speechless.

And hard as fuck.

Darnell sat there staring as that sashaying ass disappeared behind the bar. Then he glanced back at his friends.

Assholes.

Mack raised a brow, grinning. "Unavailable, huh?"

Madison smirked, and as she opened her mouth to sass him, he began to smile, silencing them both.

When he finally fucked that little firecracker, it was going to be hot as hell. Because he would.

# CHAPTER SIX

Finally, her shift was nearly over. Amber wanted to slump to the ground. Not because she was tired from working her shift but because she'd used up all her energy fighting her attraction to Darnell.

Being horny was exhausting, apparently.

Mack was gorgeous. So was Tristan, for that matter.

But Darnell and his annoyingly sexy smirks and powerful, dark body were hot as sin. And he knew it.

She might have won the first-round tonight, leaving him stunned, but she had a feeling she was going to pay for it. His scorching gaze had followed her all night, taking her already aroused core from needing to pleading.

*Damn him.*

She hated to admit it, but he was tempting her more than any other man had in recent times. She'd clenched her thighs together more times than she cared to remember and was in desperate need of release.

Her Black Stallion would be working hard when she finally got home. Thank goodness she had charged it.

"Go," Brad said. "It was busy this morning. I can handle things until the next shift starts in thirty."

She wasn't about to argue.

"You sure?" Amber asked, tossing her apron in the washing basket.

"Yes, go." He waved her off.

"Thanks, Brad," Amber said, reaching for her purse and jacket. "See you tomorrow."

He waved without looking up, and she headed for the exit. The castle would be quiet, aside from the skeleton staff that worked during daylight hours. Not that they saw it in the castle. That deadly stuff was blocked by the protective shields on the windows and gave them complete freedom to walk around risk-free. It was ten in the morning, and her usual routine was to have something to eat, relax, and be in bed by midday. Then she'd head to yoga or a run around six or seven in the evening when she woke.

Running around the castle grounds was a little more intimidating than any typical suburb. Here, she was surrounded by elite Moretti warriors.

Great eye candy, sure.

But they were also fast and powerful.

At least at yoga, she was with the girls who took their fitness a lot less seriously while still getting the benefit of walking through the training center and perusing all the biceps and abs.

God, she needed an orgasm.

"Daydreaming about me between your legs, hot stuff?" a voice said beside her as she stepped into the hallway.

Amber leaped into the air and squealed. "Jesus," she cried.

"I prefer God when you're screaming with pleasure, but I'll accept Jesus," Darnell purred, his hand going to the small of her back as he encouraged her to keep walking.

As her pounding heart began to right itself, she patted her chest. "What are you doing?"

"Walking you home?" he said as if that was quite normal and acceptable.

But it wasn't.

Amber stopped in her tracks, and because his powerful body kept moving and his enormous arm was still wrapped around her, Darnell bowled her over.

Amber went face-first toward the floor.

"Ah!" she cried.

Seconds before she kissed the carpet, she found herself scooped up into his arms.

*Gah!* This was getting worse.

"Now it looks like I'm carrying you home," Darnell said and kept walking.

What was wrong with him?

"For the love of God, can you not take a hint?" Amber groaned.

"Fuck," Darnell suddenly grunted, stopping.

"What?" she asked.

Then realized exactly what he was referring to. Oh, God. Her short skirt was doing absolutely nothing to cover her ass. Her bare, panty-free ass. But his hand...and his thumb... Holy fucking hell.

Her heart began to pound again, her body reacting in all the right ways as Darnell's eyes locked with hers.

"I'm not... I didn't mean—"

"I know," she breathed.

Fuck.

His hand slid from her buttocks to the space under her knees. The absence of his touch was almost painful. Before she could stop herself, she was biting her lip, closing her eyes, and letting out a groan.

"Amber, fuck."

"No."

"I can smell your arousal. I'm going to fucking explode," he growled deeply.

"Yeah, well, me too," Amber said, wriggling for him to put her down.

He didn't.

Darnell glanced around them and strode to a door. He kicked it open and as it shut behind them, slid her down his body.

She was well aware that this was the first time they'd been alone since they'd met. Both horny as hell and about to make a terrible decision.

"I can't—"

He gripped her hips. Her skirt still hitched up and her pussy throbbing.

"Hands on my shoulders," he growled as he lowered her to the ground. "Leg's apart, baby."

*Oh, God. I shouldn't.*

His huge hands took possession of her thighs, and she was spread open, barely balancing on her feet. His tongue reached out as she dug her fingers into his shoulders, staring down at the incredibly erotic scene before her.

Then he licked her blazing flesh.

"Fucking hell," he growled. "You taste like dark cherries."

Darnell's long tongue slid back in and took away her intelligence in one talented and delicious sweep. From that point on, she was a bubbling mess. Trembling, Amber clung to him as his thumb rubbed her clit while he sucked and lapped at the hot, wet flesh.

"Pull your tits out," he ordered from below her.

One hand reached and pushed up her top, and like a puppet, she moved her bra out of the way.

Like a wanton hussy.

"Pinch your nipple." Darnell sucked hard on her clit as she followed his instruction, and without warning, he shoved two fingers inside her.

*Holy hell.*

Like a furnace exploding, she threw her head back as scalding pleasure rushed through her.

"Oh fuck, fuck, fuck," Amber cried.

"Yes, baby. Come on my hand. Come on my face."

She felt like she was double orgasming. The more he fucked her pussy with his fingers, while he talked, the more her body shook with release. Then he was slowly lapping at her, drawing out the last of her pleasure as her legs began to wobble.

Darnell never let go of her as he pulled her clothes back into place. He stood, towering over her with his huge, dark, intimidating, sexy frame, staring at her as he cupped her face.

The was a wildness in his eyes that made her tremble.

"Teleport us back to your apartment," he ordered, his voice gruff with an intensity she wasn't expecting.

She thought he'd be smug.

"I—"

"Amber, do as I say," he said, tugging her against him. "I'm not walking you through the castle post-orgasm and having another male scent you."

Good point.

"You can let go. I can teleport there myself."

"Amber, don't push me," Darnell growled, and while a part of her wanted to be angry, there was a sexiness to his dominant and protective display that had her wanting more of his body.

His cock.

To be clear.

She wanted him inside her, claiming every inch of her body. So she would happily take him back to her place. Focusing, she teleported them inside her small room across the castle and almost preened when he took her chin in his fingers.

"Good girl. I knew you'd taste fucking delicious."

Then he lowered his mouth to hers and owned her mouth as she melted into him. Then he stepped back, releasing her, and vanished.

What the fuck?

# CHAPTER SEVEN

Darnell panted as he reached the castle. He took one look at it, then decided to go another round. He wasn't sure if running would cure him, but the twenty-five miles so far hadn't.

Nor had the hours of boxing in the training center.

Or yoga.

But he'd had to try something.

Okay fine, he'd been at yoga for five minutes before he got up and stormed out, muttering what a waste of fucking time that was.

Unprofessional? Yes.

Casey had yelled out for him to go get laid as he picked up his shoes and slammed the door, shooting her the bird through the window in response.

Fuck, what a dumbass move.

Not giving Casey the bird—she deserved that most days for being a smartass. He meant touching Amber.

Darnell had thought of nothing since. His brain cells had fried the moment he'd tasted her and felt the way she trembled and shuddered at his touch. And *my God*, the sound of her mewls.

There was no way he was going to forget those green eyes sizzling with greed as he sucked on her pussy. The last straw was the moment he'd claimed her mouth and felt a pull he hadn't been expecting.

One that unnerved him.

Warned him.

Amber was a gorgeous woman. But not someone he could mate with.

Fuck? Yes.

Mate? No.

Darnell had no idea if that sensation was a mating bond, but he wasn't sticking his cock in to find out. Which was why he'd gotten the fuck out of there.

Can you imagine it? *Hi, Mom and Dad. Meet Amber. She's a bartender. And my mate. Remember how much you loved working bar, Dad?*

Jesus, they'd lose their minds.

He had to find someone else to play with. Sexually. And keep his distance. He didn't believe there was only one vampire for someone and all that fated mates romantic shit.

Like humans, not all vampires believed there was only *one*. Especially those of the younger generations.

Maybe things had changed in the past few hundred years now that their population had grown to over ten million? For all they knew, there could be a handful of vampires you could bond with.

Things were definitely changing.

Now they had hybrid wolves. Okay, not exactly a natural occurrence, but look at Brayden and Willow. They had procreated at an unbelievable rate never heard of in their race. Was it because she was a modern-day human?

Evolution.

Change.

Or something.

But he wasn't going to lose his brain over a single woman like every other male he'd seen. And not one who would cause his parents to wonder if he'd lost his goddamn mind about his mate selection.

Worse, he would disappoint his father in ways he never wanted to think about. It would hurt him.

Darnell was aware that his father was compensating for the way his own father had behaved, but that didn't mean he would go out of his way to hurt him.

He would find another outlet. Another... pussy, which was just as greedy and tight.

Amber was a sexy and gorgeous vampire, but there were more fish in the sea. They just might not be quite as sweet and tasty as she was.

God, he could still taste her on this tongue.

If it wasn't for that damn bond tugging at his senses, he'd absolutely fuck her.

He wasn't exactly lacking in options. Females were attracted to his tall, bulky dark-skinned body. Since his promotion to one of the coveted SLC roles, the interest level had skyrocketed to an all-time high.

But his eyes had been on Amber.

Mostly her ass.

Then last night, he'd seen her tits, and fucking hell, they were perfection. Perfect peaks, mouthwatering nipples, and sized just right for his large hands.

Goddamn it.

*Just fuck her and get it over with.*

The risk was too great. His beliefs were only a theory and not one he was willing to risk. Once a bond was triggered, that was it. It was a lifelong commitment.

As far as he understood.

So all he had to do was keep his cock out of her.

Darnell might believe there was more than one mate for a vampire, but he didn't believe you could outthink biology. He'd seen vamps end their lives after losing their mate.

In time, he'd meet someone worthy that his father would be happy with. A scientist like Sage. A vet like Anna. A lawyer like Ginny, Callan's mate.

Amber was a bartender, and while he was sure there was way more to the sexy little vampire, bonding with her would be rubbing salt in his father's very deep and tender wound.

Which was why, even though his cock had been throbbing and Amber had been wet and ready, Darnell had teleported out of her apartment as fast as he could.

Tearing off his clothes, Darnell had turned on the shower back at his place and fisted his cock. He must have come in under ten seconds, stroking rapidly as his sperm shot down the drain.

But it hadn't been enough to extinguish the fire inside him.

Fuck, he was still having trouble taming the flame because of a redheaded firecracker who wouldn't get out of his head. The taste of her was still on his lips. The scent of her still in his senses, lingering and teasing him.

Once more, he found himself circling back to the castle. This time, he slowly jogged to the door leading directly into the training room.

It clicked open when he pressed his thumb on the scanner, and he stepped inside. The place was almost empty, save for a dozen vampires here and there. Darnell lifted his wrist and noticed the time.

*Shit.*

The king's announcement was being broadcast in less than twenty minutes.

This felt like a crucial point in their history. Never before had a Moretti king announced to their race that he was going to reveal their kind to human beings. Historically, they'd done everything in their power to remain unseen and unknown.

Now that ship had sailed.

Technology and science had allowed a number of humans to discover and capture them, and it was only a matter of time before there was a leak to or by the media.

This way, they could prepare the race.

Starting now.

Darnell jogged toward the changing rooms and tugged off his black top. A few vamps glanced at his ripped chest, and he winked at a couple of them.

Because, why not?

As he passed the female changing rooms, a body came flying out. He put on the brakes just in time and wished he hadn't.

*Damn it.*

"Oh!" the sexy voice cried as her head shot up.

Darnell's entire body flared to life, heat racing to every cell as she stood inches from him. His cock thickened, tenting his fucking shorts as he took in her wild red curls and the gray skater dress she wore with a pair of sexy as fuck Doc Martin's.

*Don't touch her.*

*Do not smell her.*

*Do not taste her.*

"Amber," Darnell purred, stepping closer despite his inner monologue, and his hands landed on her hips.

Like a fucking stupid magnet.

"What are you doing here?" she asked, her eyes roaming over his half-naked body. It was clear she was impacted. A lot. He smiled. "I mean, obviously, you work here. Just…what I meant was.. what are you doing…fuck. Can you just take your hands off me?"

No.

No, he really didn't want to.

He wanted to keep his hands on her and rub himself over her like a damn cat or something.

"I've just returned from a run." His voice came out rough.

*Great, now my brain cells have dissolved.*

They both stood there staring at each other, him holding her barely an inch from his body.

"People are staring at us. You should let me go," Amber whispered.

His eyes darted around them, and yeah, a few people were watching. "They'll just think we're fucking."

Vampires were highly sexual beings. While most of them kept this sort of thing out of the training space, it wasn't unusual to see a bit of flirting or displays of affection between mates.

Or lovers.

"We're not," Amber replied sharply.

"No."

"We didn't," she clarified.

"I know. I was there." He smirked.

She nodded again, then asked, "Why not?" Her chin lifted. "You've hounded me for weeks, then when you had me exactly where you wanted me, you left."

Her words reminded him why.

The bond.

Darnell dropped his hands and stepped away, letting out a long sigh.

Amber rolled her eyes. "Oh, I see. Get a taste of pussy and the challenge is over? You're one of those guys? I should have known."

"Okay, first, I didn't *hound* you. I pursued you. It's different. And secondly, stop. That isn't what happened," he said, his fists going to his hips.

Angry heat flushed her creamy skin. Darnell wanted to cup her cheek and suck those delicious pink lips inside his, tasting more of her. With one swift move, he could have her in his arms, wrapped around his waist, and his hand between her legs.

Panties or not, his fingers knew their way to her wet core.

She'd be panting his name in seconds.

Hell, he'd be fucking her against the changing room shower wall if he didn't give up this line of thought.

Tempting.

So goddamn tempting.

But again, woven through the rich chemistry buzzing between them was the bond, reaching out with a threatening tentacle trying to take hold. One that wouldn't let go once it did.

So he couldn't.

"Yes, it is. You know what, Darnell Miller? Thanks for the fucking orgasm, but keep away from me," Amber snapped.

Clenching his teeth, he forced himself not to say another word as she glared at him and slowly shook her head in disappointment.

"No. So not worth it," Amber added, then turned and walked away.

*What?*

*Worth what?*

"Amber, you—"

"Later, asshole," she said, flipping him the bird as she left him standing there.

Curiosity and desire fought for first place as he watched her leave. That skirt hugging her tight ass and those toned creamy legs determined as she stomped across the room.

*Groan.*

He wasn't sure keeping away from Amber was going to be as easy as he thought. Perhaps if they kept it oral. No penetration.

Because he'd been wrong. Amber Evans wasn't a firecracker; she was a bonfire.

Fuck, he was now running *really* late.

He teleported into the showers and was in the Great Hall with thirty seconds to spare.

# CHAPTER EIGHT

"God damn it," Nikolay cursed as he slid the diamond ring onto Elizabeth's finger, then tugged his phone out of his pocket.

"*Amore, mio.* It's beautif—"

"Nikolay Mikhailov," he answered, climbing off the bed where his new fiancée lay draped in a sheer green nightie.

Her breasts were now swollen, along with her belly. Pregnant with his child. And still, she opened to him so he could fuck her how he liked.

More gently than before, but no less frequent.

He no longer shared her. Nor did anyone get to lay an eye on her seductive figure. In some ways, he was furious with himself that others knew what the areola around her nipples looked like or the pucker of her ass.

Elizabeth belonged to him now.

She was the mother of his unborn child and would soon be Mrs. Mikhailov.

"Two of the vampires got loose," Alexi grunted into the phone. "The male was stronger than Kane once he fully recovered from the serum. He grabbed the blonde female. They're gone."

*Fuck.*

It had taken them days to find these vampires, and it wasn't pretty. As it turned out, the serum harmed humans too. So they'd been through a few bodies until they stumbled across a vampire.

And yeah, they had fangs.

Their only tactic was hunting at night because… well, vampires. Other than that, there were no identifying features they could tell.

Aside from one thing.

If Xander Tomassi's notes from BioZen were correct, it appeared that all vampires were quite the specimen. They had near-perfect bodies and were quite beautiful.

*Apologies to all the gorgeous humans out there waking up with a headache.*

The discovery was a bit of a kink in their plan. Knowing the serum could be used on their race and that they would be arming people could work against them.

Also, vampires could purchase it and arm themselves.

No doubt they would try.

Unless they were dumb.

Which he had no reason to believe they were.

Still, it wasn't deadly, and there were far worse weapons in the world. And hey, it might increase sales.

"Add more locks on the door," Nikolay ordered.

"It didn't stop him for a second," Alexi replied. "They busted through it like it was made of Lego."

*Jesus.*

He'd seen Kane and the other soldiers in action, but they were what BioZen had called hybrids. Half human and half vampire. Nikolay hadn't been sure if that meant they'd only have half the power.

An assumption but not necessarily a fact.

BioZen had held them, so it was fucking possible. There was still a lot of data to sieve through, and Elizabeth was helping him. Perhaps they would find something.

"And the others?"

"Still out of it," Alexi said. "If you plan to get video footage, I'd come down now."

He glanced back at Elizabeth, who was admiring her diamond.

"Stay there. I will have Demetri bring me," he grunted. "I will be there in twenty minutes. Set up the camera. And Alexi, ensure there is no way for anyone to identify our location."

"Yes, Pakhan."

Nikolay tossed the phone on the top of his dresser and fisted his cock. Elizabeth's eyes lifted to his.

"Spread your legs, fiancée."

"Are you leaving?" she asked, sliding down the pillows as her legs fell open.

Nikolay climbed onto the bed between them and palmed her thighs as he took in her wet pussy.

"Yes, but I have five minutes. Put your fingers inside yourself. The one with your ring. I want to see the diamond glittering alongside your juices."

"I want your cock. You promised me," she moaned, sliding her middle finger inside herself.

Fuck, she was the dirtiest, sexiest bitch he'd ever fucked. And now he'd have her forever.

He cupped one of her breasts, flicking the nipple with his thumb while he began to stroke his cock.

"Push me, Elizabeth, and you will only wait longer," Nikolay growled. "You know the rules."

Her hips lifted into the air, and she moaned, "But I'm going to be your wife."

He gripped her chin. "You belong to me. You have from the moment I took you. Now, as my wife, you will continue to pleasure me when and how I want."

He was stroking faster now, tempted to pull her hand away and thrust inside. But she needed to learn. Not much had changed.

He was still in charge.

"Nikolay," she panted, her eyes wide as his hand slid around her throat.

"Now come like a good girl. Come while I spill my seed onto your pussy."

Like a bolt of lightning, his demand worked. It always did. She played the victim, but he'd never seen a woman come as much as she did.

Her head flung back, and her moans filled the bedroom as he released her neck and sat up, stroking out his orgasm. Each stream marking her as her diamond-clad hand rubbed her clit.

Fucking beautiful.

He ripped her hand away and planted his face inside her pussy as she screamed. His tongue pressed inside her, his finger reaching under her and sliding deep inside her ass.

"Come again," he said, lifting his face for a split second, then going back in again. Tongue deep, one finger ass-fucking her, the other on her clit.

"Oh, my God," she screamed again.

Yes, he was.

She should remember that.

After he returned from making this video and sending it to the vampire king, he would get her mouth on his cock, and if she kept quiet, he would give her his cock.

Then he would work through more of the files and find out how to contain these vampires and control Vincent Moretti. His partners were getting antsy over the government crackdown on their businesses and distribution channels.

It had caused a lot of issues.

His response that they were a bunch of pussies and the reminder they were gangsters hadn't been received well.

But honestly, the fuck were they sitting around moaning for?

"I figure the officials who were working for you were doing so because you had something over them." he had said to mob boss Enzo Romano.

"Of course."

"Then double down. Jesus, do I need to tell you how to do your job or come down there myself and shoot a few cops?"

"If you want to start a war, go right ahead, Mikhailov," Enzo had snarled. "I'll remind you of the terms of these agreements. The products have a rite of passage in my city. You do not."

He would let that go.

After all, he'd been in NYC for months with only the odd, very mild threat. He wouldn't return the same courtesy in Russia.

"When are you returning home?" Enzo had asked.

"When I fucking feel like it. Ensure security is tight in your manufacturing plant. We need to control the cops and get these products made and distributed to warehouses worldwide."

The slowdown of production was a problem. It was halting his plans. So far, they only had enough serum to arm the gangs. Not to begin selling. And there was no point in shocking the world until he had a product available.

Supply and demand and all that.

The government contacts he had around the world knew nothing. He'd kept his questions vague, but they didn't know why there was a global crackdown.

They thought it was drugs.

This action had full support from the White House, Number 10 Downing Street, the Kremlin, Parliament Hill, etc., so Nikolay assumed the world leaders were aware of the existence of vampires.

And the serum.

"What aren't you telling us, Mikhailov?" Romano had asked.

A lot.

# CHAPTER NINE

$A$mber knew she had no one to blame but herself.

Or maybe her hormones.

Actually, she wasn't beyond blaming her vagina and claiming it had a mind of its own because it seemed like it when she was around Darnell.

One second after nearly plowing into the big vampire *again,* her lady parts had sat up and started dancing. Like an addict. One orgasm, and she could almost hear it chanting *more more more.*

Because, yes, the man had skills with his mouth.

Oh, and those thick fingers. Jesus, mother of Mary, he knew what to do with them. It was like he had a map of her body and knew all the corners to take.

Well, too bad it wasn't happening again.

How dare he just disappear?

It wasn't even about leaving her in a heightened state of arousal; it had been rude.

Like he'd tapped Amber Evans and now she was no longer a challenge. She'd come across this sort of thing before. The more she said no to a male's advances, the more interested they were. Vampire or human.

Just another notch on their bedposts.

Still, it was weird he gave up before actually penetrating her. Maybe he hadn't been that interested after all?

It shouldn't bother her so much. It wasn't like Darnell was her mate. But his abrupt departure had felt a lot like being abandoned.

Yes, she'd been triggered.

Psychology 101.

Darnell had taken her back to her childhood pain of being abandoned by her parents. Her mom might have died, but she read once that losing a parent, whether they packed a bag and walked out or died of a terrible disease, was the same thing. Children's minds experienced both situations as abandonment.

Annoying, really.

Amber didn't want to feel anything about Darnell. Why she cared so much she didn't know. But she did. Right now, she wanted to slap his handsome face and tell him he couldn't shove his tongue in her pussy, make her scream and then leave.

But he had.

Did he not, for a second, wonder how she felt standing there in her apartment alone, wet from his mouth and her juices and trembling with unmet need?

Her core was primed and ready for his cock. Amber had felt how thick and hard he was.

So why the hell had he disappeared?

She might never get an answer, but if she'd had any doubt about whether he meant to leave, Darnell had cleared that up when they bumped into each other in the training room.

*No, we're not fucking.*

No. They. Were. Not.

And never would.

Amber had slipped off the wagon, so to speak, and now she was going to focus on building her life and following her dreams.

If Darnell so much as winked at her, she would toss a drink over his head.

It was time to get a career plan and focus on growing her friendships. The girls were right. Ginny was awesome. Tonight, before she'd bumped into Darnell, they'd shared a meal while the boys, Casey, and Charlotte were doing warrior stuff, as Madison called it.

Then—*WOW*—they had asked if she wanted to meet Princess Willow and baby Isabella.

*Yes,* was the answer.

So, they had wandered across the castle to the royal wing and waited to be led through what seemed like ten layers of tough security. Then, finally, Amber got to meet the princess.

"Come on in, ladies," Willow said, bouncing Isabella on her chest.

"I hope you don't mind us visiting," Anna said, "I wanted to introduce you to a couple of new faces."

"Virginia, right?" Brianna asked, jumping up from the sofa. "You're Callan's mate."

"Yes, it's a pleasure to meet you both. And please, call me Ginny."

"And this is Amber," Madison said, nudging her shoulder. "Darnell's favorite barmaid."

"The new SLC?" Willow asked, handing the baby to Madison.

"Oh, she's so gorgeous," Amber said, leaning over to gaze into her round face. And diverting the conversation from Darnell. "Those blue eyes. Wow."

"Just like her daddy." Willow preened. "And look at all her dark hair."

Madison had fluffed it with her fingers and made soft baby noises. "Who's a beautiful little princess? Are you going to grow up to be a little warrior?"

"I think we're all just hoping Isabella is allowed out to see the night sky before her eighteenth birthday." Brianna snorted.

Willow had let out a laugh as she sat on one of the dark tan sofas. They all followed suit, finding a seat in the large living room.

"Why is she not allowed out?" Amber asked, frowning.

"Because her father is the most overprotective, powerful vampire in the world. Isn't that right, sweetheart?" Brianna cooed from Madison's other side, dropping a kiss on Isabella's forehead.

The room went quiet, and Amber glanced around nervously.

Brianna looked up and rolled her eyes. "Yeah, yeah, I know."

Madison snorted.

"Brianna is Craig's mate. Have you met him?" Willow asked Amber.

She shook her head. "Not officially, although I have seen him one time. He came marching in, grabbed someone, and marched out. He's kind of scary."

Brianna giggled.

"That sounds like him. Ever wondered what humans were like in the caveman years? Exhibit A." The princess laughed.

"Hey!" Brianna cried.

"Fight me. You know it's true." Willow shrugged.

Amber had found herself grinning as the two women bantered. She knew they'd previously been humans and not that long ago. Now here they were, Moretti royalty. What an incredible story of changing your life.

Which gave her hope.

If you had a vision and belief in yourself, Amber believed anything was possible. She hadn't survived so far to give up now. She was determined to make something of herself.

It didn't pass her by that she was also sitting in the royal wing, making friends with these amazing females.

Yet again, Amber sensed she'd found her place and was determined not to let anyone sabotage it.

Certainly not a gorgeous, dark-skinned warrior.

She should never have let her guard down last night. Only to have him disappear on her.

Jesus, what a douche canoe.

"Fine, but I love my caveman." Brianna had shrugged. "And back to the protective daddy thing. I am not looking forward to having our own offspring. It's a daily struggle to convince Craig that I'm safe, let alone a little mini-me."

"We'll need to get your special Craig restraints made when you get pregnant." Willow nodded.

"Ooh, kinky." Brianna and Anna giggled.

"Not everything is about sex, Bri," Willow replied.

"Yes, it is," they all cried, laughing.

Amber settled into the cushions as talk of babies and mates continued. Maybe she'd meet her mate working for the Moretti's here in Maine? It was possible. She might even have a baby of her own bouncing on her lap one day.

Amber knew who it wouldn't be.

And she wasn't thinking about him.

Even though she was a little hurt and angry with Darnell, it was important to remember he was a part of this exclusive group, so she had to keep things civil between them.

Civil yet not sexual.

Amber acknowledged she had let her body take control this morning in a weak moment—one she couldn't regret because what a damn orgasm—but it wouldn't happen again.

In saying that, she also didn't regret calling him an asshole.

But Darnell was an important member of this social group and the king's army.

If this were the place she could finally feel at home and build relationships with genuinely good people, she'd put up with him until some other female grabbed his attention.

Then he would leave her alone.

Meantime, Amber wasn't going to let his charm or hot body distract her. Nor could she keep bantering with him. Others were picking up on their sexual chemistry, and that had to end.

This was so important to her.

Not many people could understand the loneliness she'd endured during her life. Something she still felt.

You could be surrounded by people and still feel desperately alone.

Even as an adult.

Amber wanted a family.

She might have lost her parents, but she could build a family of people she cared about—a found family, as they were called—and nothing would get in the way of her doing that.

"Did someone forget to invite us to the party?" a beautiful, regal voice said from behind her.

When Amber had turned and saw Kate Moretti, the Queen, standing there, she nearly lost her damn mind.

Then Brayden and the king appeared.

*Holy shit.*

"Oh, is it time already?" Willow asked.

"Yes. Sorry, ladies. You might want to prepare for Vincent's speech in the Great Hall," Brayden said, lifting Isabella into his arms.

Amber nearly swooned, watching the huge warrior holding the beautiful princess cocooned in his arms. As if knowing he was her daddy, Isabella snuggled into his chest.

It nearly brought tears to her eyes.

"Ugh, gets me every time," Willow said, walking over to them as Brayden lifted his free arm for her to slip under. "So glad I went home with you that night."

His glowering stare sent a flush through Amber, even if his eyes were on Willow. "You had no choice, mate."

"That's what you think." The princess smirked, but nobody could mistake the love in their eyes.

It was so intense, it was almost uncomfortable.

"Blah, blah. Can we please get prepared," Vincent mumbled, and Amber's mouth parted in surprise.

"Vincent," Kate chastised.

Amber snorted.

Then.

The.

King.

Grinned.

At.

Her.

*Holy hell.*

Which was why, after that mind-blowing moment, as Amber had raced back to the training room to retrieve her phone, she hadn't been paying attention.

Then she'd run into Darnell.

Again.

Now, she slipped into the Great Hall and found a seat at the back of the room.

Alone.

# CHAPTER TEN

"My fellow vampires," the king began, and a shiver ran up Darnell's spine.

Vincent, Kate, Brayden, and Willow were all seated on gold and black thrones on the stage, and it was a rare and powerful image.

Darnell glanced around, spotting Sage and Ari in the front row alongside Craig, Brianna, and several other close friends of the royal family.

Brianna held Isabella, who was nodding off in her arms. Sage held some kind of action figure as Lucas Moretti chewed its head off while sitting on her knee.

The children's presence out in public like this was rare. The royal family guarded their young like a dragon did its gold.

Having both Princess Isabella and Prince Lucas present for this occasion spoke of its historical importance.

It was the first step in preparing the vampire race for coming out, so to speak. To humans.

They'd feared this moment all their lives. Their parents had warned them about it and taught them how to remain hidden and how to react if they were ever exposed.

It was almost in their DNA to hide.

Working with the Moretti's in the castle had given Darnell a freedom he'd never known growing up. Heck, most vampires would never know it. There, they could be who they were without any concern. Show a fang, vamp speed across the room, lift a two-hundred-pound vampire in the air. No problem.

The only thing frowned upon was teleporting here and there. It was a hazard. The castle was huge, but thousands worked and lived there.

Today was the first step in all that changing.

Very few people in the room and only a handful outside knew what the king was about to announce.

Rumors had been flying over the past six hours since the notice of the broadcast went out. Vampires from all around the world would be tuning in.

Darnell felt privileged to be in his position and know what was happening, but with that came a heavy responsibility.

He'd had moments lying on his bed during the day thinking *what the fuck* and wondering how this would all play out. But he also had something many of the other ten million vampires on earth didn't.

Power.

As a warrior, he was trained to defend himself *and* he was close to the royal family. To some degree, he had influence, or at least a voice to express his concerns or ideas.

Sometimes, that's all people wanted. To be heard. Especially when they were scared. And there would be many who were very scared after today.

They had reason to be.

There would be chaos and confusion among their race, and no one knew how the humans would react.

Darnell didn't have high hopes it would be positive. Hell, they'd already seen glimpses of their ugly natures with Anna and Callan being kidnapped and experimented on by BioZen in the not-so-distant past.

Yet again, there were threats and news of missing vampires.

Assholes.

As long as that fucking serum was in their enemies' hands, they all remained in danger.

"Tonight, I speak to you from the Moretti Castle in Maine alongside my family," Vincent continued. "My father, King Francis, and my grandfather, King Gio, all anticipated making this speech one day. Neither of them ever did. I have long suspected that I would be the one. With modern technology, where every human on the planet carries a camera in their pockets, and scientific advances, it was inevitable we could no longer remain hidden in plain sight."

Around him, vampires glanced at one another, stiffened, and shifted in their seats.

Heavy dread rolled through Darnell.

"For a while now, I have been working with a small group of world leaders to prepare humanity to learn about our race. Yes, that's right. Human leaders. They have visited my home, they have met vampires and dined at my table."

Whispers filled the room.

Vincent lifted a hand, and silence ensued.

"So let me get straight to the point," Vincent said, taking Kate's hand. Willow grabbed Brayden's, and he squeezed her fingers. "I will soon announce our existence to humanity."

The king stopped talking as the noise in the Great Hall erupted.

There was no point in trying to contain it. Even on the other side of screens worldwide, people would be reacting. Not listening.

After a long moment, Vincent continued. "Your fears are founded. We have not had enough time. However, circumstances beyond my control have forced my hand. I believe it is in our best interest to reveal ourselves, which is why I am speaking with you today."

*Jesus.*

*Holy shit, I can't believe he's doing this.*

*No, fuck.*

*This is bad.*

*Fuck, I need to ring my parents.*

Vincent's voice boomed across the hall. "I understand your panic, so let me keep sharing. What we hoped to prepare was a set of guidelines, laws, and processes to guide us all and reassure both races as we announced our existence. The fact we have done so for fifteen hundred years won't be lost to many of you, but we have made our own laws within them without their input."

Good point.

They had silently respected most human laws, and it worked. At least, Darnell thought it did.

"That won't fly once we are known, I understand that. They will fear us and want to control us. I won't let that happen," Vincent continued.

Darnell wondered how much knowledge the king intended to share about the strength their bodies wielded. Or their minds. If humans stopped for a second to consider this and how they'd lived peacefully among them despite their abilities, it might give them pause.

There was no fucking way humanity could be trusted with the same. They were far too unstable and destructive at this point in their evolution.

Humans were the worst predators on the planet by far.

"This decision has not been made lightly or without consideration. At the bottom of your screen, you will see free calling numbers and links to resources with answers to your questions. Teams of people are ready to support you.

Our warriors are ready to defend our race," Vincent continued.

Darnell glanced around at the pale faces. Many turning to their friends or coworkers looking for reassurance.

*Where is Amber?*

She might be angry with him, and he might be trying to stay away, but thoughts of her had been simmering in the back of his mind the entire time.

He'd just been trying to fight it.

Now, seeing how nervous the tough warriors looked, Darnell was worried about her.

"Remember who you are. You each have Moretti blood in your DNA," Vincent said, and Darnell was sure he sat up straighter. "More powerful than humans, with abilities they do not have."

Very true.

"We are not identifiable out on the streets, so please do not become victims. Look out for each other, reach out for help, and know that I will do everything in my power to ensure this world respects and honors every single one of you."

A bold statement but a diplomatic one.

Humans don't even respect their own race. Look at all the damn wars.

Still, words were important in keeping people calm, and that was what the king was doing now. Informing. Calming. Preparing.

"I have one last request. You have remained hidden all your lives. No human alive is aware of our ability to telepath or teleport. These skills could save your life," Vincent said.

Not if you were shot with the serum, but Darnell knew they weren't sharing that little nugget of information.

"Sharing blood so you can telepath with people outside your intimate circles and family members isn't typical for us, I know, but I would encourage you to do this now. It will allow us to communicate more broadly with one another. This is not a dictate but a recommendation."

Murmurs of agreement sounded in the Great Hall, and he watched the king survey the crowd.

It was a bold request.

Vampires had to ingest another's blood and share their own to be able to telepath with another. Once done, it was permanent. However it wasn't done lightly. Not for any reason other than it was intimate. Not quite the same as kissing, for example, but more so than giving out your phone number.

God, he sucked at analogies.

Let's just say blood sharing could be sexual. With someone you were attracted to, it heightened the experience. So it had those connotations. With family members, you did it when you were young, much like cuddling. It wasn't sexual.

It had been part of the induction when he'd been sworn in as an SLC. But as far as he knew, the only ones who could telepath with Vincent were the prince and his queen.

Darnell wondered if that was going to change.

His eyes drifted further around the vast space, seeking the female he couldn't stop thinking about. She was here. He could... *fuck*.

He could sense her.

As if just thinking about her, he felt the tug in his chest like an invisible wire.

"To answer some of the many questions you will have, my team has created a video, which will be available after this. Let me leave you with this quote from Carl Sagan. 'The universe is not required to be in perfect harmony with human ambition.'" Vincent stared into the camera in front of him for a long moment. "Goodnight."

*Wow.*

Large screens around the Great Room lit up with the video's opening screen.

"Dude, did you know?" one of his team asked.

"Yes." Darnell nodded at the half-dozen faces of his team staring at him. "Watch the video, and I can answer your questions after."

"Of course he did. He's an SLC," someone from behind muttered.

"Fuck, man. This is insane," another said as the audio kicked in.

It was going to be a long night.

And a long road ahead.

THE VIDEO WAS short. Twelve minutes. It gave answers to all the questions anyone could imagine, but Darnell knew people would want to talk it out. Better they did it here with support than go off alone and freak out.

"Let's find a spot to chat," he said to his team, and stood watching the room begin to empty.

Kind of.

Vampires were hovering, looking stunned and unsure of what to do next.

That's where the SLCs stepped in. Darnell watched his colleagues herd their teams into corners and different spots. Some headed out the main doors while Kurt perched on a table, and a few dozen vamps circled around him.

Lance had pushed open a side exit and headed outside.

Where the fuck was Amber?

Tristan nodded at him across a handful of people, and an idea came to him.

"Follow me," he said to his crew and wandered over to his buddy. "You want to tag team this? Head to Max Bar and get some beers?"

"Fuck, yes." Tristan slapped him on the shoulder, then called to his team, "Let's go, gang."

As they walked through the huge entrance of the castle, he spotted the gray skater dress he'd had his hands on an hour ago. Amber's determined expression was gone, and she looked pale and lost.

His chest tightened.

*Goddamn it.*

He hated seeing her like that. The pull to go to her and wrap her in his arms was palpable.

"Leave her," Tristan said under his breath. "Not today."

Darnell frowned. "What?"

"Don't fuck with her today, man. Not after that."

"Dude. I was going to see if she was okay," he said. "Maybe..."

"You want to invite her to join us?" Tris asked.

"Yeah..." Darnell said, glancing over his shoulder. "Yeah, fuck. Dumb idea."

He should stay away.

She wanted nothing to do with him.

But tonight wasn't the time to be thinking about such things. Like all of them, Amber needed support. As far as he was aware, she had no one in the castle except the females, who would be with their mates.

She stood alone, looking like a lost sheep, and it was fucking killing him.

Tristan slowed. "Maybe not. Come on."

"Go on ahead. We'll meet you there in a couple of minutes." Darnell slapped a couple of his warriors on the shoulder, and they continued toward the bar.

He and Tristan crossed the space to where Amber stood, scrolling on her phone.

"Hey," he said.

Her head shot up. Looking between the two of them, she gave them a wonky smile. "Oh, hey."

Darnell saw the fear and uncertainty in her eyes. He crossed his arms to stop from reaching for her and telling her everything was going to be okay.

Which was a lie.

It probably wouldn't be.

"You okay, Amber?" Tristan asked.

*Hey, that's my line.*

She laughed uncomfortably, then thumbed over her shoulder. "I mean, as much as any of us. I was just—"

No, she wasn't.

"We're heading to Max Bar. Come with us?" Darnell asked. Regardless of what had happened between them, he wanted to ensure she was supported.

Which didn't make him a saint.

Or responsible for her because he'd had his mouth on her pussy this morning.

*If it's the damn mating bond...*

Whatever it was, he wasn't leaving her alone at a time like this. He would fight the bond and keep his distance tomorrow.

"Not in the mood for partying, guys. I have a day off, so I might head out for a run." Amber shrugged.

She was a loner.

He'd noticed how independent she was since arriving at the castle, but watching her decline their support and choose to deal with her fear alone spoke of a life of solitude on a whole other level.

One that might not have been of her choosing.

Like he was a damn shrink now.

What she didn't know about him was he didn't give up easily.

"No partying. We're doing a session with our teams. Q&A-type thing. You might want to listen in. Pink lemonade on me," Darnell said, nudging his chin down the hallway to the bar.

"Come on," Tristan encouraged.

Darnell shrugged as Amber narrowed her eyes at him in question. "Can't promise I won't have you doing push-ups, but we want to make sure you're okay."

"Oh," she replied, glancing down at her phone.

"Because that's what friends do," Darnell added to clarify he wasn't doing this to hit on her.

The boundary would be helpful in keeping the damn bond at bay. Hopefully.

Although even now, he wanted to slip her hand in his.

"Fine," she said, pocketing her phone into her dress pocket. "But no pushups. And I want wedges."

"She fights tough. We should recruit her," Tristan said, looping an arm around Amber's shoulder.

Then he shot Darnell a wink and walked off with her.

*Not mine.*

Yeah, she fucking was.

He had to find a way around this because there was no way he could abandon her right now.

But he also wouldn't bond with her and hurt his father.

# CHAPTER ELEVEN

*We just want to make sure you're okay. Because that's what friends do.* Amber had nearly burst into tears when Darnell had said those words to her.

She'd been standing aimlessly at the entrance of the castle, wondering what the hell to do. The king's announcement had floored her. She had no one to call, no one she could talk things through with.

Sure, she'd made friends in the castle, but no one she was close enough to call on yet. After all, they were all dealing with this like she was. In any case, they'd be with their mates.

Leaving her… alone.

Like always.

Amber wasn't having a pity party. She was simply aware of the emptiness of her life.

Of all the people to offer support, she wasn't expecting it to be Darnell. She could almost feel his eyes burning into her back as Tristan walked down the corridor with his thick, muscular arm wrapped around her.

Oh, and a bunch of females were shooting them questioning glances.

"They're going to start a rumor." She smiled up at Tristan."

"Let them." He winked.

"Okay, I don't think she's going to run away." Darnell tugged his arm off her shoulders.

Amber fought a giggle. Was he jealous?

"She might. Maybe we should tie her up," Tristan said.

A shot of arousal spread through her body as her eyes collided with Darnell's.

They both looked away.

"Don't say shit like that, man," Darnell groaned, nudging his friend through the doors and into the bar.

Tristan chuckled, and right before her eyes, the two playful warriors turned into completely different people as they faced their teams.

"Right, let's push these tables together and gather around," Darnell instructed the lieutenants.

Amber found herself in awe of the senior warrior, a shiver running through her at the power in his voice.

Damn, he was sexy.

"Ya'll know Amber. She works behind the bar and is our special guest for a few hours," Darnell said, then glanced down at her and winked. "Amber, this is…everyone."

She shook her head at him, then took in all the new and familiar faces staring back at her. She felt tiny standing beside Darnell and Tristan. Because she was. They had a good foot on her and way more pounds.

Of muscle.

There was no sign of fat on either of them.

"Hey," she said. "What an insane moment, huh? Please ask all the dumb questions so I don't have to."

"No dumb questions here," Tristan said.

"Bazza will ask them, don't worry," one vampire said.

"Fuck off," Bazza said, flipping him the bird.

Next minute, Darnell was dragging a stool over and lifting her onto it. Like she was a prop.

*Jesus.* The power in his arms.

"Right. Hit us with it. Tris and I will tag team the answers," Darnell said, pointing at one of the vamps in the back. "Jeremy. Go."

"When is the king going to do the big reveal?" Jeremy asked.

"There is no confirmed date. Next question," Tristan said and pointed at another vampire.

Darnell dipped his eyes to her, and despite knowing everyone was watching them when their eyes connected, the world around them disappeared.

*You okay?* he mouthed.

Amber nodded gratefully and added a small smile. His eyes softened for a moment, sending a warm flush through her. Then he turned his attention back to the room.

Wow.

What would it feel like to be the special woman in his life? Because for a second, she felt like she was and almost swooned.

Who the hell swooned in the twenty-first century?

Certainly not her.

But all his cheekiness and power had dissipated for that single moment, and she'd felt important, like she mattered, for the first time since her parents had died.

It was so overwhelming she almost wanted to cry.

To feel loved and wanted—it felt like it was so unattainable for so long—but Darnell had given her hope. Not with him. He had been clear he wasn't interested. Perhaps that was his way of showing his friends he cared.

Either way, it had slipped past her barriers and struck her heart with such rich emotion, Amber was floored.

And distracted.

She had forgotten to pay attention to all the questions. She tuned back in.

"Bazza, just ask," Darnell ordered as if the moment between them hadn't happened. As if he'd felt nothing.

Which was okay. It had been special to her.

And yet... as he stood close to her, she felt this live spark sizzling between them. She knew it was him because, on her other side, Tristan was rolling up his sleeves—and yes, hot damn forearms—but no sizzle.

"Fine. Here's my question. Will we be rounded up like animals?" Bazza asked, and everyone groaned. But Amber saw concern on their faces. It was something all of them had been warned about growing up.

So it wasn't a dumb question at all.

"We'll go to war if they attempt it," Darnell replied. "As the king said, he's already in talks with global leaders, and there is a common agreement is in place to integrate our race with humans."

"Remember, you are warriors. It will be our job to defend our race if that happens," Tristan shared.

That sounded promising.

"But some will want to. You have to know that," someone said.

"Yes. But it doesn't mean we or the human leaders will allow it. The media will lose their minds with fear-mongering—we all know that's how they make money. Clicks. So for a time, we will have to stand strong and let the initial reaction pass," Darnell said. "Another thing to remember is that humans will be as scared as we are. Perhaps more so."

That was true.

What with all their books and movies, their heads were already filled with nonsense. And some truths. But they wouldn't know fact from fiction up front. It was the initial reaction they were all afraid of.

Amber was glad her mom wasn't alive to see this. She had always been very afraid. Ironically, it was humans who had been the cause of her death.

Assholes.

"There are more of them than us. Eight fucking billion. To our ten million," Jeremy said.

"True, but we can teleport. We cannot be held against our will," Darnell said firmly.

"Tungsten," a female warrior pointed out.

"Seen any Tungsten prisons lately?" Tristan asked. "Let me get you a quote. It isn't cheap to build one."

"Wars aren't cheap, but humans seem to find the money to fund them when threatened," the warrior replied.

That's for sure. And seemed to profit from them. The war machine was a business, so they needed to consider all these things.

Amber wondered what that meant for her.

Would the SLCs move around the world, taking her friends? At times like these, being alone felt very vulnerable.

What if the royal family were evacuated?

Often, they would close the castles down, like they had the Italian one recently, keeping them maintained with skeleton staff.

Meaning she would be out of a job.

She didn't want to go back to a job in the human world. The freedom working here gave her was amazing. And the friendships she was building would fade away.

Amber chewed her bottom lip, feeling herself slipping into the worst-case scenario.

"All good points," Darnell responded. "The truth is, we don't know how they will react, but I think it's safe to say we will see every reaction we can conceive of. Our job will be to remain calm, not react, and prove we are not a threat."

"Proven by the fifteen hundred years we've existed already," Jeremy said, shaking his head.

Amber let out a sigh, and Darnell's hand shot out to her thigh. Shocked, she glanced up at him, and he briskly removed his hand.

As if it had been an accident.

"I'll, um, I'll go get those pink lemonades," she said, slipping off the stool.

What the hell was that?

AMBER WENT BEHIND the bar and pulled out a few glasses, scooping some ice into each. She grabbed the soda gun and filled them with lemonade right to the top.

Then she poured in a little raspberry.

And added a slice of lime and recycled paper straws.

Like she was on automatic robot barmaid mode.

*What the hell was that?*

Maybe she was overthinking, but that knee touch? It had been… something.

Amber filled a tray with the glasses, walked around the bar, and came to a screaming halt.

"I wanted to explain," Darnell said, holding up his hands and looking deathly serious.

"I have drinks," she said at the same time.

He placed the tray on the counter, cupped her elbow, and guided her into a dark corner at the edge of the bar.

"What's going on?" Amber asked, pretending she didn't have a clue what could be wrong.

I mean, it's not like it was the first time he'd touched her. It was more the way he'd done it. Like he was concerned. Like he was consoling her.

Like an automatic response to a mate.

And it had freaked them both out.

"I shouldn't have touched you," Darnell said, looking genuinely apologetic. This was a different man from the one who'd been flirting with her for weeks.

"Before or yesterday?" she asked, curious how he would answer.

He stared at her for a moment. "What answer would you like?"

*Oh.*

She wasn't expecting that.

In some ways, it was a little offensive, but there was a connection between them they were both trying to avoid. Giving him the benefit of the doubt, Amber pushed away her irritation and remembered that this male had come to her rescue earlier.

Today was a difficult time for all of them, and Darnell was a protector. She might be reading too much into it.

Probably.

How pathetic. She was so sad and lonely that she thought this man who had *licked and left* her this morning cared for her more than he was admitting.

Good one.

Amber inwardly shook her head at herself.

Pathetic.

However, Darnell had proven to be a kind, thoughtful male over the past few hours, and she didn't have many people who cared about her. When he and Tristan had invited her to join, she nearly cried.

It was a kindness.

Nothing more.

They both needed to put this awkwardness between them aside and be friends. Wasn't that what she'd been planning before the king had thrown them all a curve ball today?

Amber had seen beyond his smirking flirtation to a male who was worthy, a good leader, and a caring friend. She might end up being one of them.

"Neither," Amber said, and it was Darnell's turn to frown. She placed a hand on his forearm. "Listen, I want to thank you for including me tonight. I'm new here. I don't know anyone, and this is all kind of scary." She wrapped her arms around herself. "So let's forget about all the other stuff."

"I can't forget it, Amber. I don't want to forget it," he said thickly.

Oh. He'd surprised her again, and this time, he was looking at her in a way that sent a tingle right through her.

"No, well, you know," she almost whispered.

"I don't. That's the fucking thing. I don't know why I reached for you just now." He ran a hand over his short, dark hair. "I'm really trying hard here, Amber."

*Don't jump to conclusions.*

Sexual attraction didn't mean this was anything more than it was.

Also, he'd just admitted he was trying, which meant he didn't want her as anything more than a friend.

She decided to help him out and shot him a kind smile. "I think you're a good guy. Even if you don't want anyone knowing."

"I'm not that good," he muttered, doing another sweep of his head, looking flustered by this entire conversation.

"I didn't say you were a saint." She gave him a lopsided smile.

The way he'd made her come with his mouth? Hell, no. The man was no saint.

"Good. Don't confuse me with someone wearing a halo. I still want to fuck you, Amber." Flames licked at the edges of those deep blue eyes, making the lascivious thoughts in his mind very clear.

*Not helping.*

He was confusing the hell out of her, but she needed to keep them on track.

"All I was saying was I think you're just a good friend. I could do with one of those," she admitted, revealing a slither of vulnerability.

Her eyes dipped, and Darnell stepped closer, lifting his hand to tuck a lock of hair behind her ear. "I'm your friend, Amber,"

Her hand lifted before she knew what she was doing, and her fingers were suddenly interlinked with his as he ran them across her cheekbone.

His hooded gaze locked with hers. "Problem is, I can't seem to keep my hands off you," he rasped.

*Oh, God.*

Arousal flooded Amber's sex as her heart pounded. Mesmerized by the sexual power rolling off this enormous warrior, her mouth parted. Darnell's plump lips lowered to hers…

"Hey, motherfuckers!" Casey called, jolting them out of the moment. "Who's ready to party?"

"There you are," Charlotte added, stepping into the shadows as she and Darnell parted like two kids caught doing something wrong.

Were they?

"I made pink lemonades," Amber said, turning to point at her tray.

"Babe, unless you're adding tequila to that shit, we need something far stronger after today," Casey said. "The girls are headed into town. Coming?"

*They came for her?*

"She's coming." Charlotte smirked as Maddison and Anna appeared behind them.

"I thought you'd all be with your guys?" Amber asked, glancing from face to face.

"Nah," Casey said, tugging her away from Darnell. "They're busy tonight with their teams. As he should be."

Amber turned and saw the last embers fading from Darnell's eyes as he collected himself.

"I'm taking a break." His voice was still rough. Then his gaze dropped to hers. "You can stay with us."

Amber bit her lip.

She wanted to.

Too much.

Which was why she had to leave.

"Thanks. I think I could do with some tequila, so I'll catch up later, friend."

"You bet," Darnell replied. "Friend."

The last word was a growl.

"Okay, I feel like we missed something big here," Anna said as they walked out of the bar.

"Darnell was going to kiss her, and I intervened," Charlotte said.

Amber gasped. "You saw that?

Charlotte stopped them from kissing. Why would she do that? Maybe it was for the best. No, it was. But she had wanted him to kiss her. Hell, she wanted to turn around, run back, and throw herself at his enormous, broad chest.

He'd catch her.

And maybe he'd drag her back to his room and...

*I still want to fuck you.*

Yeah, that.

Which meant that Char had saved them from going down the wrong path once more. Because clearly they were both terrible at this friend's thing.

"Char!" Maddison complained.

"I'm Team Damber," Anna said. "So, yeah, why?"

"Meh. I think she can do better." Casey shrugged.

"Isn't he like one of your best friends?" Amber asked, confused.

"Yes. He's a good friend, but not sure I want any of my friends fucking him," Casey said, running her eyes up and down Amber's body. "You want to get changed?"

Amber glanced down. She was still wearing her skater dress. "Yes. Wait. Why not?"

And also, she'd called her a friend.

Casey wasn't someone who let people into her life easily. Anyone could see that.

So Amber felt a little warmth in her chest.

But still, it was weird Casey had said that about her friend. The Darnell that Amber had seen today was a good male. Surely his friends knew that.

"He's a scoundrel. A playboy. A fuck boy. You seem like someone who wants more than that." Casey narrowed her eyes. "Darnell is the guy you want as your friend. Or saving your ass out in the field. That's it."

Okay, so she did know him.

And Amber's instincts were right. It was better to remain his friend. She needed to think of him as a big brother… Yeah, nah. That was never going to happen.

She was very, very attracted to him, and it would take a while to get past that.

"What she said." Charlotte nodded. "Let's go via your place and meet Ginny out front. She's organizing one of the SUVs."

Anna looped her arm through Amber's and leaned in, whispering, "I'm still Team Damber. Ben kidnapped me when we met, and I fell in love with him."

"He, what?" Amber giggled.

"Yup. But have you seen his dimples?" Anna shrugged, winking at her.

"Okay, sure, you have a point. But kidnapping?"

"Long story. I'll tell you all about it one day. But let's stay focused on his dimples and blue eyes." She giggled. "I swear, Amber, you have to look beyond their rascal history and let them show you who they are."

Well, he'd done that.

Once, which left her panting and wanting. Then today, that he could be a good friend. She knew which one she should choose.

Unfortunately, her body was in complete disagreement.

# CHAPTER TWELVE

"Jesus, that was intense." Craig flopped down on the sofa, pulling Brianna onto his lap, where she nestled into his chest.

Brayden ran his hand up and down Isabella's tiny back and realized he was making little cooing noises.

Willow, who was standing next to him, glanced up. "I love you," she said, resting her head on his arm.

Was there a word more powerful than love? Because that's how he felt about his mate and their baby princess.

He would kill for them.

Destroy planets to keep them safe if that's what it took.

They were his everything.

He and Willow had created this little precious bundle in his arms with their shared DNA, and fucking hell, she was a miracle. The first natural-born Moretti princess. Someone had recently pointed that out to him, and yeah, maybe it was a big deal.

"Focus, people," Craig said, his hand resting on Bri's ass.

"Anyone want some plasma?" Willow asked as Kate, Vincent, Ari, and Sage walked into the room.

"Lucas is with his nanny," Kate said. "Let me get it, Willow. I know how exhausting being a new mom is. Go sit down."

"Thanks, Kate," Willow said.

Brayden watched her walk over and melt into the sofa.

Damn.

Was he not doing enough?

There was a fucking lot going on, but he would ask her later. If there was anything Willow needed, he would ensure she had it.

"I don't want to put Isabella to bed yet," Brayden said, joining them on the sofa. "Will it mess her sleep cycle up too much?"

Willow ran her hand over Isabella's head. "No. I swear she sleeps more deeply in your arms than anywhere. She will probably nod off."

Fucking hell. Brayden's chest swelled to the size of the solar system.

"Yeah, he bores me to tears as well." Vincent sat in the armchair across from him.

Brayden silently laughed, his chest vibrating.

Ari shot him a smirk.

Not everyone got the king's sense of humor, but he'd grown up with the guy, so he knew when Vincent was joking and when he was serious.

And when he was being a straight-up asshole.

Tonight, his brother needed a safe space to be himself after what he'd had to do.

Willow needed to give him a break for once.

*Don't harass him tonight, sweetheart.*

*I wasn't going to,* Willow telepathed back. *Tomorrow, though...*

They shared a quick smile.

"You did well, Vincent," Ari said, wrapping an arm around Sage's shoulders. "The kings before you would be proud. Hell, I'm proud of you."

"I am too, brother," Brayden said.

Vincent slowly nodded, taking the glass of plasma from Kate as she sat down beside Willow and also handed her a glass.

"I think they liked the video," Brianna said to the king. "So far, there are very few comments on VampNet."

"It's awesome, Bri," Willow said.

"The princess is right. The video is excellent, Brianna," Vincent said, leaning forward on his elbows. "At a guess, I'd say people are still processing. Tomorrow and the next few day's emotions will run wild."

"You can't control that," Ari said.

His uncle was right. There was only so much they could do, and as far as Brayden was concerned, the king had done a good job preparing their vampires for the days and weeks to come.

"We can't, but the teams are ready around the globe to give support and to step in if anyone gets out of control," Brayden said.

It was a horrible thought, but people could go either way. In general, vampires were less unstable than humans, for want of a better word.

Perhaps it was genetic.

Perhaps it was because they were predators and felt less powerless than the other intelligent race they shared the planet with. That didn't mean all were, but the likelihood of them losing their minds and doing something stupid was slim.

In some ways, they'd been prepared for this all their lives. Whereas humans wouldn't see this coming.

They were expecting aliens, not blood-sucking vampires who had lived next door and worked in the cubicle next to them at their night job.

Or served them Maccas at the drive-through.

Or treated them in the ER.

They were everywhere.

In saying that, Brayden had his warriors armed and alert in case any vampires acted out. Which meant he, Craig, and the SLCs were unlikely to get much sleep over the next few days while they monitored the situation.

Thank fuck they'd doubled their numbers.

For centuries, it had been Tom, Lance, Kurt, and Marcus working with him and Craig. Then Ben had joined. Alex had won the coveted position during the Vampire Games, at which point it became clear they needed more SLCs, and Brayden had made the call to appoint Darnell and Tristan.

Honestly, he'd have Charlotte in the team, too, if she wanted the role. But she didn't, and he had to respect that.

Not every SLC had to be the most powerful fucking vampire on the planet. It wasn't the sixteen hundred's anymore. Other skills were just as valuable. Plus guns.

In any case, Charlotte was a highly trained warrior and had given Alex a run for his money in the games. Never say never. Brayden would let her settle into her new relationship with Marcus and approach her one day.

Now, he had his eyes on a few other vampires who had arrived in the castle. The new world they were stepping into meant they needed a stronger defense and a broader team.

There were options.

One's he was keeping to himself for now.

"Give it to us, Vincent. When are you going to make the announcement?" Craig asked.

The king sat up straight. "Honestly, I'm not sure. I want clarity on these missing vampires. I need to speak to James Calder and a few of the other leaders. Then I think we need to get a bit more information on what progress the mega-mafia has made."

"It's never going to be the right time," Ari said.

"No. It won't. But if I can do one thing, it's eliminating as much risk as possible before I do this," Vincent said. "You all know as well as I do vampires are going to die when this happens. It's my job to protect them. Every single one of them."

A ripple of the king's power ran through the room, and Brayden felt Isabella stir in his arms.

Wow.

What the hell?

Willow leaned into him as Brayden glanced down to see if Isabella was okay. Her eyes flickered open, saw him, and closed again.

Then he looked at Vincent. Kate was leaning forward, rubbing his arm.

Had the king leaked power?

Was he that concerned about the race?

Brayden had seen the Moretti power transfer from their father to Vincent the moment he died. It was an almost ethereal moment. One he'd never asked his brother about. And it was far more tangible than he'd realized.

He glanced at Ari, who was staring intently at Vincent.

His uncle knew something. Of course, he did. He was one of the originals. But the damn stubborn vampire wouldn't talk.

If they'd been in private, he would have challenged him, but Craig and Brianna did not know about the power of the Moretti blood.

Only those who had the name knew. Which included Sage and Ari now.

As the prince, he could help his brother and alleviate some of that pressure. He wanted him to know that while the crown sat on his head, he wasn't alone.

"It's all our job, Vincent. Me, Craig, Ari. Every single warrior in your army to protect them. Not just you."

"*Our* army," the king growled gently.

He never let him forget he was the Moretti prince and once heir to the throne.

"And me," Sage said quietly.

All eyes turned her way.

"I don't want anyone to get excited, but I've been testing an antidote and maybe—"

"You've done it?" Vincent jumped to his feet.

Isabella's eyes flew open, and she began to scream. Willow let out a groan and reached for her. Brayden handed her over and let his mate take their daughter.

"No. I said don't get excited." Sage held up her hand, shooting Brayden an apologetic look. "Maybe. It needs testing first."

"Then let's fucking test it," Craig said.

"Let her explain," Ari said firmly.

"Shoot me with it and test it. Actually, no. There's a guy at the deli who leers at Bri. Let's test it on him," Craig said and laughed when Brianna slapped his chest.

Kate giggled.

"I don't want to test it on a vampire yet. Give me a few more days." Sage let her smile fall away. "I wouldn't usually say something this early, but given the circumstances…"

"I encouraged her," Ari confessed. "We need hope right now, and frankly, my beautiful mate is a genius."

"Ari, stop." Sage blushed.

"If you have created an antidote, I would agree. On the genius thing." Brayden winked at Sage.

"Wink at my mate one more time, nephew, and you will not be producing any future offspring," Ari growled.

Brayden laughed.

"I will come by tomorrow, and you can talk me through it," Vincent said. "Hope is exactly what we need. If I can share that with the race before making the public announcement, we will be in a much better position."

"We still need to produce it," Sage said.

"Just so happens we will have a bunch of manufacturing facilities we can commandeer." Craig smirked. "When we find them."

"Now that's wishful thinking." Ari shook his head, laughing. "Listen, if we end up in a war with the mafias, it will be incredibly destructive. Many lives will be lost. We can't stop them, but we can weaken them."

"Give me a few rocket launchers, and I'll stop them," Craig offered.

He wasn't wrong.

But neither was Ari.

"Ari has a point. If we can prove we have an antidote, we can start fucking with Nikolay. His business model will be drastically impaired if we can vaccinate our entire population." Brayden glanced at Sage. "Is that how it will work?"

He had jumped to a conclusion.

But like the others, he was eager to get ahead of this Russian gangster and protect their race.

"Possibly. But at this stage, the testing I'm doing is more about countering its effects. Much like you do with snake bite venom. Creating a vaccine is a much bigger job," Sage responded.

"But not impossible," Vincent stated.

"Impossible in two weeks," Sage said firmly.

"Unless we say it is." Brayden smiled and glanced at the king.

He grinned back at him.

Yup, they were both thinking the same thing.

"I'm not following." Sage looked confused.

"I am, and it's a dangerous path to take, boys," Ari said darkly. "You need to think this through."

Sometimes, fiction was just as powerful if your enemy believed you had a tool at your disposal. Ari was right; it was a risk but worth considering in their strategy. After all, the mafia were masters at games, so they needed to start thinking like them.

Vincent stood. "Keep working with your team as fast as you can, Sage. Come on, my love."

Kate stood and collected the glasses.

"Leave them, Kate," Willow said. "Brayden will tidy them up."

Brayden laughed and kissed his mate, glancing down at Isabella, who had quietened almost immediately in her mother's arms. He was pretty sure it was Willow who had the Midas touch with their little girl. But Brayden was well aware that Willow thought his doting father's behavior was sexy.

And who was he to interfere with that?

Did he need to take his shirt off when he nursed their daughter in the morning? No.

Did it guarantee him sweet sex afterward? Hell, yes.

And now, as he caught the seductive glint in Willow's eyes, that was precisely his plan.

"Party's over," Brayden declared, standing. "I'm taking my girls to bed. Get out of my house."

"Ten rocket launchers. That's all I'd need," Craig said as he lifted Brianna in his arms and stood simultaneously.

"Keep thinking about those rockets, baby. And take me to bed too." Brianna giggled, wrapping her arms around his neck.

"Fuck, yes. Later's," Craig said and teleported away.

Things might be about to turn to shit, but Brayden loved his family and his life.

He'd do whatever it took to protect them all.

# CHAPTER THIRTEEN

Darnell found himself walking into the Operations room for no good reason. Tristan was with him. They hadn't discussed heading this way, but their feet had kept walking in the same direction.

And what do you know, Alex, Ben, Kurt, and Marcus were boots up on the desk kicking back.

"Hey," Darnell said, pulling up a chair and straddling it.

"How'd your teams take the news?" Kurt asked.

"We tag-teamed it," Tristan replied, nodding his way. "Got a lot of the curly questions out of the way faster."

"Smart." Marcus nodded and took a swig of his water.

"Overall, I'd say they're wary but not panicking," Darnell said, leaning against a desk. "Your teams?"

"About the same." Alex swiped on his phone, glancing up.

Darnell narrowed his eyes as he took in the warriors. Something was going on. They looked like someone had killed their cat.

Were they that stressed about the king's message?

He glanced at Tristan to see if he had a clue what was going on. Then it clicked.

*Oh, my fucking God.*

Not that he could judge. His own mind was elsewhere… with a certain someone.

"The girls went into town," Darnell stated.

"Yup."

"They did."

"Yeah."

His lips stretched into a smile. What a pack of brooding fucking males. He pushed away from the desk and stood. "Well, guess I'll see you all tomorrow."

Five pairs of eyes lifted to his. Big, brooding eyes.

"Unless you pathetic bastards want to get your ass into my Hummer and come into town with me," he added.

Tables and chairs scraped as boots dropped to the floor.

"Asshole." Kurt nudged him as he walked past. "Hurry the fuck up."

Darnell let out a booming laugh as Tristan snickered and got tackled around the neck by Ben.

"DO WE KNOW where they went?" Tristan asked from the shotgun position.

"Turn right here," Marcus replied, holding up his phone.

"Dude. If you're GPS-tracking your mate, I'm not keeping that secret from Charlotte." Darnell glanced at him in the rearview mirror.

"Eyes on the road," Marcus growled. "Then you have nothing to tell."

"Risky." Mack laughed. They'd bumped into him on the way out, and he'd been totally keen to join them.

"We did it," Alex confessed. "When we found out about the serum. If Casey gets taken, I want to be able to find her as fast as possible. She agreed."

Yeah, that made sense.

Darnell imagined Amber being shot with that shit—he'd witnessed it happen firsthand to the warriors in New York City—and the thought of her being incapacitated and in the hands of their enemy was not okay.

*Amber.*

He hadn't stopped thinking about her since she walked out of the bar. Even with all the intense questions from his team when he'd continued the meeting, all he could think about was how close he'd been to claiming that sexy mouth of hers.

And how he knew the moment it did, there would be no stopping.

The intensity between them was growing stronger. His willpower weakening.

God, he could have throttled Casey and Charlotte for showing up when they did. Yes, he could have got rid of them, but the joy in Amber's eyes when she saw her friends had come for her had surprised him.

There was no way he was going to interfere with that. He knew the value of friendships. Amber had come to Maine alone. That was clear. At least as far as he knew.

The question was, how alone was his sexy little vampire?

*I think you're a good friend. I could do with one of those.*

And why?

She was a beautiful young female. Where were her other girlfriends? Her family?

Had she run from a male who had abused her?

Amber had a story, and he would put money on it being part of the reason she'd actively rejected him for so long.

Whoever hurt her, he wanted a few minutes alone with their neck.

"Fine, but if Charlotte tries to torture the information out of me, I'm not lying," Darnell said to Marcus, confident that the female would not be happy to be tracked. He turned the enormous Hummer into a parking lot. "I take it they're at Main Street Bar."

"Bingo," Alex said, holding up his phone.

"Do they know we're coming?" Mack asked, and when there was only silence, the vampire laughed loudly. "So, how is this going to go? Because I want front-row seats if your females are going to kick your ass."

The guy had a point.

What would Amber think of him rocking up after the moment between them?

Had he really intended to wander around town until he found her? Just to check she was okay?

Apparently, the answer was yes.

They had unfinished business.

He still hadn't come to terms with the way he'd reacted when he heard the deep, shaky sigh leave her body during their team meeting. Reaching out to her in front of everyone might've appeared like a friendly touch of comfort, but Darnell knew differently.

*That damn thread.*

It had been the mating bond at work.

His need to comfort her when he'd heard her stress had created a reaction in his body before his brain could work. It was natural to protect and possess the female who was your mate.

Darnell hadn't realized how powerful it was.

He thought it was just sexual.

But now he realized it was way more.

It was the reason he couldn't walk past her outside the Great Hall tonight. Why he couldn't leave her alone to deal with the king's news. The reason he'd grabbed the fucking stool and planted her right beside him as he answered questions.

And the reason he'd reached out to her when he knew she was anguished.

Jesus fucking Christ.

It was the reason he was climbing out of his Hummer and going in search of her now. Darnell needed to know she was okay.

*Liar. You need to be the one protecting and reassuring her.*

But it had to be a friendship.

If he wasn't prepared to take her home as his mate—and he couldn't do that to his father—he had to find a way to protect her while not letting the mating bond take full control.

"Leave it with me," Ben said, climbing out of the Hummer.

"This is going to be good," Tristan said, clambering out of the vehicle as Kurt, Alex, Marcus, and Ben strode across the road to the bar.

"My money's on the females," Mack said.

"No one's betting against you, buddy." Darnell laughed, the car alarm beeping behind them as they followed the Moretti warriors into Main Street Bar.

NINETIES ROCK MUSIC pumped out of the speakers. The bar was busy for a Wednesday night. Not that Darnell was a regular, but he'd been here enough times to know the vibe.

There wasn't an obvious dance floor, but an uncarpeted area drew those ready to shake their booty. And what do you know, some of those booties belonged to a few familiar-looking females.

And shaking they were.

Which was why all seven of the warriors were standing there glaring. This wasn't going to end well.

Casey spotted them first.

"Fuck," Alex muttered under his breath.

"Told ya." Mack snorted.

Then Charlotte did a double take when she noticed Casey had stopped dancing. She did the same, and then her arms crossed and head tilted.

Oh, boy.

Behind her, Madison twirled and came to a halt. "Woah," she exclaimed.

"Babe." Ben started to cross the room to Anna, who had stepped up next to Madison, but Kurt stopped him. "Let them come to us. They're basically wild animals right now."

Darnell rubbed a hand over his mouth to stop his smile while he sought out Amber. She wasn't with them. Had she changed her mind and remained at the castle?

Casey slowly walked over to them. At that moment, they *did* look like a fucking girl gang as Charlotte, Anna, and Madison flanked her. Ginny was smirking right behind them.

"Males."

"Females," Alex replied firmly.

"What brings you here?" Casey was clearly the spokesperson for the gang.

"Mostly sex," Marcus replied, smirking at Charlotte.

She snorted.

It didn't look good for him.

"Girls." Casey glanced to her left and right. "Is this an acceptable answer?"

"Absolutely not. It's dancing *and* sex. Or no sex at all," Anna replied.

"Sweetheart, you know I don't dance." Ben winked. "But I'll toss you over my shoulder and show you my best moves."

"Gag," Casey replied.

The blush on Anna's face said she was sold.

Weak.

She was letting the gang down.

"No dancing," Alex replied firmly.

"Shame," Casey said, shooting her mate a seductive glance before turning her back on him and reaching her arms out like the cult leader she was becoming. "Come on, girls."

"Fuck this," Kurt growled. "Madison, get your fucking sexy ass over here."

Next minute, his hands were on her hips, and giggles filled the air as their lips locked. Ben had Anna over his shoulder, and Alex had fisted Casey's hair.

"You will be punished for that," Alex growled.

"Give it your best shot," the female warrior purred.

Pushovers.

"Do not even try it," Charlotte said, planting her hands on her hips as Marcus approached.

"I wouldn't dare." Marcus smirked, then Darnell heard him whisper. "Run."

The powerful female warrior took off, her laughter an echo as Marcus slapped Mack on the shoulder and said, "And you underestimated us."

Then he was gone.

Darnell had to admit, he couldn't work out who had won. The females had played them, but the males thought they had conquered.

It was all very confusing.

"Damn," Mack said. "Please tell me there's a stock of females like that in these parts because I'm going to need approximately three of them."

Tristan laughed.

"Tonight," Mack clarified.

"I like your style." Darnell laughed. "Let's get some drinks."

Then he heard the giggle, and his body stiffened.

The hell?

"Go on ahead," he told his two friends as he scanned the room.

Across the other side, bright green eyes surrounded by a haphazard mess of rusty red curls met his.

Then swiftly darted away.

Amber wasn't surprised to see him, so had obviously spotted them as they'd arrived.

Yet she hadn't come over, and the reason was clear.

Darnell stood in the middle of the bar, watching Amber lean over a tall glass of something golden, sipping from the straw while chatting to a man sitting opposite her.

Who the hell was this guy?

He could only see the man's back, but she seemed to be giggling and flirting with him. Darnell's fists clenched as he fought to keep his feet where they were.

*Don't kill the human.*

Then she threw her head back and laughed. Jesus, she was fucking beautiful. The vein in her neck pulsed as her neck arched, and Darnell's cock thickened against the dark denim he wore.

When his fangs pressed at his gums, and his mouth salivated, itching to taste her, he wasn't surprised to find himself standing at the table beside her without remembering how he got there.

*Fuck, I hope I didn't teleport.*

"Darnell," she gasped.

"Introduce me to your friend," he ordered without taking his eyes off her.

*What am I doing? Walk away. You can't claim this female.*

Hurt and disappoint his father? He couldn't.

"This is John. We just—"

"Hi, John. Take a hike. Now," Darnell said firmly, his eyes on Amber.

"Excuse me?" John replied, sounding offended.

"Hey!" Amber began to get to her feet.

Darnell turned to the guy, finally. John was human, as he'd expected. Six feet on a good day, which meant Darnell had at least four inches on him.

And fifty pounds.

Fifty pounds of vampire muscle.

Along with a mating bond that was tugging at him with a ferocity he was struggling to ignore.

If the guy had any sense of survival, he'd take one look at Darnell's build and hightail it. Hell, his T-shirt sleeves were stretched, struggling to contain his enormous biceps, so if John wasn't smart enough to figure it out, there was no hope for him.

Unless he was one of those karate fucking kids who thought they could take down a mountain like him with one swift knock to the neck.

Yup. That would work.

If he was human.

Which he wasn't.

John would be kissing the carpet before he got his arm in the air.

God, he hoped he tried.

"Darnell," Amber said again.

"Amber," he replied, his eyes on John. "Say goodbye to your friend."

"How about we ask the lady?" John asked.

Wow. Maybe the guy had some balls, after all.

He had to respect that, even if it wouldn't get him anywhere tonight.

Not with his girl.

*My girl?*

Shit.

"Good idea, John." Darnell turned to Amber and almost groaned when he took in her little one-shouldered black dress, which cinched at her waist.

And barely covered her ass.

*Fucking hell.*

Did this woman want the entire universe to see her damn peach?

"John wants to know if you'd like to go home with him tonight and enjoy some vanilla sex and *maybe* an orgasm if he can be bothered rubbing your clit. No guarantee, though," Darnell asked, and while the guy was *what the fucking* Amber's mouth fell open.

She slapped his arm.

"Is this your ex?" John asked, tossing back his drink and slamming it down on the table.

"No," Amber said. "He's a protective *friend*."

Fuck that.

*No, not fuck that. Yes, to friends, remember?*

"Who thinks you deserve a good-quality orgasm," Darnell said, shrugging. Which he'd already proven himself worthy of. Or had she forgotten?

Maybe she needed reminding.

"Well, your friend is right. I do want to fuck you. But he's wrong about one thing," John, with the bigger balls than he'd given him credit for, said. "I'll lick your pussy and give you the best damn orgasm of your life."

Bad move, John.

John with no more balls.

A growl slid from deep within his chest, and Amber, who knew all about predatory vampires, let out a gasp.

"If you want this human to live, you will come with me right now." Darnell ignored the man and wrapped his arm around her back, gripping her hip.

She nodded and quickly grabbed her black purse.

"Go home, John," Amber said as they walked away, ignoring his protests. Big green eyes looked up at him pleadingly. "Please don't hurt him."

*Hmmph.*

"Darnell!" Amber cried.

"Give me a moment," he growled.

Fucking hell, the fact his hand wasn't around the guy's neck was a miracle.

But she wouldn't understand that. Amber didn't seem to be aware of the mating bond, or if she was, she was better at ignoring it than he was.

"Where are we going?" she asked as he shot Tristan a nod to indicate they were leaving and pushed through the front door.

He drew in a long breath of fresh air.

"To my car," Darnell said, tugging her across the road, not giving a fuck about jay walking or any other human law.

When they reached the Hummer, he pressed the alarm, opened the driver's side door, lifted her, and planted her on the fucking seat.

Panting, she stared at him. "Now what?"

Darnell took a step closer, parting her legs. "Now you fucking kiss me."

# CHAPTER FOURTEEN

This vampire was giving her whiplash.

One minute Darnell had his head between her legs, then he was telling her they weren't going to fuck, and the next he was threatening another man and dragging her out of a bar, and demanding she kiss him.

"Stop," Amber said, holding up her hand.

"I'm warning you, Amber. Now is not the time," Darnell growled, his mouth inches from hers.

"Put your fangs away, warrior," Amber said.

Darnell licked his lips, nudging his canines. God, she really wanted him to kiss her.

"I won't bite you," he said, tugging her hips closer to his hard cock.

"Promise?" she asked, her lids lowering as her core burned at the thought of his mouth over her vein and those sharp incisors piercing her.

While his cock entered her.

Darnell froze, and his eyes widened. Simultaneously, their eyes dipped to find her hand over his cock.

"Oh, I didn't—"

"Yes. You did," he growled, and five seconds later, he had her in the backseat, and the door slammed closed behind them as his enormous body lay over her. "You want to play, little firecracker? Then it's time to see what you've got."

*Oh, fuck.*

"Wearing little skirts like this, I bet you have no... oh, you *do* have panties on tonight," Darnell rasped.

Her body jolted, then arched as his fingers glided along the seam of her thong.

"Barely."

"I thought we were just friends," she whispered, her heart pounding. It was worth one last attempt.

"You grab all your friend's cocks, baby?"

No. No, she did not.

With a snap, her thong was torn off, and Darnell's thick, talented fingers slid through her hot, wet flesh.

*Oh, God.*

Her mouth parted, ready for his full, dark lips on hers. To taste him, to be owned by him. To be filled by him.

In every way possible.

"Fuck, you're drenched." Darnell's voice was so rich with arousal, she moaned. Then he slid a finger inside her pussy, and she lost all control, arching into the pleasure of his touch.

His own growl escaped as he gripped her neck, lifting her to his face and then slammed his mouth down on hers.

*Holy hell.*

Sweeping his tongue inside and dominating her, Darnell consumed her hungrily as she swallowed down hints of smoky malt. Her hands flew to his bulky shoulders, and just for a second, she glimpsed her pale skin against his dark, glossy muscles.

It was... beautiful.

He truly was a stunning creature. Powerful, sexual, intoxicating. He towered over her in both height and width, yet he was handling her with care while simultaneously pleasuring her. His bright blue eyes, which seemed almost ethereal, were only enhanced by the thick, long eyelashes surrounding them.

And when they locked on hers, she was trapped in a jail she never wanted out of. Not if it felt like this.

His jaw was square, his lips full and kissable.

And holy hell, he was lying on top of her, fucking her with his hand and kissing the life out of her.

Amber needed more.

She would work out how to *just* be friends with this vampire afterward. Right now, they both wanted each other.

"I'm about to pass the edge of no return here, Amber. If you want to run, you have two seconds. I can't promise I won't chase you, but you need to tell me right fucking now if you want me to stop."

Stop?

God, no.

His thumb swiped her clit, and she cried out. "I, oh, God, that feels so amazing."

"One second and my cock is replacing my hand, baby." He cupped the back of her head, their eyes blazing at one another. "You want me to fuck this pussy?"

"Yes."

"Good girl," he rasped as his finger slid out and Darnell took his jeans and t-shirt off with vamp speed while she lifted and removed her dress.

When he pressed a hand on the leather seat beside her and she got her first glimpse of him naked, her entire body reacted.

As in exploded with arousal.

This man was a god. Every dark inch of him molded with layers of toned muscle. Amber's hand lifted and ran over his skin in complete awe of his physique.

"Like what you see?" He smirked.

She didn't have the ability to deal with his arrogance right now because, frankly, he had every right to be confident from what she could see.

Instead, Amber mumbled something about *very much* and licked her lips as she continued running her fingers across his pecs and down over ropes of abs. Then she felt the heavy thickness of his cock between her legs.

"Baby, I'd love to take our time here, but we're in the parking lot," he growled playfully, nipping at her bottom lip. "My blacked-out windows will soon steam up."

Right. Shit. They were in a car.

"Then fuck me. Hard. Fast. And don't hold back. I want it all," she said, lifting her eyes to his.

Because if they were doing this once, she wanted the full experience. All of it.

"I thought you'd never ask." He smirked, pressing the head of his cock at her entrance.

She moaned as his head pressed in. "Yes, God. And after this, we go back to friends."

"Sure," he groaned as his cock slid in an inch. "Jesus, you're tight."

No, he was big.

Thick, hot, swollen.

Amber panted with every inch, digging her nails into his arms.

"Gonna need you to relax, baby." Darnell lifted her hips and slid out, then back in a little further. "So fucking hot and tight. Baby, you cannot feel this good."

He was right. It was too good.

But there was no way she was stopping. It would take a nuclear war to tear them apart. Their moans filled the vehicle as he filled her inch by inch.

"More," Amber cried, arching her breasts against his chest, wanting all of him. "Deeper."

Darnell's eyes locked with hers and he gripped her face. Then he slammed into her in one swift move.

*Oh, my God!*

They both roared, and she was left breathless as his cock filled every inch of her.

"Fuck, fuck," Darnell cried while she began to tremble. "You okay?"

"Yes," she almost whispered. "Go."

Only then did he begin to thrust, his thick roped cock moving within her, finally addressing the needy ache she'd endured for weeks.

Stroke after stroke.

But it soon became clear Darnell was too large for the space as they were limited in their movement.

"Come here," he said, scooping her in his arms.

Sitting on the back seat, he spread his legs wide and positioned her around him.

In this position, his length inside her deepened, and Amber let out a pleasured cry.

"Ride me, baby." Darnell cupped her breasts. "I want these in my mouth while you fuck my cock with your pussy."

Christ, she could barely fit over his huge thighs, but she was a vampire, so one thing she had was core and body strength.

Amber leveraged herself into position, lifted her hips, and finally found her rhythm.

"That's it, baby. Oh, yeah," he said, reaching his tongue to tease her nipples as she bounced up and down on him.

*Jesus.*

When one of his hands slid between them and rubbed her swollen clit, their eyes met.

"Wait," she huffed.

"No. Come, baby. I want to watch you fall apart around me."

Circling in just the right way as she rode him, Darnell gave her zero choice. Amber knew she had no willpower to stop her orgasm from spreading through her body.

Then he took one of her nipples in his mouth, and she was history.

"Darnell!" she cried.

He took over her hips, pushing her down deeper on his cock as her orgasm shuddered around him.

"I'm coming," he growled, lifting his face to hers.

She felt his hot seed fill her.

"Amber! Jesus fucking Christ." Darnell threw his head back and clenched his powerful hands as he stroked her pussy up and down his cock.

When his head lifted, Darnell threaded a hand through her hair, and a shudder went through her as their eyes locked. The last of their orgasms released as he clamped his mouth to hers.

This vampire.

He was different.

Amber couldn't say why, but being in his arms, connected like this, she never wanted to move.

She felt safe and protected for the first time in her life. It was such an overwhelming emotion, she could only imagine it wasn't real.

As their heartbeats slowly returned to their normal rate, they lapped at one another, sweat sticking them together. Amber remained pressed against his chest, taking in the last few moments.

Darnell had one arm wrapped around her, the other still in her hair, and one word kept playing over and over in her head.

Home.

She pressed her eyes closed, taking a second to relish this most magical feeling.

And then her survival skills kicked in.

*Run.*

*Stay, and he'll only reject you.*

Amber pulled her lips from his and stared into his startling blue eyes.

"Well, fuck. If I knew it was going to be that good, I would have doubled down on my pursuit." He smirked, squeezing her ass.

"Consider me well pursued." Amber smiled and began to wiggle loose of his grip.

"Hey, take a moment." His smile faded.

Amber glanced around them. "We're in a car, remember?"

Plus, she had this overwhelming desire to get home and cry. Amber had just had the best sex of her life with a man she could only be friends with and who felt like home. Plus, the race was about to expose themselves to humanity.

The ground below her was shifting.

Her life was already lacking in foundation. She was terrified that once the earthquake came, she'd fall into an abyss.

Alone.

DARNELL GUIDED THE Hummer back into the Moretti underground parking garage and slowly reversed into his personal park. His eyes darted to the female in the passenger seat.

"I didn't know this was here," Amber said.

"The garage?" Darnell asked, and when she nodded, he asked the question that had been on his mind for days. "You've not been here long. Where did you come from?"

She shrugged and began to climb out of the Hummer.

She froze as his hand shot out, and he held her arm. "What?"

"You going to fuck me and run?" He raised a single brow.

"Will that hurt your feelings?" she asked.

*Wow.*

"Yeah, maybe it will," Darnell replied, resting his forearm on the steering wheel.

What the hell was her deal?

Was she so unaware of the mating bond that was alive and well and threatening to drown them in this intense sexual attraction? His need to claim and protect her was knocking on the inside of his head like a sledgehammer.

Yet Amber was halfway out the fucking door.

Was he wrong?

Surely he wasn't the only one feeling this.

Not that he'd changed his mind. Claiming Amber wasn't an option. He'd wait to meet a mate his family would accept. Every time he even contemplated them finding out about Amber, Darnell imagined the surprise on his father's face.

She relaxed back into the seat. "I'm pretty sure the small talk is supposed to come first."

He rolled his eyes.

Thing was, he was curious about this female. She was, after all, one of his potential mates. You didn't meet them every day and... and he wanted to know why she had shown up in the castle with no apparent links to anyone.

Alone and vulnerable.

"Come on, tell me about you. If we're going to be friends, that's what people do," he pushed.

Amber busied herself plaiting her hair into a side plait and shrugged some more.

*Wow, she was literally gaslighting him.*

"Jesus, woman. If you were human, I'd be accusing you of adultery right about now." He laughed, "Or thinking you're a spy."

"I'm a server at a bar." Amber frowned at him.

"Yeah, I'm not buying it," he teased, trying to open her up.

"You're a dick. Come on. Let's go. I need to get some shuteye before my shift tomorrow," Amber said, closing down even more.

He drew in a slow breath. "Baby, give me something. I just fucked you. I want to know you. Tell me, where did you grow up?" Darnell tried one last time.

This time, she huffed. "A lot of places, okay? Everywhere and nowhere."

He stared at her, but she wouldn't return his gaze.

But clear as day, he saw the pain on her face. Not only pain, there was also shame. It took everything not to pull her into his arms and demand the entire story. But her walls were huge.

Maybe it was a good thing.

Fucking Amber had surpassed every single expectation he'd had. The moment he'd completely sheathed himself inside her, he had never wanted to leave her body. He'd expected that feeling to pass once he'd come, but it hadn't.

Now, she was closing down, leaving a cold emptiness between them where such luscious pleasure had been.

And yet, Darnell could sense the threads of their bond weaving between them, creating a connection they were both clearly rejecting.

Which was just as well.

Except he didn't think it was.

Fuck.

# CHAPTER FIFTEEN

Brayden stood with his arms crossed, one hand on his chin as he stared up at the screen.

"What do you think?" he asked, his eyes drifting to Ari, who was standing in almost the same stance.

Ari drew in a deep breath and dropped his arms. "I think they're telling the truth, and we need to advise the king immediately."

*Yeah.*

Ari's team, made up of Oliver, Elijah, Logan, and Jason, had taken the Moretti helicopter to NYC to investigate the missing vampires. Things had taken a surprising turn when they got a 111-call–the vampire emergency line–from two of their kind who claimed to have been taken. Then escaped.

Ari had sent Oliver and Logan to meet with them while the others continued.

When they'd met with the male and female, who were shaken but not harmed, they'd only been able to give them sparse details about the place and the people who had held them due to being in the serum coma and quickly teleporting to freedom.

The male had awoken and, before making a run for it, had shaken awake the closest female. Then taken her with him.

Fast thinking on his behalf, but now he was racked with guilt for not helping the others.

Oliver had reassured them the Moretti warriors would be moving fast to get them out.

And they would.

But the words the male had overheard as they'd teleported through the building during their escape were playing out in Brayden's brain.

A threat to the king.

A threat to the entire Moretti royal family.

"Want us to bring them in?" Oli asked over the video.

"Yes. Let's get the medical team to look them over." Craig nodded. "I'll have some of my crew interrogate them further while your team stays on the ground following the lead."

They'd given some details on the location that may be helpful.

"Agreed. Logan, you escort them back. Oli, stay with your guys," Ari instructed.

"Roger that," Oliver said and disconnected the call.

"We need to move you," Craig said.

Brayden cursed and recalled Oliver's words.

*They said they were going to destroy Vincent Moretti. That they knew where he lived, and once he was eliminated, the race would die.*

He didn't know where they got that idea. Technically, when Lucas was born, he became the heir to the throne. What Brayden had witnessed with Vincent upon their father's death appeared to be a transfer of the Moretti power.

Could a toddler handle that type of power if Vincent died? Or would it go to him as the next most senior Moretti?

Fuck that.

Brayden had never desired to be king.

If they were right, Brayden would have three deaths on his hands: Vincent's, Kate's, and Lucas's. Kate would never survive the loss.

It wasn't going to happen.

These humans needed to be stopped.

"I promised Willow I wouldn't. Isabella is too small," he said, running a hand through his hair. "And I can't be separated from them."

"Bray," Ari slid his hands into his pockets. "This place is compromised. You know that. Kate and Willow are too vulnerable with their young. And the king needs to be in a secure location. We can still speak to him on video."

Fuck.

*Fuckkkkk.*

"Would you? If it was Sage?" Brayden challenged his uncle.

The dark shadow that crossed Ari's face, the way his jaw tensed, gave him the answer he already knew.

"And you? How about we send Brianna with them?" Brayden challenged his commander.

Craig held up his hands.

"Brayden," Craig said firmly in a tone he'd rarely heard from his best friend, "you have two choices. Send them and stay here. Or go with them. Technically, you should go with them."

Fuck that.

There were always more choices.

He'd send Kate, Lucas, and Vincent and keep his girls by his side. But with the royal guard following the king and queen, it would only make his girls more vulnerable.

Which wasn't acceptable.

"Actually, there is a third option," Ari said. "One I've often contemplated should something like this occur."

It was unsurprising, given he had fifteen hundred years of thinking under his belt. Ari Moretti had been the commander of Brayden's grandfather and father's army.

Hell, he'd learned all he knew from his uncle. How to wield a sword, and how to strategize war. So his ears were wide open.

Once Ari shared his idea, Brayden slowly nodded.

"I'll speak to the king. I wouldn't want to act until it's absolutely necessary. But I agree this is the best course of action."

"Agreed," Craig said.

"Prepare the SLCs. Tell them they can keep their mates with them. If the king agrees, we are evacuating the castle. Essential staff, mates, and warriors only."

"And the medical and science teams," Ari said. "They need to keep working."

Brayden nodded.

Then he strode across the room and into the castle halls to find Vincent.

# CHAPTER SIXTEEN

Amber stood in the shower as warm water flowed over her shoulders. Her hands ran over her breasts, her nipples hard. She let her thumb press against the light pink nubs and closed her eyes as arousal rushed through her body.

She was aching in delicious ways, but despite the powerful orgasm she'd had, she wasn't fulfilled.

Not because Darnell had been a bad lover. Quite the opposite. She needed more of him.

More of his cock. More of his talented mouth. More of the way he made her feel desired, protected, and beautiful.

Like an addict, she craved him.

And damn, those ocean-blue eyes. They saw right through her, ripping apart her defenses and discovering her secrets.

*Baby, give me something. Where did you grow up?*

Great damn question.

California if you wanted a location.

When? The moment her father had walked through the front door and out into the sun. That's when her heart had broken, her family had disappeared, and she'd been left alone in this world to look after herself.

To defend herself.

Initially, Amber hadn't considered that her life ahead could be so cruel. Vampires didn't go into foster care, but her parents had always told her if something happened to them, she should reach out to her mom's second cousin, Mallory.

After a day of crying her heart out, she had.

Mallory had arranged for her to live with them. They'd taken care of everything. Sold the house and most of the furniture and moved her bed and clothes into their home in Virginia.

While Amber had been grieving and broken, she'd thought she was cared for and safe. She also thought the money from her family estate had gone into an account for her. Money she would get when she was twenty-one.

Brian and Mallory Whitlock told her they were taking some money from her inheritance to pay for her expenses. Amber was a kid but figured it made sense. She wasn't their child, and life was expensive, so all the adults said.

But she'd been wrong.

Very, very wrong.

Brian and Mallory only saw her as a financial opportunity. Fancy new cars showed up a few months after she moved in, and then they all went to Disneyland at Christmas.

When the new armchairs and an enormous TV arrived weeks later, her younger cousin asked, "Dad, are we rich now?"

That was the moment Amber got the first weird feeling in her tummy. Her life had changed from that moment on. Or at least after she enquired about her inheritance.

"Can I please see my bank account?" she asked the Whitlock's.

"It's fine," Mallory replied. "We'll look after that for you. You'll get it when you're grown up."

"But how much is it?" she pressed.

"Not as much as you think. A few thousand," Mallory snapped.

A few thousand?

Amber was sure houses were worth more than that. She searched online when they thought she was doing homework days later. It took her a while, but she found the listing and learned her parent's house had sold for way more than a few thousand.

A whole lot more.

Unless they had a huge mortgage, there should have been fifty times that. Her dad had always been sensible with money, so Amber had no reason to believe they were in financial trouble.

Nor did she have any way to prove it.

But as a kid who was costing the Whitlock's money to look after her, she didn't feel she was in any position to inquire further.

The next year, things began to change.

Brian lost his job, although Amber thought she heard him say he'd resigned because *fuck his boss, they didn't need his money anymore,* and the food in the pantry began to shrink.

She was told over and over what a cost she was to them and that they might not be able to afford to keep her for much longer.

It was a terrifying feeling.

"What about my parent's money?" she cried one night when things escalated.

"How much do you think it costs to live?" Brian yelled at her. "This house, the mortgage, the heat. You kids eat a lot."

Amber crossed her arms, partly in protection, as Brian was a big vampire. "But that money was for me. To cover my expenses. Not the entire family."

That was the wrong thing to say.

"You selfish little girl. You're not part of this family and never have been. We took you in out of the kindness of our hearts. This is how you repay us?" Mallory chastised her. "Your mother would be ashamed."

Amber stood shaking, tears pouring down her face.

"Pack your bags. You can find somewhere else to go," Brian said.

Horror almost crippled her.

Sobbing, she cried, "I'm sorry. Please don't make me leave. You can have all the money."

"There's no money left." Brian laughed angrily. "Actually, there're some crumbs. Mallory, send her to my brother. He needs the money and can take the bitch."

Ronald?

Amber had met him once and didn't like him.

Her eyes widened in fear. "No. Please. He's scary. I can't live there."

She sobbed as they put her on a bus and sent her to West Virginia. To a small town called Oak Hill, with a population of only ten thousand people.

She was thirteen.

Ronald was a single vampire who only showered once a week, according to her records. Tall, lanky, and creepy-looking. He had long hair, beady- eyes, and barely spoke a word to her.

He told her two things when she arrived. "You sleep on the couch and keep out of my way, and we'll get along just fine."

So she had. While he went to the pub, got drunk, dragged women home, fucked them, and spent the day sleeping. He had a job at a gas station a few nights a week, but the money he received from the Whitlock's soon disappeared.

Amber thought about running away, but Ronald kept out of her way as much as she did him. So with a roof over her head, she tried to make the most of it.

She taught herself as much as she could on the library computers before they closed each night in the absence of any schooling. She also learned how to cook because Ronald's idea of food was spam and anything else cheap in a tin.

His specialty was beer and beans.

Just what every growing girl needed.

Amber grew vegetables in the yard and did her best to get as much nutrition as possible. When she was old enough, or rather when the fake ID said she was old enough, she got a job in the bar.

The same one Ronald went to.

Most of the time, he barely spoke to her.

He never celebrated her birthday–no one did. He spent the holidays at the bar with his pals or in some female's bed.

Amber tried to make friends, but she couldn't go to school because she was a vampire, and they were the only ones in the small town. It must have looked weird, her living with Ronald all those years, but it still hurt when the young people teased her about him being her kinky sugar daddy.

When she was old enough to understand what that meant, Amber found it odd because a) gross, and b) he had no sugar in the pantry, let alone any kind of wealth.

In some ways, she was grateful to Ronald. The one thing he did not do was touch her. Oh, she saw him look as she began to blossom, but he never tried a thing.

So she grew up isolated and alone, hungry for connection, love, and companionship.

After all these years, she wasn't sure she was capable of giving or receiving those things.

Amber never understood why Ronald let her live with him, but he did. She would never call it home. Not now and not then.

He never gave her a bedroom, and the sofa remained her only semi-private space from the moment he tossed her a pillow and blanket the day she arrived. She kept her belongings in the corner under the coffee table. Her clothes were stuffed underneath the sofa.

That was it.

Amber didn't have a home. Ronald hadn't been a parent.

So when someone asked her where she grew up, the answer was simple: in the living room of her parent's house in that single moment when her father had killed himself.

The rest of the time, she had simply been surviving.

Still, her childhood ended abruptly the day after turning twenty-one. Amber woke to Ronald standing over her.

"You need to leave," he announced.

Amber sat up and rubbed her eyes. "What?"

"Lou-Anne is moving in. You need to leave," Ronald repeated.

"Who the hell is Lou-Anne?" she asked.

"The woman I'm going to marry. You need to leave today." Then he left the house, and to this day, she'd never seen him again.

Amber had been saving small amounts of cash for a few months, so she had enough money to get to New York on the bus and get a room in a hostel.

She invested in some cheap makeup and clothes, and a girl she shared the room with, Marci, who was studying to be a hairdresser, cut her hair and taught her how to tame her wild frizz.

It was transformative.

She quickly found a job in a bar, and the tips sure were bigger in NYC than Oak Hill. But so was the cost of living.

People came and went from the hostel, but Amber stayed. She hated the place, but it was better than anything she'd had since her parents died.

She didn't try to make friends. Amber had decided long ago that she was going to better herself. Bar work paid the bills and kept her alive while she tried to find work in a kitchen.

Amber wanted to be a chef.

Fortunately, a vampire named Jamaica—probably not his real name—managed the hostel. He segregated the rooms with blacked-out windows, saying they were for night workers. NYC was the best place to be as a vampire. The city that never sleeps. No one questioned her. No one suspected a thing.

She got to know Jamaica over the years, and he let her use the kitchen in his separate area to cook. It was a real kitchen compared to the one back in Oak Hill. Whenever she had a night off, Amber tried out different recipes and always left Jamaica samples as a thank you.

It was a win-win.

But soon, her dream felt like it was disappearing. Interview after interview, she was declined because she had no education or experience in a restaurant.

Then one night, the sleazy new manager at the bar she worked at slid his hand up her skirt and told her if she didn't let him fuck her, she would lose her job.

Here's the thing about being alone. There's no one to buy gifts for, no family events to attend, no weddings, no funerals, no Christmas, no friend's dinners or parties, no movie tickets…nothing.

No people, no expense.

So, Amber saved a little bit of cash.

Enough to tell the manager to keep his dick in his pants, and when he tried to force her, she used some of her vampire strength to grip his neck and said, "Try it, motherfucker, and make my day."

He squealed like a pig, and she removed her apron, tossed it at him, and left him on the busy Saturday evening to deal with the crowds alone.

She didn't regret it, but she found herself living in NYC with no job, no prospects, and nobody to help her.

She was alone.

And being alone in NYC was hard.

After a few days of moping, Amber took herself to the New York Public Library, returned some of the cooking books she'd borrowed, and logged into VampNet.

That was the moment her life changed.

There on the screen was the vacant bar server job at Max Bar in the Moretti castle.

Did she want to move to Maine?

Did she want to work for the royal family?

Amber had been looking for a job in a kitchen, but now she was desperate. Her money wouldn't last much longer. On a whim, she applied and decided to let fate take her on a journey.

After all, what did she have to lose?

Plus, the idea of being around her kind, vampires, seemed kind of nice. And serving her king also sent warm fuzzies through her.

Finding out that she was successful was bittersweet. It felt like her dream of becoming a chef was getting further and further away, but then she met Madison and Anna the first night she arrived.

They were fun, friendly, and sassy.

And Amber felt like she clicked with them but was a little scared to get her hopes up.

To be honest, she felt like a complete fraud, pretending she was like any other female vampire talking about hair and guys. Inside, she had been screaming *they don't really like me,* but they returned the next day and the next day, propping up the bar to chat with her.

Then they invited her to yoga.

Cool, calm, and completely not collected, she said *sure.*

That was the day she saw Darnell.

And he saw her.

"Five o'clock. Our newest SLC has eyes for Miss Amber," Maddison drawled.

"No, thanks," Amber said, shooting the gorgeous man an uninterested look.

She was anything but uninterested. He was the sexiest man she'd ever laid eyes on.

"Darnell is a friend of ours. Go for it. He's cheeky, but I mean, look at him." Anna giggled as they pushed through the doors to the yoga class.

Even more reason not to.

"I'm having a break from men right now," she lied.

Amber wasn't a virgin, but the way her body had reacted to him that first night, she should have known he was different.

But now, as the water ran down her body, Amber wasn't sure she would ever want another male.

She slid her fingers between her legs and let out a moan. Circling her swollen clit, she closed her eyes and imagined it was her dark warrior.

They could never do that again.

He would only ask more questions.

She didn't want anyone knowing about her past. She liked how things were progressing with making friends. Heck, being invited to the bar with the girls last night was amazing.

They'd come looking for her after the king's announcement and included her. That was not something she'd had before. Fucking Darnell and messing all that up was a dumb decision.

The castle felt like home, and she was happy.

She didn't feel safe yet, but she would.

*You felt safe in Darnell's arms last night.*

That wasn't real.

It was probably some post-sex brain disorder or something.

No, Amber was going to stick with her plan. And who knew? A job in the Moretti kitchen might come up one day. She could volunteer and see if they might one day consider her.

All she needed was a chance.

Still, that didn't mean she wouldn't crave her warrior god every time she saw him. She would. But the way he made her feel scared the living crap out of her, so Amber swore to herself she wouldn't give in to him again.

She arched into her fingers, remembering his lips claiming her mouth as his cock filled her so thoroughly.

"Yes, yes. Hmmfphh," Amber cried as her legs trembled and pleasure flushed through her.

If only she could cook up a double batch of willpower.

# CHAPTER SEVENTEEN

Nikolay smirked as he sent the email. The fact that all the vampires they'd taken had now escaped was irrelevant.

He loved that he was fucking with Vincent Moretti.

Especially as the officials continued to cause issues around their production of the serum. The last he'd heard from the mob bosses, the cops had tried to force their way in, but without search warrants, they'd had no luck.

At a guess, it was a little hard to get search warrants when no one knew about vampires. So even those at the top were hamstrung.

So sad.

Never mind.

The video he'd made, watching the vampires he'd captured unconscious as he lifted their lips and flicked their canines, was going to upset a few of those fanged fuckers.

A risk, but Nikolay liked to live on the edge.

He wanted a way to kill them.

He'd find it. If the myths about daylight were true, it could be fun. At this point, they hadn't been able to catch and hold one long enough to test it.

Right now, though, he had to focus on ensuring the production of the serum remained on track and protected by the people trying to get in their way.

Elizabeth, with her experience in the pharmaceutical space, was a valuable asset. Sure, she might be an accountant, but she understood how a manufacturing business was structured.

She was setting up an LLC and similar in other countries to start trading once the product was ready.

Damn, their baby would be smart and powerful with both their genes. Hopefully, it was a boy. Someone he could hand over his empire and lead the Russian mafia when he was ready to retire.

If he lived that long.

His life was always at risk, but it wasn't worth focusing on, or it would make him crazy.

*Ping.*

Message read.

Nikolay grinned, and his cock hardened. Power was a fucking aphrodisiac.

The little vampire king wouldn't expect the visit he had planned for them. Alexis had talked him into it, and he'd added his own idea into the mix.

One that was going to start a war.

But they were already at war. Now it was about to get real. Plus, it would send a strong message that while they were human, the mobs were a powerful force to be reckoned with.

Because things had changed.

Nikolay had found the information he was after.

Tungsten.

The world was about to change completely. If leaders already knew about vampires and he needed to let them into his business profits, he would.

Reluctantly.

It would become a vampire versus human war with him at the helm. Vincent Moretti would be a fool to underestimate him.

# CHAPTER EIGHTEEN

"Evacuate the entire population of the castle?" Darnell asked, his stance wide and arms crossed.

Craig nodded.

"Mates can stay. Tom and I are working out a list of essential employees." Craig said. "Anyone not army personnel or on this list, including your mates, must evacuate."

*Jesus.*

"For how long?" Kurt asked.

"I understand why, but for thousands of them, this is their home," Lance said, shaking his head.

"Which is why we need to do it now. We have no idea when Nikolay plans to act. The more notice we can give people, the better," Craig explained.

Darnell stared at the floor. Did Amber have somewhere to go?

As a bartender, her role wouldn't be essential, even if the warriors thought otherwise. She'd be sent away, and he had no idea where she would go.

*Tell me where you grew up.*

*A lot of places, okay? Everywhere and nowhere.*

She had no one. He knew it in his bones.

Darnell might not plan to mate her, but there was no way he was letting his could-be-mate go off into the world alone and unprotected.

Shit.

"What's the timeline?" Marcus asked.

"Forty-eight hours. The castle needs to be cleared after that. I want your teams leading this," Craig said. "We'll arrange shuttles to take key people to the LA and New York Moretti properties. Those who qualify."

Craig glanced at Tom.

"Yup. On it. Getting quotes now. But they'll have to load up outside the castle gates. We can't have that many unvetted shuttles coming inside." Tom shook his head as if he thought the whole thing was as crazy as the rest of them.

"Agreed," Craig grumbled.

*Fuck*

What was he going to do?

"So, essential personnel. What is that?" Darnell enquired, chewing the inside of his cheek.

"Aside from military, the science and medical team, skeleton kitchen and housekeeping crew for the royal family, and a few key technical experts."

No bartenders.

"Anyone with a job that can be done digitally fits into the secondary category, which we're qualifying now," Tom shared.

Again, no bartenders.

"Mates stay," Darnell said out loud for no reason. It wasn't a question, but his brain was whirling.

"We can't separate mates, you know that." Alex frowned at him. "We'd lose our minds."

"Yeah." Darnell shook his head. "Yeah, of course."

"So, focusing back on the royal family," Craig said. "We have intel which says the castle could be attacked."

"Not to question your authority," Ben said. "but why the fuck aren't we moving the royal family?"

The room went quiet.

"The king and prince made the call," Craig said, his hands on his hips.

Wow.

Darnell was surprised Vincent and Brayden had made this call. It would be much easier to move them stealthily, surrounded by warriors, and get them out of the country.

After all, they had properties all over the world, but this was the only one known to humans.

"As you say, mates can't be separated. The prince being apart from his princesses isn't going to happen. Bray and Ari have gone over and over this. I'm reluctant to agree, but I do," Craig confessed.

"Yeah, fuck. I get it," Marcus said, rubbing his face.

"True." Kurt kicked his boot on the floor.

"We have a secure, nearly impossible-to-infiltrate bunker for them should an attack occur," Craig said, referring to the one connected to the king and queen's wing. "Our job is to evacuate staff while protecting the royals from any incoming threat."

Logan joined them. "Hey, guys."

"Welcome back," Craig said. "Everything go smoothly?"

Craig had told them about the two vampires who had escaped, and that Logan was flying back to Maine with them.

"Yeah, they're pretty rattled," Logan said, fist-bumping Ben, "but they're with Dr. Abbot now, and then Sage will test their blood."

Right.

To test the serum.

Whenever anyone got jabbed with that shit, they tested it. It was the only way they could keep track of any changes the humans might be making to it.

Which was just fucking terrifying.

"Oli still in NYC?" Ben asked, enquiring about his best friend.

"Yeah, he's with Elijah and Jason," Logan said, collapsing into a seat. "Tracking the location from the intel we got so far."

"Is it a long shot?" Darnell asked.

"Big fucking long shot." Logan nodded.

"But one worth taking when a threat to the king is hanging in the air," Craig barked. "Tom, get that list done and meet me in an hour. The rest of you brief your teams, and then we'll put out a castle-wide alert. Two hours. Until then, this remains confidential."

"Can we tell our mates?" Kurt asked.

Craig nodded. "Strictly confidential. And only because if they lose their minds, so will you. I need you all clear-headed. Understand?"

*Yes, sirs* sounded, and they all got to their feet.

"Fuck, I'm glad I'm unmated," Mack said as they all stood.

He watched the other warriors lift their phones to their ears and teleport.

"Ditto, buddy." Logan high-fived him.

Both males were huge and muscular playboy vampires, getting a lot of female attention right now. Logan's dark edge—part of the assassin's creed, he figured—added an extra layer of interest.

But then again, Mack had that wolf gene, which was like an aphrodisiac. He'd heard they were into a lot of group sex. Wherever. Whenever.

The castle might be emptying, but one day, Amber could return. To what? A bunch of horny powerful warriors who were as handsome as fuck, and ready to celebrate their success.

Because they would defend their king.

What if she didn't return?

Fuck!

Darnell cursed and kicked a chair.

"You all right, man?" Logan asked.

*Good-looking asshole.*

"Yeah, I'm… I have something I need to do," Darnell said, striding across the room.

He couldn't let Amber walk out of his life.

Recalling the look in her eyes when he'd spotted her after the king's announcement, Darnell knew she was vulnerable, and he couldn't do anything.

Amber might be strong, but it was his job…

*Shit.*

Fucking bond.

Still, he wasn't letting any other man take care of her, he thought, as he stomped his way to the door.

Right now.

It was just for now.

He might never know her story. Not with the shame he saw on her face last night. Amber had taken off so damn fast after that it had felt weird. He'd walked a circuit of the castle twice before finally talking himself out of going to her apartment and demanding answers.

He'd promised they'd be friends and had no right to push her to spill her entire life story.

A sense that she was his, whether he liked it or not, was taking hold in his chest, and he didn't fucking like it.

No, he did like it.

He just didn't fucking like it.

Jesus.

*Bang.*

"You good, SLC?" Craig asked as he bounced off his chest.

"Shit. Fuck." Darnell shook himself out of his daze. How the fuck had he walked right into the fucking commander?

*Because your head is in the goddamn clouds.*

"No. Just—"

"You disagree with the king?"

"No, it's not that—"

"If I had my way, I'd lock them all up in a fucking house in Italy, and no one would know where they were."

Darnell let out a dry laugh. "Yeah, except me now."

"Italy is a big place," Craig muttered. "So what's going on?"

His eyes darted around the room as the stupidest decision of his life took place inside his head. One he had no idea how would play out.

Or how he was going to convince Amber to go along with. But the words fell out, and he hoped it wouldn't destroy everything he'd worked for.

Or get back to his family.

But…he had to try.

"I've met someone. Kind of," Darnell said, rubbing the back of his neck.

"Congratulations. Tell Bri. She's more into these conversations than me," Craig said, narrowing his eyes. Then he shrugged, and the corners of his lips lifted. "Or Ben."

Darnell snorted.

"Sure. No, it's…" *Fuck.* "I think she's my mate."

"Jesus." Craig dropped his smirk and crossed his arms. "Terrible fucking timing, Darnell. Is she or is she not?"

"Yes?"

"Yes? Or yes!" Craig pushed.

He cursed.

"This isn't for tickets to Broadway, son. This is a potential attack on the king's residence. Staying will put her in harm's way. Unless she's your mate, and unless you think you won't be able to function without her, she has to evacuate."

"So I get to decide?" he asked tentatively.

Craig planted his hands on his hips, his voice darkening. "You are an SLC. A trusted king's warrior. Yes. But choose wisely."

He glanced down at his boots and nodded.

"Speak," Craig ordered with force.

Fair enough too. What he was asking was serious. This was his out. He could shrug it off and never bring it up again.

Or he could lie to his commanding officer.

And the royal family.

Motherfucking fucker.

He visualized watching Amber be put in a van and driven away to god knows where. Away from him. And never seeing her again.

The bond existed.

He just hadn't acted on it.

Nor would he.

But would anyone really know?

He had to keep her safe, and they could figure it out afterward.

But a touch of the truth wouldn't hurt…

"She is. I know she is. I just don't want to bond with her," Darnell confessed.

"Why the fuck not?" Craig frowned.

"It's complicated." Darnell sighed.

Booming laughter filled the room as the commander threw his head back. "Oh, yeah, she most definitely is your mate, then. Tell Tom, get her on the list and you might as well just acknowledge it." Craig kept chuckling.

No, that wasn't his plan.

But he'd go along with it.

At least he'd shared his doubt and laid the foundation for reversing this when the castle was repopulated.

"Yeah, probably," he said, nodding.

"Get it over with. I need you focused. Trust me when I say rejecting the bond only fucks with your brain. Plus, the sex is amazing." Craig grinned.

The sex was already amazing.

"Sure. Cool. Thanks, Craig," Darnell said and began to walk away.

"One more thing. We'll have to allocate jobs to all the females, so find out her skill set and get her to speak to Tom after we've evacuated," the commander instructed.

*Crap.*

He had a feeling Amber would be furious with him. If she even wanted to stay.

Getting her to fake being his mate was a tall order. But he wasn't letting her leave. She would have to understand that.

He nodded and went off to find Amber.

# CHAPTER NINETEEN

Amber tugged on a fitted white crop top that showed the outline of her breasts and gazed into the mirror.

It was probably too much. But she liked how it showed off the skin above the waistline of her jeans when she put on her jacket. Just a hint.

It was sexy without being too obvious.

Amber didn't have time to slide on her jacket before someone knocked at her door. She walked over and opened it, surprised to find Darnell standing there, gripping the top of the doorframe with one arm.

*Woah.*

Speaking of skin peeking out.

This level of hotness should be illegal.

His T-shirt was lifted, showing the gap between it and his gray sweatpants. She pressed her nails into her hand to stop herself from reaching out and running her fingers over the defined rims of his abs.

Her mouth watered, and the rest of her body reacted in all the ways she hoped it wouldn't the next time she saw him. Apparently, that was wishful thinking.

"Amber," Darnell purred, dropping his arm.

"Hi," she replied as her eyes darted up to his.

"Can I come in?"

She stood back and nodded. Darnell walked in, dropping a kiss on her neck below her ear.

A shiver ran through her, and he smirked. Damn him for knowing how much he affected her.

"How are you?" he asked, glancing around her room curiously.

Suddenly, she felt extremely self-conscious. She didn't own much. This was the first bedroom since her early childhood that had felt like hers. So it was sparse and lacked any kind of personality. He was probably looking for photos of her friends and family or signs of hobbies.

He wouldn't find any.

She did have a small photo of her parents inside her top drawer. Seeing them every day was too painful, so she kept it in there to pull out when she had the privacy and space to feel and cry.

It wasn't completely sparse, though. Amber did have some cooking books, a laptop, a mobile phone, her wardrobe, and personal items. And a set of cooking knives she'd invested in before leaving New York. Still boxed up and on the floor.

But she was more curious about what Darnell was doing here.

Did he want to talk about what they'd done?

If he was worried that she hoped it would happen again, she was happy to assure him she wasn't. Friends were all she wanted.

Except that body of his would be as hard as hell to stop desiring.

And if he could start wearing some contacts which dulled those sparkling blue eyes, it would be helpful.

Also, stop looking at her.

Stop smiling.

Stop being all sexy and powerful.

And yeah… friends. Easy.

"I'm good. I have to start work in an hour," Amber said to encourage him to keep this visit short and sweet. "If you want to talk about last night, it's fine—"

"No. That's not why I'm here." Darnell ran his hand over his face. "Well… yes, it is."

He took her hand and led her to the bed, where they both sat.

"Are you pregnant?" She smirked at him.

"Yeah, twins. Smart ass." He nudged her with his shoulder playfully.

He turned, and the seriousness of his expression had her heart pounding.

What the hell was going on?

If he wanted to keep what happened between them confidential, she was fine with that. He didn't need to make a huge fuss about it.

"Last night. Look, any other time, I would leave this. Hell, I never planned to even say anything," Darnell said, not making any sense.

A sense of dread spread through her.

Amber stood, not wanting to hear any rejection or whatever he might have to say.

"There's no need," she snapped. "I have no expectations. I thought I made that quite clear when I left last night. It's not like I lingered hoping for a second date."

"It wasn't a first date," Darnell said, then shook his head. "Not the point. Right."

Jesus, what an asshole.

"Exactly. We're two friends who have a sexual attraction and fucked. The end," she said and crossed her arms.

So go.

Leave.

I don't care.

Damn it, she did care. It might have just been sex to him, but there had been something more for her. A sense of being wanted and feeling safe. She didn't want him to destroy that.

His words would undo it all.

Darnell stared at her blankly. After a moment, it began to get uncomfortable. Those blue eyes had a power that got under her skin and saw the real her.

*Please don't.*

The part of her she was trying to hide from the world. Trying to portray that she was fine. But he saw her, and she hated it.

"Truth time, firecracker," he rasped. "Did you feel nothing when we fucked?"

"No, I—"

He reached out and slid a finger through the belt loop of her jeans, tugging her between his legs. Amber stumbled, but he grabbed her hips and held her firmly.

Had he felt something like she had?

A rush of nerves had her shivering as a flush of heat rushed over her.

No. It couldn't be. He probably wanted more sex.

Staring down at him, she placed her hands on his shoulders and drew in an unsteady breath. "Is that what this is? You want to fuck me again?"

"More than anything," Darnell answered, taking one of her hands and placing it over his hard cock. "Constantly. If I could tie you up and have you as my sex toy, Amber, I absolutely would."

*Oh.*

Heat rushed to her core, and her face warmed with arousal.

"You'd like that, would you?" He smirked. "To be wet and ready for me to lick you, slide my cock inside you, my fingers, a dildo, whenever I wanted. Have you strapped up, chains hooked to your nipples and clit?"

"Stop," she breathed as her pussy throbbed.

"Oh, baby. I can make your fantasies come true." He ran his fingers over the denim, and she pressed into him.

Next minute, her zipper was lowering, and her jeans were falling to the floor before his mouth was on her pussy.

So much for talking.

But this was what they did.

They fucked.

"Jesus," she cried.

"Pull those tits out," he ordered as his tongue pushed through her folds.

Amber tugged up her tight bra top.

Darnell let out a sexy groan. "Fuck, I love your breasts. This is exactly what I'd do. Take you when I wanted." He lifted her hips with his powerful arms and lay back on the bed, positioning her over his face.

"Darnell," she cried, unable to grasp anything but thin air.

"I've got you. I've got your pussy." He continued ravishing her. "Pinch your nipples."

Just as her orgasm was about to rush to the surface, he pulled her away from his mouth and lifted her once more. Standing on the bed, he placed her on top of the headboard.

Amber swallowed, completely aroused and at his mercy.

"Arms up," Darnell ordered, and she reached them above her head. "I would tie you here and make you wait all night, getting wetter and hornier for me as you anticipated my arrival."

*Oh, God.*

He lapped at her mouth, and her tongue snaked out, wanting him to touch her, relieve her.

But he only teased her.

"Then I'd undress," he said, tugging his sweatpants and T-shirt off to reveal his huge, dark, muscular body and

enormous erection. "And stroke myself"—which he did—
"until I decided I wanted to sink into you."

*Do it, do it.*

*Please, God, do it.*

"You should," Amber said, beginning to reach for him.

"Uh-uh. Hands up," Darnell growled. "If I had
restraints, and we had time, I would show you just how
much pleasure this could be."

His fingers slid through her pussy, his mouth lowering
to suck on one of her nipples as he stroked his cock.

"Darnell, please," she begged.

"And I would slip in like this," he said, pressing those
fat fingers inside her as she cried out. Thrusting once,
twice, three times.

Then he pulled out.

*Ugh.*

"And stop as I pleased. You are mine to fuck, to tease,
to consume." Darnell kneeled, licking her pussy. "To
torture."

His fingers rolled her nipple harshly. Amber cried out,
somehow keeping her arms in place above her head.

This male was dominating her.

Controlling her.

And she, *ugh,* loved it.

"Every fucking day," Darnell rasped, standing once
more. Then he thrust his cock inside her.

She let out a guttural cry as he stilled.

His thick, swollen cock throbbing inside her.

"Would you like that, baby?"

"Yes, yes, yes," she cried.

"This needy pussy would be begging for me all night."
He thrust once. "With no toys or naughty little hands to
touch it."

"No." She clenched around his cock, trying to get him
to move.

"Or maybe I would leave a toy inside you that I could control during the day." Darnell circled her sensitive clit, and she trembled with neediness while he remained pulsing and not moving.

What a sadist.

"Darnell, please. Fuck me. Please."

"Would you like me to tease you? Bring you close to orgasm so you're dripping wet and foaming at the mouth for me when my cock walks through the door?"

Like now?

Because she was dripping wet.

He gripped her neck, and she gasped.

"Tell me, Amber," Darnell growled, slowly pulling his cock out and then slamming it inside her so she nearly screamed. "Is this naughty, needy cunt mine?"

"Yes," she cried.

"Say it again."

"Yes."

A million times, yes.

*Just fuck me and let me come.*

"Yes, yes, it is." Darnell thrust harder now. Faster. "Your body is mine. Your orgasms are mine. Your pleasure is mine."

Pressing his body flush against her, he reached up to grip her wrists as he slammed into her over and over.

"Come, little firecracker. Suck me with your hot, wet pussy and come on my cock," he rumbled.

With pleasure.

That was all she needed. Her body shattered into a million pieces. As his hot seed filled her, something in the back of her mind, a knowing that his dirty talk had more truth to it than she was acknowledging.

Darnell was claiming her.

Sexually, yes, he was a dominant warrior, but there was more to this, and it terrified her.

Yet she wasn't sure she could say no to him.

DARNELL WRAPPED HIS arms around Amber and lowered her to the bed. She was jelly.

This hadn't been his plan.

He'd come here to talk.

To propose the fake mate idea to her.

But one look at her sexy fucking body and those green eyes and his cock had taken over.

And it wanted complete and utter dominance.

It surprised him that Amber had completely submitted. Even now, as he held her while their juices dripped down his legs, she seemed to be letting him remain in control.

Good.

He wasn't sure he was exaggerating about wanting her as his sex slave. Having her hot and ready when he came home each day was not so much a fantasy as a guttural need with this female.

Was this how the mating bond expressed itself?

Hotter and sexier than anything he'd ever experienced?

Then, Jesus.

It was going to be hard to fight.

As long as his fangs stayed put, they were both okay.

But regular hot sex like that? Yes fucking please.

Did Amber know how those green orbs made him hard when she looked at him so doe-eyed? The way she ran her gaze over his body and licked her lips made him want to push her to her knees and force open her mouth so he could fuck that pretty face.

Or the way the curve of her sexy breasts screamed for him to slide his cock between them and come on her throat.

She didn't.

Darnell wasn't sure if Amber was aware of the bond threading its way through both their lives and tugging them together like a clearly woven seal of fate.

It didn't matter.

He'd decided he was keeping her *for now.*

Unfortunately, he couldn't keep her chained in his room for sexual pleasure twenty-four-seven, but Darnell was not letting this female evacuate the castle.

She was staying here with him. And that was that.

Now he had to convince her.

Without telling her they were mates.

If she didn't know, that was a good thing. It was unlikely she didn't have the same beliefs about it as he did. Darnell was in the minority. A little like human atheists, he supposed.

He would remain in control and keep them as lovers.

Not mates.

And ensure his family never found out.

He didn't think this evacuation would last long. The mafia would strike hard and fast if their past efforts were anything to go by.

Then…their lives would return to normal.

Friends.

Who didn't fuck.

How he would then unbind himself from the addiction of Amber Evans, he wasn't sure. But Darnell decided he would work that out afterward.

Maybe he'd ask to be stationed elsewhere for a few months.

"I don't have long," Amber said in his arms. "I have to get to work."

His mouth found hers. The kiss a lazy, sexy caress.

"I honestly didn't come here to fuck you, but that was a nice bonus," Darnell said. "I need to tell you something highly confidential."

She lifted her head, her eyes widening. "What?"

"Our world is about to change. Massively," he said, preparing her. This was going to be a lot of information and probably scare her. Darnell knew how vulnerable she was, so while he wanted to go slow, scaring her a little might work in his favor.

"Is there a date? Is the king going to tell the humans now?" she asked, chewing her lip.

Darnell sat them up and reached for the blanket to cover her. To give her a sense of protection.

"No," he said as her big eyes held his. "Only the senior warriors in the castle and our mates know about this, so when I say it's top secret, I mean it."

"Okay." Amber nodded.

"The castle is being evacuated except for key personnel," Darnell said. He didn't mention the king staying because unless she agreed, that bit of information was way too classified.

"What? When?" she cried, alarmed.

"Two days. Less," he said, shifting to wrap his body around her. "And Amber? I'm not letting you go."

Wait, he needed to word that better.

"Listen, the whole sex toy thing was an incredible turn-on, but you know you can't actually do that, right?" She frowned. "I think the humans call it kidnapping. Oh, and so do vampires."

Darnell's lips stretched into a soft smile. "Yes, baby, I know I can't kidnap you. Unfortunately."

She shook her head and then sobered. "Oh, my God. So we have to leave. Well… you won't."

"Nor will you," he said firmly.

"I won't?" She frowned in confusion.

"No. Listen to me, Amber. I want you to stay," Darnell said.

"How?" she asked. "And why?"

"Well, I think the why is pretty obvious." He smirked and ran a finger along her creamy skin. It was easier for Amber to think this was all about sex than to accept his help. Or to know they were probably mates. "The *how* is simple. I told Craig you were my mate."

"You WHAT?" Amber cried, sitting up straight.

"Mate," he repeated. "All you have to do is pretend you're my mate, and you can stay here in the castle. With me."

With me. That was important. She needed to understand how this would work.

She wriggled out from under the blanket and jumped off the bed. "I can't do that." She waved her arms in the air. "I barely know you."

"Says the naked woman with my come dripping down her legs." Darnell leaned against the headboard and smiled.

Amber's eyes dropped to her body, and she ran into the bathroom, calling out through the open door. "I still can't do it."

A minute later, he heard the toilet flush.

Still naked, she stood in the doorway and crossed her arms, glaring at him.

"Hearing you pee was far sexier than I imagined it would be." Darnell laughed as Amber huffed and dressed.

"I'm going to smell of sex at work," she grunted, pulling out a new pair of panties and sliding them on.

Darnell watched, his cock hardening again.

She glared at him, then pointed at his groin. "Control that thing."

He moved to the edge of the bed and stood. "Drop to your knees and put it in your mouth."

"I. Have. Work," Amber repeated like he was a little simple.

"Well, that's the only way this *thing* will be controlled." He smirked, kissing her harshly on the mouth. "Pack your bags after work. I'll move you into my rooms when I'm done."

"What? No, I-I haven't said yes," she stammered.

"I wasn't asking, Amber. You are *not* leaving," he growled.

"You can't—"

He smothered her words with his mouth, pulling her hard against his body. "I just did. You are mine. Don't make me take it a step further."

Shit.

He knew she didn't understand his words, but the more he thought about her leaving, the more angsty he became. The bond was strengthening.

"But people will know," she said quietly.

No, they wouldn't. He was sure of it.

They all knew the two of them were dancing around each other. Now they had to make a show of it.

How hard could it be?

"Then we'll have to be very convincing," Darnell said, cupping her face. "The fact my cock wants to spend twenty-four-seven inside your pussy will help."

She swallowed.

"So you'll do it?" he asked.

She chewed her lip for a long moment.

"So let me get this straight. If I don't, I will have to leave?"

Darnell nodded.

"If I stay, we pretend we're mates, and I can stay here with my friends and my job?"

"Unlikely, the bar will remain open, but you'll be tasked with other work," he shared. "Don't forget the passionate sex."

More chewing of the lip.

"Afterward, we can tell them we were mistaken," Darnell explained. "Then you can carry on with your life."

"And I can here in my room?"

"No," Darnell growled before he could stop himself. "Mates would never sleep apart."

"Then we'll have to take turns on the couch. Sex is one thing. Sleeping together every day is another." Amber frowned, her eyes drifting away in thought.

Darnell kept his smile to himself. He planned to fuck her to exhaustion every morning after a hard night's work, so where she slept would be the least of her worries.

But it *would* be in his arms.

"Pack your bags, mate," he said, slamming a kiss on her lips and heading out to find his team.

# CHAPTER TWENTY

Amber made her way down to the Great Hall after sneaking out. That's right, she was now living with a male.

Her fake bonded mate.

It was official not long after she had agreed.

Darnell had requested a meeting with Brayden Moretti, and he'd responded within the hour. With little preparation, they'd taken off through the castle and ended up at the royal wing, where the prince's security had led them inside to a small room.

They were given refreshments, and Amber nearly chickened out a dozen times while they waited.

"Uh-uh," Darnell said at one point when she suddenly spun around, his hand grabbing her wrist and tugging her back.

"We can't lie," she whispered.

"Amber, you *are* mine," Darnell growled in her ear.

Even to her, his words sounded like the truth. She knew it wasn't, but his comment earlier was still racing around in her mind, making her wonder what he meant exactly.

*You are mine. Don't make me take it a step further.*

A step further?

How much further could they go?

He'd fucked her to within an inch of her life, and as he'd pointed out, she'd also peed in front of him. Or at least within his hearing. She'd never done that with another being in her life.

Save her mom and dad, probably.

It was too late now. Brayden had walked in.

"SLC Miller, what can I do for you?" the prince asked, shooting Amber a glance.

Amber leaned into Darnell without realizing as he introduced her.

"This is Amber Evans. She's... well, she's my mate," Darnell said.

The prince's brows lifted. "Is that right?"

Amber nodded.

"Is this male your mate?" he asked her.

Amber nodded again.

"Use your words, Amber," Brayden ordered, his eyes drifting to Darnell and back.

"Yes, sir. He is," she said and was surprised when a) lightning didn't strike her, and b) it felt less of a lie than she expected.

Weird.

Brayden's lips stretched into a smile. "This is new."

"Yes, Amber has been...reluctant, should we say." Darnell's voice was rich with amusement.

She turned and glared at him.

"Ah, yes. I remember it well." The prince laughed. "Obviously, you don't need my permission to mate, but I assume you're here because of the circumstances we are in."

"Correct," Darnell answered.

"I appreciate the courtesy. Obviously, there's no way I would expect Amber to be parted from you, so make arrangements for her to stay. Let Craig and Tom know."

Darnell nodded. "Thank you, captain."

Brayden took a step and slapped him on the shoulder. "Congratulations. And, Amber, welcome to what I guess you could call a very exclusive inner circle in our race."

Oh.

"Thank you, my lord." She lowered her eyes, feeling a rush of emotion come over her.

He'd welcomed her into a group of honorable and respected vampires. Those she wanted to befriend. The very circle she had sat in with Willow Moretti and all the others recently, hoping these vampires would be a social circle she could be a real part of.

Now, Darnell had secured that for her.

Temporarily.

It was an enormous risk because if they found out she was lying, they wouldn't be so kind to her. Darnell had promised they'd part amicably after this and remain friends.

It would be fine.

She could do this.

Because he was right. Where was she going to go? With no other job and a need to keep working to earn and live, Amber had no backup plan.

Plus, if she was being honest, he was very hard to say no to. Especially naked, with an erection pointing at her.

Also, this did align with her plans. Staying in the castle and remaining with her friends. They could all bond further with this experience.

If they thought she was Darnell's mate, it would temporarily make them accept her more.

Then, after, *oops*.

Surely anyone could make that mistake.

They'd blame their powerful chemistry.

Except she couldn't fight the sense of dread that remained as Darnell had led her from the royal rooms.

God. They had deceived the prince. They were going to lie to their friends. If it all came crashing down, she'd lose them, and that would be worse than never having them at all.

As it turned out, lying wasn't the only challenging part of being Darnell's mate. He'd taken it upon himself to hold her hand everywhere they went.

It was weird.

She wasn't used to having someone in her space.

Or living with someone.

So tonight, while Darnell had been in the shower, she'd snuck out. Childish, sure. But she needed some time out.

Even if it was just for a five-minute walk.

*Amber, where the fuck are you?*

Oh, yes, and they'd had to share blood, which meant Darnell could now telepath her. As if the image of his burly hunky body wasn't enough to drive her insane, he was now in her head.

Amber sighed.

*Walking into the Great Hall. See you when you get here, matey.*

She heard his growl.

*It's mate. Not fucking matey.*

She giggled. Then felt a pang of guilt. She wasn't entirely sure why Darnell was doing this for her, but she appreciated it.

Sex, yes. But she had a feeling he cared. Or there was something she wasn't getting. Maybe he felt sorry for her. Amber decided it wasn't worth trying to psychoanalyze. The partnership worked for them both.

They both enjoyed mind-blowing sex, and she got to stay here with her friends.

Which was a bigger deal than even she had realized.

Last night, the castle had emptied, and it had been quite emotional. Vampires were crying and hugging one another. Some were even angry. But it had been a highly coordinated event and was done quickly.

Now, it felt like they were rattling around in the enormous structure. She was sure their footsteps echoed.

It was eerie.

Now, she was about to find out why they had evacuated. Darnell had refused to tell her, saying that it was up to the royal family to share when ready. That time was now, apparently, as they'd all been called to the Great Hall for an announcement by Captain Brayden Moretti and Commander Craig Giordano, who had issued the evacuation.

"Amber!" Madison called, waving from where the group was seated.

Well, some of the warriors were seated, some leaning against the backs of chairs and walls. The girls on their laps, beside them or, in Brianna's case, standing between Craig's legs while he cradled her hip.

What would it be like to truly be mated? To trust someone so much, they were basically a walking sofa you could just lean on. To know they were there for you, no matter what. Twenty-four-seven.

And would die for you.

Heck, these males would even kill for you.

And likely had.

"Hey," Amber said, sliding into a seat beside Madison.

"Babe, I heard the news. Congratulations," Madison said, grinning like crazy.

Amber frowned. "What?"

She caught Casey looking at her strangely.

"You. Darnell. Mating. It's amazing," Anna said, leaning forward to catch her eye.

Oh. Shit.

"Yes," she said, and even to her own ears, it sounded fake as hell. "So amazing. He's, you know, so amazing."

Crap. Way too many *amazing's*.

"Sounds…amazing," Casey deadpanned.

"Hmmm," Amber replied, trying to keep her mouth shut now.

"When did you know?" Casey asked, leaning her hip on the wall. "Must have been fast?"

"So fast." Amber nodded, forcing her smile as Madison, Anna, and Casey listened and no doubt expected some romantic story. Which she didn't have. "But when you know, you know."

God, she was terrible at this.

"Yeah, apparently. And where's your mate right now?" Casey continued.

Amber swallowed.

"He's, um." *In the shower, and I guess if I were his mate, I would probably be in there too, but I'm dodging him because all this hand-holding and public affection is freaking me the hell out, and while I want to shag his brains out, I can't handle the way he looks at me like maybe I* am *his mate, and then that would be really, really bad.* "On—"

"Right here," Darnell said, lifting her out of her seat and plonking her down on his knee as he sat. Then he kissed her right on the lips, lingering as he smirked and asked, "Miss me, baby?"

Actually, she had.

In that *we need to lie together* kind of way.

Play, she did like him touching her. More than she should.

"Hmm, a lot." Amber nodded, rubbing her lips together awkwardly.

Casey snorted and pushed off the wall.

Darnell shot her a look, and she shrugged. Then he glared at Casey.

Oh, boy. It didn't look like she was buying it at all.

"You guys are gorgeous together," Anna preened, then squeaked when Ben tugged her back against him.

Were they?

This was the most intimate she'd ever been with a man. Sex was one thing, but she'd never been cuddly or affectionate. Nor had a male with her.

Nor any human men she'd slept with.

So far, their agreement to tag team sleep on the sofa hadn't worked out well. Amber had woken up this afternoon with her huge black warrior wrapped around her. Before she could stop herself, she'd wiggled her ass against his cock.

Talk about fast reflexes.

He'd been inside her minutes later.

Darnell was right. This wasn't a bad deal. She got to have delicious sex with a hot guy—her words, not his—and remain in the castle with her friends.

They just had to unravel it. How hard could that be? Surely people were mistaken about mates from time to time.

What did she know? She'd spent most of her life in Oak Hill.

"Whoop, gotta go," Craig said as the prince strode into the hall.

Amber watched him kiss Brianna, slap her ass, and step into line with the huge vampire prince. The two progressed to the front of the room and jumped onto the stage.

Who needed steps when you were a vampire?

Both wore black pants, boots, and Moretti bomber jackets—the royal army uniform. The same one the vampire underneath her was wearing.

And the surrounding warriors.

She noticed that Casey and Charlotte wore black leggings, smaller boots, and tank tops under their Moretti jackets, so there seemed to be some flexibility with the outfits they could choose.

But without a doubt, they were all elite warriors.

Craig and Brayden stood a few feet apart and stared out across the crowd of people as everyone took their seats.

Even with the evacuation, there were still hundreds of people in the room. Mostly military personnel, but a few civilians like her.

"Vampires," Brayden started finally, and the already quiet room hushed to silence. "In normal times, my brother would be addressing you, but this is a matter of security. Therefore, as your captain, not your prince, I have ordered the evacuation of the Maine Moretti castle."

Security?

Amber's eyes widened, and Darnell gripped her hips as if to offer some reassurance. Then he pulled her against his chest.

But she wasn't relaxed.

He had mentioned no danger.

Goddamn him.

"Your presence here means you are a member of the royal army or an essential employee."

"Or the mate of one of the above," Craig added.

*Or a liar like me.*

Brayden glanced around, almost appearing to make eye contact with everyone.

"Where's Ari?" Darnell asked Marcus.

"With the king and rest of the family," Marcus said quietly.

What the fuck?

"It's okay," Darnell said to her neck.

*Tell me what the hell is going on? Are we safe?*

*The safest place is right here with me,* Darnell replied, but she wasn't sure if that was true.

If something happened, his job was to protect the king. Every vampire knew the SLCs' jobs and lives were committed to that. As his fake mate, Amber would be alone in a dangerous situation.

Damn him.

"We have received intel that the king's life is being threatened, and they know the location of this castle,"

Brayden continued. "At this time, we cannot relocate to another country, so I made the decision, for the safety of our citizens, to evacuate them."

*Oh, my God.*

"Instead, we will reinforce this location while the Moretti royal family remains in lockdown," Craig added.

"Sans me." Brayden shrugged, and a few timber laughs sounded out.

Amber tried to wriggle out of Darnell's hold, but he wouldn't let her go. Panic began to slice through her, heating her from head to toe.

How could he trick her into staying here when it sounded like they could be attacked?

Who was going to kill, or rather try to kill, the king?

Her arm went up before she knew what she was doing, and the prince glanced her way.

"We're not doing Q&A, Amber," he said.

"Okay, but I think it would be good to know if, like, someone is going to attack us. Is it the government? What if they bomb us?" she cried.

"Babe," Darnell growled and tightened his hold.

She slapped at his hands, but it did absolutely nothing.

"Is someone going to bomb us?" Madison asked Kurt.

"No, Jesus," Kurt groaned. "Ladies, please. Let Brayden finish."

The prince cursed as the room erupted into noise with all kinds of conspiracy theories flying.

"Christ, Amber. Could you not have waited?" Darnell ran a hand over his face.

"Why didn't you tell me I was in danger?" she hissed. "You lied."

"I didn't li—"

"Enough!" Brayden yelled, his voice booming to all corners of the Great Hall with a vibration of power she'd never felt before.

Everyone immediately fell silent.

"Woah," Casey whispered.

"Your question is fair, Amber. Albeit premature. First, no, the US government is not about to attack us. Nor is any other government. This is a new enemy, and the details are classified." Brayden's voice was clear and dominant as he again seemed to look at every face in the crowd. "Remember, we are a powerful race. Our army is strong. We have withstood enemies before, and we will again. My decision to remain here is, I admit, selfish. The prince and princess are too little and vulnerable to be moved. This castle has our strongest defense; therefore, there is no better place to fight from *if* it comes to that."

Craig moved an inch, attracting everyone's attention.

"While we safeguard the royal family from inside these walls, our teams will be working proactively in the field to eliminate the threat," the commander said.

Brayden crossed his arms, looking so intimidating and powerful that it nearly took Amber's breath away.

"We do not know how long this will take. Days, weeks, potentially months. Unlikely the latter," Craig continued. "So to keep this monster of a place running, those of you in essential jobs, please know you are appreciated. Mates, you will need to sign up for the vacated roles we have identified."

Amber chewed her bottom lip.

What would she end up doing?

While in fucking danger. She was furious with Darnell.

"Please ensure you're up to date with the correct procedures in case of an emergency," Craig added. "Head immediately to your rooms if there is an amber alert. Come here if it's a red alert. Warriors, you know your roles."

The murmurs shifted gears as reality sunk in.

Amber took notes to read up on what she needed to do. Like those things on airplanes, no one ever read the emergency forms.

"Mates of military personnel, and I cannot stress this enough," Brayden said, "you must check in telepathically with your partners immediately to let them know you're safe. I want them to focus on the job, not worrying about you. Got it?"

Around her, people were nodding.

Darnell pinched her.

*Oh, yeah.*

"Uh, huh? Yup," Amber said too loudly, and Casey shot her a look, rolling her eyes.

"Any questions, speak to your team leaders or Tom and his team," Craig said.

"Our goal is to get things back to normal as quickly as possible, but the priority is to keep the king safe," Brayden clarified. "Thank you all for remaining here and playing a key role."

Whatever. Amber had been lied to.

Which maybe she deserved as she was also lying.

Karma was a bitch.

# CHAPTER TWENTY-ONE

A few hours later, Brayden stood behind Vincent's desk and watched the video for the fourth time. Ari stood beside him with his enormous arms crossed.

"Let's look at the facts," his uncle said. "From what we can see, none of the vampires appear harmed. It's theatrics for the camera."

"I hope one of them woke and bit the fucker," Vincent snarled.

Brayden smiled briefly.

"Don't let him rile you," Ari said. "We know the serum only lasts a short time and that they have the ability to escape immediately after."

But in the meantime?

Those humans had their hands all over them. And the mafia weren't known for being decent people.

Fucking assholes.

Brayden walked around the desk to the bookshelf, where a photo of his deceased parents sat. He picked it up and stared into his father's face.

What would King Frances do?

He'd been a much more bloodthirsty king, but then again, those times had called for it.

"Nikolay is playing with us. Like a cat with a mouse," Brayden said, turning.

Vincent watched him thoughtfully. "What do you suggest?"

Returning the photo to the shelf, Brayden lowered himself into the leather armchair in front of his brother's desk and tapped his fingers on the arm. He watched Ari as the ancient vampire walked around to the side of the desk and slid his hands into his pockets.

Then he rocked back on his heels.

They were all thinking as hard as each other.

"We have evacuated. We continue with our plans and wait for them to come. This could be a distraction. Or it could be an information-gathering mission," Brayden said. "They won't get through our defenses. Hell, let's use it to defuse Craig. We might have to rebuild a few walls and explain a few bodies, but if they come for us, it's our right to defend ourselves."

Vincent nodded. "I will update Calder," he said, referring to the U.S. President. "Out of courtesy."

"We have teams out around the area and in key parts of Portland, so we will know before they arrive," Brayden added. "There will be bodies. I'm not taking prisoners here. They threaten your life or the lives of our children, they can meet their fucking maker."

"Agreed," Ari said darkly.

"How is Sage going?" the king asked.

"She is making progress. I think she will want to speak to you again very soon. But I will leave that to her," Ari said, his lips stretching into a slight smile.

That sounded positive. And they all needed good news right now.

Vincent stood. "Having a vaccine or antidote will change this war."

"Sage knows that. She feels pressure every day, which doesn't help her to stay focused. Vincent, I will protect

Sage above all else. So check in with me if you have to, but try to leave her to her work," Ari said.

Brayden watched his brother turn and stare out into the dark night. It had certainly been a trying time since he'd taken the throne in the late eighteen hundreds. Together, they had watched the world change.

And fast.

Life was moving faster, even for them as near immortals.

"I'm trying to be patient." Vincent sighed.

"I understand." Ari nodded.

"Ignore the video. Don't reply. We will prepare for their attempt to invade the castle and continue to find where they are manufacturing the serum and disrupting their plans," Brayden said, standing. "This is confirmation they are feeling the pressure."

"I'll update you after I've spoken to POTUS," Vincent said.

"And I'll break the good news to Craig." Brayden grinned.

"No Goddamn rocket launches."

"I can't promise anything." Brayden laughed as Ari shook his head, grinning.

# CHAPTER TWENTY-TWO

"You could have told me." Amber tried to tug her hand out of Darnell's for the tenth time.

God, she was infuriating at times.

"You won't be in any danger. I'll make sure of it," he replied, striding down the corridor. "And stop trying to let go of my hand and start pretending you're my mate."

"No one is around. Let go," she hissed. "I'm mad at you."

Really? He hadn't noticed.

Darnell rolled his eyes.

When her mouth opened one more time, he snapped. Pushing her up against the wall as they abruptly stopped walking, he placed his forearm on the plaster above her. "Would you like me to fuck the anger out of you?"

Because he would.

Hell, he wanted to. Darnell was angry himself after finding Amber had left while he was in the shower. He had a bunch of mad he needed to get off his chest, and pounding her pussy sounded like an excellent plan.

"Are you going to fuck me out here in the open? Is that what mates do?" Amber ground out.

"Don't tempt me," he growled.

"Why did you lie to me?" She put her hands on his chest and pushed.

Darnell raised a brow, and she tsked, leaning her head back against the wall in resignation.

Damn, he wanted to kiss her.

But that was different from fucking. Kissing her softly and relishing the dark cherry taste that was Amber Evans was a whole other thing.

It was…affectionate.

"I didn't lie. I omitted some information," Darnell said, giving in to temptation and leaning down to suck her bottom lip. "Happy to let you take your frustration out on my cock."

Amber returned her eyes to his. "How kind of you."

He snorted and released her.

Taking her hand and ignoring her groan, he led them down to the employees' room, where a meal was being served.

The large restaurant that usually catered to the citizens of Castle Moretti was temporarily closed, but its kitchen was still functioning. So meals would periodically be served to those still in residence.

Max Bar was closed, as he suspected.

Amber waved at the females sitting across the room. Darnell spotted Logan, Mack, Callan, Tristan, and Kurt and gave them a nod. Then he grabbed two plates and went to hand Amber one.

She already had one in her hand.

"I'm your *fake* mate, not handicapped," Amber muttered.

"God, you're terrible at this."

"God, you're rude," Amber retorted.

Darnell chuckled as she spooned some salad and chicken onto her plate. "Eat more than that, Jesus," he said, scooping a large helping of potato mash and some type of beef onto his.

She sighed and glared at him. Her green eyes were full of fire. "Okay, let's get one thing very clear, warrior. No one, and I mean no one, has told me what to do since I was very little. And I'm not going to let anyone start now. Consider this a boundary."

Without taking his eyes from hers, he slopped a spoonful of mash on her plate. Then dropped the metal spoon and slapped her ass. "Come on. Let's go see our friends."

Man, this was much more fun than he had anticipated.

AN HOUR LATER, Darnell lounged on the sofa in the employees' room, his arm behind Amber. It had taken her a little while, but she'd eventually softened and leaned into him.

Mostly because Casey, who had shown up not long after they had with Alex, was watching them like a hawk.

It was like she saw right through their lie.

He had to get her off the scent. She was like a dog with a bone when she sensed bullshit. Which made her a great warrior, but Darnell needed her to let this go.

Everyone else had just accepted it. Including the prince.

"What job did you end up getting assigned?" Darnell shifted and turned his body into Amber's.

"Tom put me in housekeeping, but I asked to work in the kitchen," she replied.

"Oh, yeah? You going to poison me?" he teased.

She broke into a smile, which he knew she regretted when her pretty green eyes darted away. Forcing it down, she glanced at him again and lowered her voice. "I might. But if you give me the bed, I could consider a truce."

*Oh, baby, you're never sleeping on the couch.* She hadn't today, and she wouldn't any other day.

"Deal," he lied.

Not that vampires could be poisoned, but he liked that she was joking around with him.

"Want to get out of here?" he asked.

"Yeah. I might go for a run. Yoga is canceled, so I need to stretch my body."

Darnell stood, and they said their goodbyes. When they reached his rooms, he pulled off his Moretti jacket and tossed it on the armchair it normally landed on.

"This place needs sorting out. It's a mess," Amber said, her hands on her hips as she glanced around.

"Go crazy." He swept out his arms.

"I'm not your housekeeper," she snipped.

"Then I don't know what to tell you. Don't trip over my big ass boots, I guess." He laughed.

When he continued undressing and pulling on his shorts and a T-shirt, Amber started with the, *what are you fucking doing?*

"We're going for a run," he said, crouching to tie his shoelaces. "You getting changed?"

"Not *we*. Me. We aren't chained together. This is a fake relationship, not a prisoner situation." She propped her fists on her hips.

Darnell stood, walked around her, and plugged his phone into the charger.

Then he turned.

He'd had enough of the banter between them. Now it was his turn to set some boundaries.

"Here's how this is going to go," Darnell began, and her brows lifted slowly. "If I think an activity is something mates would do together, we're doing it. Together. If I think your life could be at risk, I'm going with you."

Her mouth opened, but he stepped toward her, and she quickly shut it.

"If I want to fuck you, you will spread your pretty legs." His hand cupped her hip and tugged her against him.

Amber palmed his pecs, and fire flared to life in those emerald globes.

"If I want you on your knees and my cock in your mouth, you will do it." His voice was thick now, his shorts tenting.

When she swallowed, the corner of his mouth lifted.

"You're wet, aren't you?"

"No," she tried to say, but it came out a jiggered whisper.

She was.

When his eyes dropped, he found hard nipples pointing at him.

"Let's see what this mouth can do." Darnell cupped her face. "Down on the floor."

"I—"

"You're wet and aching, so if you want me to do something about it, get on your knees, *mate.*" He pinched one of her nipples hard.

Amber let out a loud moan and dropped to the floor. Then his cock was in her hand, his shorts bunching under it from where she had quickly tugged them down, and she began to stroke.

Watching her lick her lips was hot as fuck.

"In your mouth, baby," Darnell moaned. "Fuck, I need you to suck me right goddamn now."

"I'm not swallowing," Amber said as she leaned forward and wrapped him in her hot, wet mouth.

*Holy hell.*

Pleasure shot up his shaft, and his brain lost most of its cognition as she worked him up and down. Whether she'd had lots of practice or it came naturally to her, Darnell had no idea, but damn, she knew what she was doing.

He steadied himself, widening his legs and gripping her hair, speeding her up and pushing himself deeper.

Next time they did this, he wanted her naked. He wanted to watch her breasts bounce as her mouth worked him and that sexy saliva leaked from her mouth.

He could fight the bond all he liked, but when they came together physically like this, it was the most real he'd ever felt.

He wasn't joking when he said he could fuck her twenty-four-seven. Amber appeared to want him just as much.

And just as often.

As her mouth caressed his shaft, the mating bond tugged at his senses, and his fangs itched to release.

It was only the image of his father's face, the memory of the pain he'd shared of his own father shaming him, that gave him the willpower to push the bond away.

He wouldn't do it.

Every day, he wanted Amber more. But he loved his family and needed to remember what was at stake.

He could do both.

Keep her safe.

Fuck her until they'd exhausted one another.

Then let her go.

He would find himself a beautiful mate and make his dad proud.

Amber gagged, and his balls tightened. Lord, this female was so damn sexy. Darnell gripped her face, pushed her back on her heels, and fucked her throat deep.

When her eyes widened, he let up.

"You gonna swallow?" he rasped.

Amber shook her head.

Fair enough. Not all females enjoyed it. But he wasn't stopping there. Darnell pulled out and ripped open her top as he stroked his cock.

There was something thoroughly carnal and erotic about shooting his sperm onto her generous breasts as she watched with complete, utter lust.

"Good girl," he growled.

Lifting her to her feet, he swirled his fingers through the white come on her chest and thumbed a nipple.

A moan escaped her.

"Don't wipe it off. Get on the bed naked and spread your legs," he ordered, ripping off her top with one swift move.

And yeah, he didn't miss the dark, seductive smile in her eyes.

## CHAPTER TWENTY-THREE

No matter how hard Amber tried, she woke up in Darnell's arms every day. She'd even snuck out of bed, curled up on the sofa, and woken up wrapped in his dark, muscular deliciousness.

Because as much as she complained, she had to admit—only to herself—that she slept amazingly in his bed.

In his arms.

He would never understand the gift that was. While Ronald had never touched her, every day, she'd worried he might. Not a lot, but it meant she never felt completely safe.

Nor at the hostel.

Now, with Darnell, even if it was fake, she was relaxed.

In truth, pretending to be his mate wasn't all bad. The sex was amazing.

Darnell thrived on taking it to the extreme. She had expected him to do the bare minimum, but oh no, if they were walking somewhere, he held her hand or wrapped an arm around her. Even if no one was there. If they sat, he tugged her onto his lap, and his cock was always semi-hard.

That was where she had trouble differentiating truth from fiction.

Sure, it was a physical reaction, but it was beginning to feel real between them. Her body reacted every time and obeyed his every order. All day and all night.

His dominance had her wet even with a simple glance. Last night, she'd been brushing her teeth, and their eyes had met in the mirror. Next minute, she was up on the counter, and his mouth was on her pussy.

Life was not miserable.

He never let her shower alone, and at this point, she wasn't complaining. Sex shower with Darnell was... otherworldly.

He'd opened a package in front of her yesterday, and in it was a large pink vibrator. When her mouth had fallen open, he'd told her not to get too excited and pulled his cock out to show that he was bigger.

Which he was.

Still, she pretended to be unsure and ended up on her back with his mouth on hers.

The moment the buzzing dildo slid through her wet folds, she'd been toast. Crying out as Darnell teased her for what felt like hours. He finally slid his cock inside her and made her hold it on her clit while he slammed into her.

Amber came so hard she nearly turned inside out.

"What a good little pretend mate slut," Darnell muttered into her hair, and *damn him,* it made her want him again. So she spun around and mounted him, unsurprised to find him already hard again. Then rode him right there on the floor.

For a moment afterward, when he lifted her onto the bed and she lay in his arms, a warm glow enveloped her.

It was a feeling so foreign but so right, and she'd tried to hold on to it. But it had faded away to nothing. Then Darnell had kissed her shoulder and whispered, "Sleep well, baby."

Every day, she reminded herself that what they had was fake. But the lies they told felt less like lies and more like half-truths.

At least to her.

Life in the castle was strange now, more so for those who had lived here longer. Amber quite liked it. Luck had been on her side when Tom agreed she could swap her role. She had longed to secure a job in a kitchen, and here she was, working with the Moretti chefs.

Wow.

While she couldn't stray from the menu, Chef Rogers complimented her on her skills and even thanked her for being so great to work with the first day.

"Not going to lie, Amber. I was not looking forward to having inexperienced people in my kitchen," Chef Rogers said. "But you have picked everything up quickly and shown excellent initiative."

She preened. "Thank you, Chef."

"I might not give you back after," he warned with a wink before returning to work.

Was that a possibility?

Amber didn't want to get her hopes up, but she would do whatever it took to get out of serving patrons in a bar and learning more from amazing masters like Chef Rogers.

The next day after her shift, she asked if she could test a recipe, and he hesitated before asking to take a look at it.

"Interesting." He nodded. "Go ahead. Go light on the ingredients so we don't run out of anything. And leave me a sample."

She danced on the spot and almost hugged him. "Thank you. I will."

As he walked out, he called. "And clean up!"

"Yes, Chef."

What a dream come true.

She glanced around the Michelin Star-worthy kitchen and tugged up her sleeves then began to gather her ingredients. Firing up a fry pan, she added some oil, tossed in the chopped onions, and sliced some garlic.

Taking notes as she went, she continued playing and trying different combinations. Time disappeared in a blur of creativity and delicious aromas.

A few hours later, she leaned over a plate and spooned it into her mouth.

"So this is where my mate is hiding," a dark, sexy voice purred, jolting her out of her fog.

Amber's head shot up.

Darnell leaning on the doorjamb, looking stupidly sexy in his Moretti uniform. His feet crossed at the ankles.

"Am I not feeding you enough?" He frowned.

"No, I just—"

He tugged the fork from her hand and stabbed a piece of the veal. She watched him lift it to his mouth and moan as he closed his lips around it.

"Jesus," Darnell said with his mouth full. "Vis is dewishous."

She smiled.

"You guys eat well in here. Tell the chef he needs to share the king's menu with the rest of us," he added.

Her smile faded.

She was the chef.

Why had he not even assumed she had cooked it?

Darnell dropped the fork and patted her ass. One of his favorite things to do, it seemed. "Come on. I know you like to run, so let's go before it gets light."

Amber pressed her lips together and nodded.

It would do no good to take offense. Why would he think she'd had been the one to create the tasty dish? She was only a barmaid in his eyes.

A slice of hurt rushed through her.

She'd been having so much fun and was proud of how it turned out. It never occurred to her that someone would assume this wasn't her work. The fact it was Darnell hurt more.

"I just need to put this away," Amber said, setting aside a sample for Chef Rogers as promised.

"You know, you should probably check if you're allowed to help yourself to those meals," Darnell said, stealing one of the potatoes she had roasted in duck fat. "Holy hell, these are good."

She slapped his hand.

"I'm allowed," she muttered and walked over to the walk-in fridge, tucking the meal away.

Amber added a note so the chef would see it when he started work during the next shift and decided not to let Darnell's ignorance get to her.

What did she expect?

She was a no-one from nowhere.

Maybe coming to work for the Moretti's would open more than one door. She'd made new friends and might end up with the career she'd always dreamed of.

Once the danger to the king was over, she could unravel this fake relationship with Darnell, and they could both get on with their lives.

# CHAPTER TWENTY-FOUR

"Bazza, keep your focus ahead of you. Trust the team backing you up," Darnell called as his team finished yet another training exercise.

These war games helped simulate what happened in the field, and right now, they were running drills, assuming the serum was in play and humans were a threat.

Despite the fact they were an enemy, the captain had been clear their goal was not to eliminate, rather to slow them down.

In other words, wound not kill.

He sensed a warrior behind him right before he was kicked in the back of his knees. But his reflexes were fast. Darnell leaped up and dropped behind her.

"Casey," he growled as she spun around.

"How do you move so fast when you weigh four million pounds?" she grumbled.

"Rude."

She snickered, and the two of them wandered away from his team. As he leaned back against the wall and drank from his water bottle, Casey lifted herself onto the table next to him. "So where's lover girl?"

Here we go.

He'd been expecting the question sooner or later. Outspoken didn't begin to describe Casey, but she cared deeply for her friends.

Despite the cynicism in her eyes, it was likely that she was worried about him.

"At work," he said.

"That happened fast."

"When you know, you know." Darnell shrugged and took another drink.

"What's her background?"

Darnell knew she meant well, but that didn't mean her interrogation didn't aggravate him.

"I don't know, Case. Why don't you make friends with her and ask for yourself?"

"We are friends. But you don't know, do you?" she asked, not missing a fucking beat. "I can smell a rat, and I want to know what you two are up to."

Goddamn her.

"Casey!" Kurt, her team leader, called. "Get your ass back over here."

Darnell shot her a look.

"Something stinks, Darnell. I'm going to find out." She leaped off the table and shot him a look as she ran off.

"Sniff away," he muttered, knowing she'd hear him.

*Fuck.*

The truth was, his plan wasn't going all that well. His cock was happy. Everyone except Casey believed them, but he was finding it harder to fight the bond now biting at his ankles like a piranha.

But Amber was safe, and he had to remember why he was doing this.

"Start at the top," he called out, walking back to his team. "Jones, you take the lead. I want to see you in and out in under five."

There was no way he'd be able to focus on what needed to be done right now, knowing Amber was out in the world without a place to live or a job.

Or someone else trying to get under her skirt.

Or being unable to do it himself.

And this is where he kept getting tripped up because while he felt the bond calling out to him like the grim fucking reaper, and he was sure it was a simple case of just saying no, he was beginning to wonder if maybe he was wrong.

Today, when he'd walked Amber to work, Darnell had watched her skip into the kitchen and high-five one of the other kitchen hands.

The guy had then followed her wiggling ass with his eyes. Amber had been so focused on talking animatedly to the chef that she'd paid no attention.

But he had.

And he'd felt murderous.

The sex was incredible, creating an intimacy between them that wouldn't be there otherwise, but having her in his home and in his arms when he woke seemed to be getting under his skin far more than sinking his cock inside her.

Which was confusing as hell.

Maybe he should let her sleep on the sofa.

*Fuck that.*

Then, as if he'd conjured his petite flaming-haired beauty, she walked into the vast room with a container in her arms.

Tonight, Amber wore a pair of black jeans and a tight black tank top that left nothing to the imagination regarding the shape and size of her breasts. *His breasts.*

He wandered over to the table Casey had been sitting on, and Amber changed course to meet him.

"Hi, I—" she started as he lifted his Moretti jacket and wrapped it around her shoulders. "What are you doing?"

"Covering you up. Have you seen how many males are in this room?" Darnell growled.

Amber glanced around. "Do they have x-ray vision?"

"What?"

"What?"

"Don't be a smart ass," he grunted.

"Then don't be stupid." She shrugged off the jacket, and he caught it as it fell to the ground.

Then put it back on her.

"What's that?" he asked, looking at the plastic Tupperware.

Her cheeks turned pink.

Cute and sexy. She was going to kill him.

"Some leftovers."

"Cool. We can walk down to the lake and eat," he said as he threaded her arms through the jacket and zipped it up. "Keep it on."

Amber sighed.

"Let me wrap this up, and we can head on out and taste tonight's delicious morsel." Darnell nodded at his team.

"Okay," she replied.

Darnell wondered why her cheeks were deepening with a blush. "Hey," he said, taking her chin. "It's normal to bring your male dinner and go on a date. Don't be embarrassed."

Her brows bunched, and she slapped him away. "I'm not. Forget it."

He laughed at her and strode over to the team. "Okay, boys. Hit the circuit for twenty laps and then hit the showers."

"Come on. Ten laps," someone called.

Darnell smirked. "I'm in a good mood. My girl brought me dinner, so yeah, ten."

He hoped the chef wouldn't get upset with Amber for helping herself to the food. It wasn't like a bar where you could pour the odd drink for yourself and a friend. Still, he liked that she was trying to play the part of his mate.

Despite everything, he didn't want to be anywhere else but with her and going on their fake date.

That didn't feel fake at all.

AFTER GRABBING A blanket and some bottles of water, they wandered down to the lake at the back of the Moretti property and settled in a soft place on the grass bank.

Amber pulled out a couple of paper plates and bamboo utensils and served the meal.

His eyes widened.

They all ate like kings, so to speak, at the castle. The SLC team was well taken care of. But his mouth fell open when she layered slices of thick roasted chicken and poured an incredibly aromatic gravy over it, adding baby carrots, more of those damn roasted potatoes, and what looked like slithers of zucchini.

"Okay, so I hope this is enough," she said, handing him the plate. "I also have some flourless rich chocolate cake with an orange zest." Her eyes lifted to his. "Oh. You aren't allergic to citrus, are you?"

"Nope." Darnell shook his head and took the plate.

"Dig in," she said and lifted her fork to her mouth. "It's so nice to be out here under the stars."

One mouthful of the chicken, and he was moaning. "Jesus, this is good."

He didn't want to offend her efforts, but he'd have to check with the chef to make sure they were taking liberties. Being an SLC had influence, and Amber might not be aware that the chef thought he had no choice but to say yes if she was asking to take home leftovers.

Because clearly, this was for the royal family.

Not that they ate spam every night. But this chicken was tender as fuck, and he could taste the herbs it was seasoned with. And orange zest… Jesus.

"Yeah, it's nice out here," he said with his mouth full. Mostly because he couldn't stop eating long enough to find his manners. "You help make this?"

Amber lifted her shoulder. "Sure."

He didn't want to embarrass her, so let it go. But he would definitely speak to the chef.

As he moved on to the chocolate cake—*flourless, by the way. And who the hell needed flour because this shit was incredible?*—Darnell leaned his arm on a knee and recalled Casey's question from earlier.

"So, firecracker, tell me about your life before meeting me," he said as an owl hooted from one of the trees.

"There's not much to say. Pretty boring. You?" she asked, wiping her mouth with a paper napkin.

Amber did this every time. She diverted the conversation back to him.

But he was done with her tactics.

"Already told you. I grew up in Chicago. My dad is a chef, and my mom is a lawyer. After I left high school, I joined the army and have worked my way up to senior lieutenant commander more recently."

"I saw you on VampNet when you were sworn in." Amber smiled at him.

"Oh, yeah?" Darnell asked, loving that she had.

She nodded, taking a bite of her cake.

"Fancy me back then, too, huh?" he teased.

She snorted. "In your dreams, warrior."

"Baby, you are in my arms while I dream these days." He reached out and pinched the side of her bottom.

Amber slapped at his hand. "Temporarily. Don't get comfortable."

Darnell dropped his plate and rubbed his stomach as he lay down and stared up at the stars. "Who knows how long this will go on for? Might be years."

She gasped. "What? It will not."

"Probably not. But would that be so bad? You don't hate living with me, do you?"

"No," she replied softly.

His eyes drifted back, watching as she packed everything away and sat beside him, crossing her legs.

"Come here." Darnell reached for her, and without hesitation, Amber stretched her body alongside his, her head on his bicep. "I could unzip those jeans and have my fingers inside you in minutes, and you wouldn't stop me."

"No," she admitted, and she wriggled with arousal.

"But you won't tell me where you grew up," he pushed, determined to get answers out of her.

Not because he should know, but because Casey had got under his skin. Whether Amber was his for now or forever, Darnell wanted to know who she was.

He cared.

And it was starting to irk him that something really fucking bad had happened to her.

"Fine. California." She sighed. "Then Virginia. There. Now you know."

"Christ, I thought you were going to say it was Hyder, Alaska, or something."

"What's wrong with Alaska?" She twisted her head to glance up at him.

"The population of Hyder is eighty-seven. Eighty-seven people. Can you imagine that? There are more people living in the castle, even with the evacuation," Darnell said, trying to lighten the topic so she'd open up more. "Okay, so now you're oversharing, and that's a joke, by the way. What do your parents do?"

"They're dead."

Oh. Fuck.

"I'm sorry." He cursed, taking her chin. "Amber, fuck, I'm sorry. When did it happen?"

She shook him off and lay her head back down, but he could feel her tensing. He felt like an asshole. No wonder she didn't want to talk about it. She was grieving.

"A long time ago," Amber replied.

*Ah, there goes that theory.*

"I was thirteen." She sighed, and he zipped his lips to see if she'd keep talking. And she did. "Mom was carjacked, then the sun got her, and Dad took his life not long after that."

Jesus.

"Baby." He wrapped his arms around her, but Amber had completely stiffened.

"Don't. It is what it is," she said coldly. "Life wasn't the same after that. I didn't have the same happy upbringing as you. Or most people."

His fists clenched, imagining the worst-case scenario. "Did someone—"

"No. I wasn't raped. No one touched me. Not physically, at least," she said. "Sometimes abuse is invisible. But people don't talk about that stuff. People don't understand it."

Fury began to bubble deep within him, but who did he aim it at? He had no target. Who were the people who had done this to her?

And what had they done?

"Tell me," he ground out.

She twisted, pointing those green globes at him and resting her chin on her hand as she lay on his pec. "How about we get to the part where you slide your fingers inside me?"

Darnell closed his eyes, hating that his cock jumped in response. And he was going to let her get away with the diversion. Yet again.

Her past was obviously painful, and he had a feeling if he pushed too hard, she would close right down.

"Fuck."

"Correct," she said, sliding a hand under his T-shirt.

Her touch had him on fire. He gripped her with both hands and pulled her on top of him, his mouth taking hers. She wrapped her arms around his head and threaded her fingers through his dark, curly hair.

He loved the way she did that. It sent pleasure all the way to the end of his cock.

"I'll fuck you," he said against her warm lips. "But we are not done talking."

"Yes, we are big boy," Amber said, reaching into his black sweats and gripping his cock.

She was right.

For now, the conversation was over.

For now.

# CHAPTER TWENTY-FIVE

As Darnell lowered her onto his engorged cock, Amber pushed down the emotions that had risen to the surface as she revisited her childhood.

Hardly arousing stuff, yet this male was able to make her hot and wet for him in seconds. The deep timber of his voice, the way he unapologetically used his strength to dominate and own her body as his wild blue eyes locked with hers.

"Wait," she said, gripping his biceps.

He was going too fast. She wasn't wet enough.

"You can take me in one," Darnell gritted out, need making his eyes crinkle. "I want to feel the way your pussy clenches me on the first pass."

God, she loved his dirty mouth.

Despite his width and length, he did fit perfectly. Snug and delicious, filling every inch and stimulating all her senses until every cell in her body was awake, alert, on fire, and wanting more.

Plus, it was easier to fuck than talk.

She didn't want to do more of that.

He now knew she didn't have an idyllic childhood. That was enough. Details wouldn't change it. It would only make him judge her.

And she liked how things were going.

Life had not been safe for Amber, so it was unusual for her to trust anyone. But she seemed to be.

One day, while they were watching TV, Darnell had tucked her under his arm while Amber scrolled through social media. She heard him laughing as her eyes flickered closed and realized she had dozed off.

When he lifted her off the sofa and shushed her as she stiffened, Amber let her eyes fall closed again and almost purred when he tucked her into bed.

Had her mother been the last one to do that?

Who knew, but when Darnell's lips landed on her forehead, then froze, she used every ounce of willpower she had not to react and pretend she was asleep.

Fucking was one thing. Even sleeping in the same bed, which appeared to be what they did now, was another.

But butterfly kisses on the forehead?

That was terrifying.

And beautiful.

But not real.

It couldn't be.

"Come here." Darnell cupped the back of her head and tugged her face down to his. His full lips surrounded hers, sucking before thrusting his tongue inside while his cock plunged in and out of her.

God, he was clever with that thing.

"Grind on me, baby," he instructed, pressing her down on him so her clit grazed along his muscles.

"Oh, shit," she cried as his mouth moved along her neck. "D! God. Shit,"

She felt him swell and thicken as she clenched him tightly. And the fireworks began.

"That's it, yes, fuck," Darnell rasped. "Fuck, Amber, fuck."

Then she felt his fangs.

*Oh, God.*

The sharp incisors sunk into her neck, and suddenly everything magnified as an erotic rush from Darnell's essence entered her. He pulled from her vein as she ground down on his cock, and their moans filled the air.

Pleasure like she'd never experienced before, overtook her as their blood merged, creating a bond that neither of them could ever undo.

*Holy fuck.*

Darnell's mouth ripped from her, their eyes locking in horror as both of their orgasms shuddered through them.


AMBER STARED INTO the mirror as she brushed her teeth, taking in the still-healing puncture wounds in her neck. She ran her fingers over them, and a shot of arousal rushed between her legs.

She glanced around at the empty room.

Every morning before bed, if they were still awake, Darnell brushed his teeth with her. Usually so he could play with her ass. Then fuck her once she'd rinsed.

But he hadn't today.

After biting her, he'd gone deathly quiet.

His only response had been a mumbled, "Shit, I'm sorry. I shouldn't have done that," as they walked quietly back to the castle.

Where he'd then disappeared.

Amber didn't feel like she had a right to know where Darnell was twenty-four-seven, but he'd made a habit of telling her from the moment they started living together.

Days.

Hardly a pattern, but still.

She changed into a white silk nightie and climbed into bed. Then turned off the lamp on her side, leaving Darnell's on.

How her life had changed.

Overnight, her whole world seemed different. She was living with a male, working in a kitchen, living her dream, and having mind-blowing sex.

Well, it had been tonight after he'd sunk his teeth into her.

It had been the most erotic moment of her life.

Until she'd seen his face.

Now, she hated how empty it made her feel. Every day she felt herself becoming a little reliant on him emotionally, and it scared her.

Because after this was over, she would be alone again.

Fake mating was better than she'd been expecting.

She wanted to tell him it was okay to bite her. Not that she'd done it before.

While biting was a mate-bonding thing, other lovers did it. It just took things to a whole other level erotically, and she could attest to that.

She had sensed his essence and was well aware it had made them closer than they'd ever meant to be.

Had it freaked Darnell out?

Surely he knew she would never expect anything from him. Even if she was enjoying their fake mating, neither of them could make it real if it wasn't.

And it wasn't.

Right?

So why did she feel she was missing a limb right now?

Why did she make dishes—yes, to impress the chef—to watch Darnell moan and lick his lips when he devoured her cooking?

Watching him destroy the chocolate cake had been so arousing tonight. His eyes fluttering as his mouth closed around it.

Amber wasn't sure why she was so aloof about it being her cooking. Almost like she had to stay in her lane. She didn't want anyone to know it was her dream, only to end up behind the bar as a nobody again.

It was better to keep these things to yourself. She wasn't sure she'd survive it if Darnell laughed at her.

Having him doubt her would…yeah, it would hurt.

When nobody believed in you, this was what happened.

And she wanted Darnell to believe she was more than a girl who served drinks. She wanted him to know that the morsels he put in his mouth were of her making. Meals she had prepared with him in mind, wanting to please him.

Not only with her body but with the heart and soul she put into her art.

Because Amber had a dream of being the chef walking into a room and everyone applauding.

Everyone needed a dream.

Right now, having the opportunity to cook in such an incredible kitchen was pure joy. Then, coming home and being ravished by her tall, dark warrior god was good enough.

She just hoped Darnell would come home.

Amber lay awake for hours, wondering where he'd gone. Wondering who he was with and why he had taken off.

Finally, she drifted into a fitful sleep.

# CHAPTER TWENTY-SIX

"Mr. Moretti," James Calder, President of the United States, said through the speaker.

Vincent adjusted the volume and leaned back in his chair. "James. Thank you for being available," he said, refusing to directly call him by his title as president as always.

Vincent was a king and ruler of his world. They tolerated human laws and respected them for the sake of fitting into this society.

But Vincent was the king.

He was born to the role and would never be knocked from his throne like these temporary politicians. That wasn't to say he didn't like the man. He did.

James was a pragmatic and sensible ally. But he wasn't ruled by a president, prime minister, king, or any other human.

Vincent ruled his species.

End of story.

Still, society required compromise, forgiveness, and agreement to live peacefully on the planet they shared. It was clear which cultures in the human population *still* hadn't figured that out.

There was historical pain, yes, but to move forward, one had to forgive.

In families. In love. In communities. In war.

Otherwise, it was simply a repetition of the same. How did that saying go? If you keep doing the same thing, you will keep getting the same result.

Anything else was simply a victim mentality designed to keep you stuck. And yeah, he knew that fucked people off, but he didn't make the rules. It was what it was.

Vincent wouldn't make the same mistake for his vampires.

"Of course. I only have ten minutes before the British royals arrive, but I wanted to speak to you first," James replied. "I have been inundated with calls and messages from UN members."

*Here we go.*

"I'm not surprised if I'm being honest. This is a huge moment in human history. Discovering we exist," Vincent said darkly. "But our race is at threat, and now that we live in modern times, we are limited in how we can deal with things."

"Please don't tell me what you did in the past," James groaned

Vincent laughed. "I won't."

What they didn't know, and would hopefully never know, was that vampires had the ability to telepath one another and manipulate human memory.

There were limits to that.

It was highly complex, and there was what they called the tipping point. Making it impossible to contain.

Right now, the number of people who knew about vampires had created a tipping point, thanks to rebel vampire Stefano Russo and BioZen's involvement. They had cleaned up as much as possible, but it was now out of hand. Vincent had hoped to take control by creating

Operation Daylight, but then the fucking mafia got involved.

Nikolay Mikhailov was probably their deadliest enemy yet.

Ironically, he was human.

The Russian had no respect for human life. Nor human laws. And he thrived on power and playing with fire.

Now, he had challenged the vampire king.

What a fucking fruit loop.

Or, as Craig liked to call him, future roadkill.

Vincent wasn't a bloodthirsty king—although he drank the stuff every day—but yeah, if the moment arose, he wouldn't hold back his commander.

Craig had full permission to destroy the human, and Vincent would deal with any political reaction.

He had a feeling there wouldn't be a serious one.

"Listen, Vincent, there is great concern in your declaration announcement. The unrest it could cause in an already volatile world is too risky," James shared.

Vincent didn't disagree, but he needed to ensure whatever they decided was in the best interest of his race.

"So what do you suggest, Calder? We've had a year of meetings, and while we've put some roadmaps in place, the process is too fucking slow."

"I agree."

"But?" Vincent asked.

"Better slow than exploding. I have enough nations at war, as you know." James sighed. "I've spoken to over a dozen heads of state, and they are all willing to put vast resources into eliminating the threat to your race."

Vincent's brows shot to his hairline. He was having a hard time believing what he was hearing. And he needed to clarify it very fucking clearly.

Because there could be no gray area.

"Let me get this straight," he said, his ancient Italian accent rising to the surface. "You're willing to eliminate the mafia. All of them? Because you know they're in partnership, right?"

"I'm aware."

"The Russians. The Italians. The Irish. The Mexicans," he spelled out.

"I know who they are, Vincent. But here's the thing. There are eight billion people on the planet. A few mean to take control by fear-mongering and being the sole producers of this serum. No one can have that much power. Over you or the governments of the world."

No.

But if you looked at it like that, the very existence of the vampire race was not dissimilar. It was only a matter of time before humans saw them as having too much power and being a danger.

Fortunately for Vincent, humans were up to their necks in their own internal human battles and concerns.

"And I won't let it happen," James said firmly, sounding like the world leader he was. "While learning about you has shaken me to the core, you have proven to be a thoughtful leader and a respectful ally. We have hundreds of years of history showing you are no threat to our race."

Wow.

He took a moment to let those words sink in. It was unlikely the president would ever say them publicly, but they meant a lot.

If only Gio and Francis, his grandfather and father, were alive today to hear them. It was an achievement he was proud of.

"So, how is this going to work?" Vincent asked. "The UN knows about us now. So do a bunch of fucking gangsters. Eventually, it's going to spread."

"Listen, it's just like the alien conversation. Even if people believe, it doesn't change anything unless someone like me makes an official announcement," the president said. "With the amount of information and misinformation, it'll just end up on Netflix or something."

Vincent let out a snort.

James was right.

A part of him relaxed as he realized they were buying themselves more time. "Then I want my team involved. We have warriors around the world who will work with your human teams and report back to me."

He heard a pen tapping.

"That's the only way this works, James. I'm not taking someone else's word for it that the serum production has been destroyed. We partner or nothing."

"Fair enough. But the UN doesn't work like that. I'm not in charge. I can't dictate."

But Vincent could.

"I can still push broadcast. Tell them these are my terms," Vincent said firmly.

It was almost like POTUS was smiling. When he spoke, Vincent heard it in his voice. Damn, the guy had been leading him there all along.

Smart.

"I'll have an answer for you by the morning," James said.

Then Vincent dropped the bomb. "Oh, by the way, a bunch of mobsters are on the way to Maine to blow us up."

"Jesus, when?" James groaned.

"Today. Tomorrow. Not sure. But we'll be taking the same strategy as the UN."

As in *boom*, you're dead.

Craig was going to be thrilled.

The president cursed. "Fuck. Just keep it low-key so we don't have to deal with local authorities and media."

"There won't be any officials involved. This is not our first rodeo, James." Vincent smiled.

When they hung up, Vincent pushed his chair back and sat for a moment, thinking.

This was a good solution.

The fact the human race was willing to take such swift action was bold and smart.

Was he happy that lives were about to be lost? No. But as James had rightly pointed out, the impact was greater than a few hundred mobsters. They'd chosen their path.

Now, they had a strategy to move forward with.

*Bray!*

*If this is an emergency, let me know. Otherwise, I'm getting dressed first.*

*It's a cover your cock meeting.*

*You are an idiot.*

Vincent let out a laugh. Finally, he was feeling optimistic.

But first, they had a battle to fight.

# CHAPTER TWENTY-SEVEN

"You know the bar is closed, right?" Casey asked, appearing in front of Darnell.

Goddamn it.

"I left a twenty on the cash register, Mother Teresa. Settle down," he said, lifting his beer to his lips.

What the hell was she doing here? And why did it have to be her who found him when he was trying to have a minute to himself to figure out what he'd just done?

Bitten Amber, that's what he'd fucking done.

One step away from bonding them together for eternity.

To make matters even worse, his father had messaged him. Darnell couldn't even bear to open it, let alone reply.

And it wasn't that he didn't give a shit about Amber. He did.

Very much.

You didn't get this close to bonding with your mate without caring. Hell, he was pretty sure he was falling in goddamn love with her.

Which was a pain in the ass.

Because he also loved his family.

What an idiot he'd been to think he could fight nature. He might not be in this situation if he'd listened to Amber, kept the *faking* for when others were around, and let her sleep on the sofa.

Instead, he was drowning his sorrows in shitty beer that couldn't even get him drunk and worrying about Amber's stupid fucking emotions.

Not that they were stupid.

He was stupid.

Stupid for not letting her leave so he didn't fall in love with her.

*Like you could have let her.*

"Good, then you can pay for my beer too." Casey walked behind the bar and grabbed one from the fridge. With a flick of the cap, she returned to his table and sat opposite him.

"Go away," he growled.

"Wow, for someone so in love, you're really grumpy."

"For someone so short, you're really annoying," Darnell grumbled.

Casey laughed.

"I miss this," she said, tossing back her beer.

"What?" Darnell snapped, not in the mood.

"Winding you up. Being mated is kind of restrictive at times. Don't get me wrong, I would kill for Alex. But you males are so protective. I can't banter with you the way we used to. He'd kill you or something."

He could try.

"Hmm," he replied instead.

"You like that with Amber? Uber protective?" she prodded.

"Guess so."

Darnell wasn't playing her game. He knew what Casey was getting at, but she wasn't prying anything out of him.

Plus, she was lying.

Alex hadn't stopped that noisy little mouth of hers one bit. Casey was still the outspoken little minx she'd always been. And one of his best friends.

Soon to be ex if she didn't fuck off in thirty seconds.

Darnell spun his bottle, glaring at her and waiting for the next dig, but it never came. Casey sat there, staring at him.

Finally, his patience snapped.

He tossed back the rest of his beer, slammed it on the table, and met her stare. "Say what you need to say, Casey, then fuck off."

"Amber is not your mate." Casey shook her head.

"Yes, she is."

Ironically, he'd be lying if they'd had this conversation three hours ago. Not anymore.

"No. She. Is. Not." She leaned forward and pointed at his eyes. "You forgot one little detail. Why are your eyes not black around the rim?"

Fuck.

He'd forgotten that. Why had the prince not called him on it? Nor any of the others.

"My eyes are dark brown, nearly black. You can't see it." But it did give him pause.

Was he wrong about Amber?

The moment his teeth had sunk into Amber's flesh tonight, he'd been sure she was his mate. The bond was there for the taking. All it needed was for Amber to bite him and take his blood during the sexual act, and they would be bound.

Instead, the shock had given him the willpower to get her back to his room and hightail it out of there.

But Casey had a point. His eyes hadn't changed, and they should have now.

So there was a small chance he was wrong about all of this. Amber might not be his mate after all.

"Jesus, Darnell, you lied to the fucking prince. There will be consequences." She shook her head.

He stood suddenly and slammed his fist on the table. "Just leave it, Casey. Amber is mine. She's just...I'm just not... just not bonding with her, okay?"

"Why the hell not?" Casey asked, flinching away from him in shock.

"It's complicated."

"Uncomplicate it. Tell me."

Darnell knew about Casey's history. She had been born to an aristocratic human male, and when his mate had turned him vampire, he'd never let go of his old-school values. All of which were excuses to control his daughter.

Giving her a few years of freedom, Casey had joined the Moretti army, and when the time was up, her father had come to retrieve her.

So she knew about family expectations.

But the thing was, his parents had never said a thing to him. Never asked anything of him. It was their beliefs and values in life he was trying to live up to.

The shame his father had endured from his drunken father had scarred him for life. *You are scum. Look at you, working bar and scrubbing floors. You no-hopers.* But his father hadn't let it weaken him. He'd worked hard and made something of himself.

Unfortunately, he'd never had the chance to prove himself.

Every day, his father donned his chef uniform proudly and said the same thing in the mirror. "I am a better man than you ever were."

They all knew he wasn't talking to himself.

But to the ghost of his dead father.

The wounds were still there despite what he'd achieved. He hadn't been able to show the man while he was alive, something he would never get over.

So how could Darnell bring home a girl and announce she was his mate? Then say, oh, yeah, she works bar.

*No.*

No fucking way.

He might never have said it out loud, but Darnell knew his father expected the best for him. Hope and expectation were very close. He was sure they hoped his mate was someone amazing.

Unspoken, yes, but that didn't mean he wasn't aware of the expectation.

Casey had her experience with her family, and she had suffered, but Darnell was sure she wouldn't understand.

She would think he had a choice.

He didn't feel like he did.

Plus, he felt like an asshole when he thought about saying it out loud. *Amber isn't good enough for me or my family.* What a jerk.

She was plenty good enough when he was walking down the hall with his hand in hers, or lying on the grass under the stars, or when he slid his cock inside her.

Plenty.

"I'm not telling you anything, Casey. I need you to keep this to yourself." He glared at her. "Just be her friend. The rest is between her and I."

"I am her friend. She's a cool chick. I just don't like that she has pulled you into something you might lose your career over," Casey said.

He ran a hand over his hair and sighed. "Honestly, she hasn't. I want her here. With me."

And he wasn't sure he would be able to let her go.

Sooner or later, he was going to have to choose.

"Shit," Casey said, and her eyes glazed over momentarily. A sure sign she was telepathing. A second later, Alex teleported in.

"What's going on?" his fellow SLC asked.

"I was trying to have a quiet beer. Your mate showed up and started harassing me," Darnell said.

As they walked into each other's arms like two muscular magnets, Darnell felt a pang of regret.

He'd left Amber on her own. After their awesome date by the lake. After the delicious meal. After making love under the stars.

After fucking biting her.

Then just left her.

Whether she was his mate or not, Amber didn't deserve this. He had chosen this. He'd talked her into this whole fake mate thing.

It was time to man up and go home.

The more he thought about her lying awake in the dark, wondering where he was, the more powerful the pull was to get home.

"Everything okay?" Alex asked, frowning at him.

"I need to get home. See you in a few hours," Darnell said, shooting Casey a warning glance.

He'd lost many hours of sleep sitting here stewing. Now, all he wanted was Amber in his arms and to know she was okay.

Alex nodded as Darnell teleported away.

Landing in his living room, relief struck him as he walked to the doorway of his bedroom and saw the small lump in his bed.

Ripping off his clothes, Darnell tossed them on the chair where his other clothes had been neatly folded. Not by him. He cursed silently, then quickly folded his discarded clothing.

Damn females. They changed you.

Sliding under the covers, he reached for Amber and felt the soft silk of her nightie under his fingertips. She let out a little moan as he pulled her against his chest.

"Darnell?" she whispered.

"Were you expecting someone else?" he teased softly.

She rolled in his arms and their eyes locked. "Where did you go?" she asked, and as he knew they would, hurt shone from them.

"Somewhere to think," he answered honestly.

Amber continued staring at him. It was as if she could see into his soul and all the truths he was trying to keep hidden.

Her fingers pressed into his pecs, and he became suddenly highly aware of every single inch of her body against his. Her thighs pressing against his. His hands cupping her soft ass. Her toes pressing into his legs, her tummy flush against his own.

Amber fit him like a jigsaw piece.

Her wild hair fell around her face, and while he knew she was scared, he wanted to tell her how brave she was.

Because he knew she had feelings for him.

If they were anywhere as close as the ones he was feeling, he was surprised she hadn't bolted.

She might not have shared much about her life, but he had a feeling love had been missing. They were wildly different. He'd been loved beyond measure.

And under different circumstances, he'd want nothing more than to fall madly in love with this gorgeous creature and spend his life pleasuring her, keeping her safe, and making her happy.

It was as if he'd known from the moment he'd met her. The need to take her under his wing as if she belong—

*Stop.*

He felt himself falling and wasn't sure he could crawl back out if he didn't hold on.

"Do you want me to leave?" Amber suddenly asked, her pupils dilated.

"No," Darnell responded immediately, tugging her closer, his hand threading through her hair. Then said again more firmly. "No."

His mouth pressed over hers, forcing her to open as he swept his tongue inside.

*No.*

*Never.*

That was the problem.

# CHAPTER TWENTY-EIGHT

*C*runch.

Nikolay ripped his fist from the wall. Blood and plaster blending and falling to the floor.

"Who did this?" he roared.

The Italian mobster sucked on his Cuban cigar, his eyes narrowing, and slowly blew out the smoke. His face would be fucking next if he didn't start talking.

And why the hell wasn't Enzo Romano as furious as he was?

Because he didn't fully understand the stakes.

"Well, that's the question, isn't it Mikhailov? People are starting to talk. The Italians. The Mexicans. Have you set us up?" Romano asked.

Nikolay's face heated as his fury rose to an all-time high.

"Have. I. Set. You. Up?" he ground out. His breath was shallow as he tried to restrain himself.

Another draw on that fucking cigar.

Then the Italian mob boss nodded. Like he was agreeing it was a nice goddamn day.

"For fuck's sake, Enzo. We are on the precipice of creating one of the most important products that will ever be manufactured, and you think I'm setting you up? Jesus, I'm trying to set us *all* up for success."

Demetri stepped into the room. Nikolay nodded at him to speak.

"The delivery is here," Demetri said in thick Russian so the Italian assholes couldn't understand. Which was probably exasperating the mistrust, but right now, Nikolay's patience was thin as fuck, so too bad.

Plus, he didn't want any of them knowing about this. The delivery Demetri was referring to was weapons.

"Good. Inspect them, and you can approve. I need to deal with this shit," Nikolay replied in his mother tongue. "Load them up and get the team ready."

"Yes, Pakhan," Demetri said, heading back out the door.

Soon, they would be heading to Maine. Portland, to be exact, and visiting his friend Vincent.

"More secrets." Enzo lifted a brow.

"We all have our businesses to run," Nikolay said, lifting his vodka and tossing back a healthy shot. "Now we've lost a manufacturing plant, which will delay our schedule. Should I start looking for different partners?"

The production line where their biggest production of the serum was finally underway had been destroyed. An explosion. Enzo had advised him that the fire chief was vague about what caused it.

The security cameras magically stopped working.

Fucking vampires.

They had to be involved.

But it did seem contrary to their behavior to date, giving Nikolay pause for thought. If they truly did know what he was up to, he wouldn't put it past the Americans to try to stop him. Even if they did see the vampires as a kind of enemy.

He pursed his lips, thinking.

If they found their other production facilities, this would be the end of his plans. Nikolay wasn't going to let that happen.

Fuck you, Vincent Moretti.

Now, he was playing dirty.

He fired off a text to Demetri. Their plans in Maine had just expanded. Now, they were really at war.

"You told us nobody else knew about vampires. So why are the officials riding our asses?" Romano asked.

Jesus, did he have to spell it out?

But then again, he did tell them that.

"Perhaps they know," he said, thinking he had nothing to lose now. The mobs had a target on their back, and he wasn't lying when he said he might need to shift tactics.

Pharmaceutical companies might be a better option. They were already set up to produce. They loved an insane profit margin, and frankly, they were as corrupt as any fucking mafia organization he knew of.

He might have to make a few phone calls.

BioZen being his first one, given he already had a contact there who would jump when he said jump.

Cash Waltmore, Director of the pharmaceutical organization.

AKA his bitch.

"Perhaps? Or they do?" Enzo growled, standing abruptly. "Start talking, Mikhailov."

"How the fuck do I know?" Nikolay said, finishing the last of his vodka. "Do I look like I sit at the UN table, Enzo?"

The two men glared at one another.

"Fuck you. You aren't cutting us out now. I may have a few other properties we could use. Give me a few days," the mob boss said.

It would take them too long to set up a new production line, but if he couldn't convince any of the pharmaceutical companies in time, this might need to be a backup.

So he agreed.

"Sure, but you might have a rat in your house. Someone is leaking information to the Feds," Nikolay said, turning the glass around and around on the condensation ring on the desk. "Get rid of them. The world is changing, Enzo. You are either with me or not. Don't let a few soldiers in your organization fuck this up."

"I can't go around shooting my gangsters."

Nikolay laughed. "That's exactly what you do."

Enzo let out a few Italian curses he recognized.

"Call me whatever you fucking want," he said, leaning forward. "But when those vampires decide to go to war with us, and they will, and you don't have the serum to protect you and your family, it will be their bodies lying in a pool of blood. Not mine."

Enzo Romano paled before him.

Finally, they were getting the fucking picture.

# CHAPTER TWENTY-NINE

"You could come running with us," Amber offered as Madison sipped her coffee across from her.

"No," Darnell said, and Amber turned to frown at him.

*I said no. I plan to fuck you down by the lake again. And I don't share.*

*Stop it,* Amber chastised him. But the truth was, she loved this new Darnell. Since he'd arrived home after his disappearing act, he'd been behaving like a real mate.

Worse, she wanted it. And was acting as if this thing between them was really just as much as he was. Because she wanted it to be. Something had changed between them at the lake. Was it because he'd bitten her? Amber was sure he'd freaked out and then worked through it.

Now…did he feel like her? Did he want to see where it went?

Because she was struggling to ignore that feeling when his teeth were in her neck, a type of essence that bonded them…

Not that she thought they were proper mates.

Unless…

No. They couldn't. When life returned to normal in the castle, they'd have to backpedal on their story and go back to their lives.

This meant Darnell would find his real mate, and she'd have to watch him be like this with another female. And all the girls he flirted with until he found his mate.

Great.

Maybe Chef Rogers would offer her a permanent job, and she wouldn't be forced to watch it every time he was in Max Bar.

Until it happened, Amber was going to lap up this feeling of having someone in her life, in her corner, and cherish it. It might be fake, but it didn't feel like it.

So hey, why not pretend for a little while longer?

"I'm up for a club run," Anna chirped, and Amber grinned.

"Jesus," Darnell said, pushing out his chair. "Come on. We have to get to work."

"You go. I've got five or ten more minutes. I'll stay and chat with the girls." As her coffee cup lifted to her lips, she felt her body being torn away. The cup landed in a clang on the saucer, and the next minute, she was in the arms of a dark, fiery-eyed warrior.

"You will let your mate walk you to work."

"Ooh, sexy," Madison purred, and Amber giggled.

"Excuse me?" Kurt growled.

Darnell's lips stretched into a smile as he lowered her to the floor and slapped her ass. "See the trouble you cause?"

Amber waved goodbye and smiled as they walked through the halls holding hands. When they reached the door leading into the restaurant kitchen, she waited as he pressed her against the wall and lowered his mouth to hers.

Arching into his passion, she let out a silky groan.

"Do not do that, or you're having a sick day," Darnell ordered darkly, but his smirk was there.

Amber giggled.

She was falling for this gorgeous vampire.

Rightly or wrongly.

Then the mood shifted, and the sparkle in his eyes darkened as a shiver ran through her body.

Her fingers lifted to his cheek, aware she never wanted to let this warrior go. "You have the most beautiful blue eyes."

"Amber." Darnell tugged her closer.

"I wish we were at home." She tiptoed up, stretching to his mouth and putting what felt like all of her into the kiss.

As if she knew this was their last moment together.

"Baby, fuck," Darnell moaned as he slid his fingers into her hair.

"Tell me this isn't fake, D. Not this," she whispered.

"Baby," he said, opening those ocean-blue eyes. "I think you can feel I'm not faking it."

That wasn't what she meant, but his cock pressed against her thigh, and his mouth completely claimed hers.

"God, I can't get enough of you," he growled.

Amber ran her fingers down his chest, inching toward the top of his black jeans.

Damn, he was sexy. Every inch of him was hard and ripped. Every single inch.

She wanted him to steal her away and hide out in a cottage somewhere with no one around for miles. Somewhere with a private lake so they could make love, look at the stars, and do more of the biting.

Much more.

She wanted another orgasm where her brain malfunctioned, and all she could feel was absolute pleasure and all of her warrior's.

Darnell drew in a breath as he let her mouth go. "Fuck this. What time is your break?"

"In four hours."

"Teleport home. Take off your panties. I want you spread and ready for me on the bed," Darnell ordered, pinching her nipple.

"Ugh, meanie. Are you going to leave me wet and needy all that time?"

"Do not say wet. Do not. Fucking hell." He ran a hand over his hair. "Maybe you do need a sick day."

"I'm a vampire. I don't get sick." Amber laughed even though her pussy was throbbing. "Go. I'll see you in four hours at home."

Home.

"Baby," Darnell purred, kissing her again, "I'm going to make your pussy come so fuc—"

Suddenly, he froze.

Darnell's head lifted as his entire body stiffened and straightened away from her. Amber raised her brows, glancing around. Then his eyes dropped to hers, and he had transformed from her sexy lover to a powerful and dangerous warrior.

"I have to go. Do not leave the castle. Stay in the restaurant until I come for you," Darnell said firmly.

"What's going on?"

"Please. Just do as I say." He grabbed her arms.

Amber nodded.

Then he kissed her harshly and took off down the hall in a sprint.

DARNELL'S COCK HAD never softened so fast in his life. Craig had ordered them all to the operations room.

Something was going down, and he knew what it was.

The Russians were here.

Or close.

Goddamn, he hated leaving Amber. Not because of the moment they were having—which just got sexier and more intense every single day—but he hated not being able to tell her anything.

Darnell could not share the classified information. If the castle was going into lockdown, only three people could order that. The king, Brayden, and the commander.

Darnell's job was to protect and follow orders.

Still, he hadn't been able to say anything. He might be holding back their bond by a fucking hair, but she was his…

His to look after.

His to protect.

His to make love to.

His to…

Hand back when this was over. And now that time was coming. The Russians would not survive this. Vincent had updated them on his conversation with POTUS, and after Craig had danced what appeared to be some kind of Irish jig, they'd been given full approval to use all force necessary.

Which didn't happen very often, judging by the looks on the other SLCs' faces.

"Hey." Darnell met up with Tristan at a fork in the hallway, and they jogged to the operations room together.

"It's happening," Tris said. "Can't wait to get rid of these fuckers."

"You and me both, brother," Darnell said, punching his fist as they slowed at the door where more warriors were piling in.

"Hey, what's up?" Mack asked as he, Callan, Logan, and Ben walked in behind them.

"Ready for some action?" Darnell smirked. Although he was pretty sure he was the only one who had a stake in this not being over.

Perhaps he and Amber could keep the fake relationship going a little longer Just so it wasn't super obvious.

Amber didn't look unhappy. Not when he woke her with his mouth. Or when he pressed his cock inside her in the shower and listened to her scream his name.

"Hand me a weapon. I'm ready to off some gangsters," Mack said, rubbing his hands together. The hybrid had been training with the teams and was a natural. Far more powerful than Darnell was expecting. No one knew what effect the wolf genes had on the vampires, but it hadn't made them weaker, that was for sure.

"I've hated these mafia assholes for a long time," Logan said, laughing. "Get in line, buddy, get in line."

"True that," Ben said.

"You're all going to get a chance, so settle down," the prince said as he strode in.

Everyone took the cue and found a spot to sit or lean, big arms crossed, boots scuffing the floor.

"We have a sighting of the mafia arriving in Portland. They'll be here within the hour at the latest, we think," Brayden said.

"Interesting they're doing this at night," Craig said, glancing at the prince.

"Or they know there is no way inside through the shutters." Logan shrugged.

The guy had a point.

"One of Craig's rockets through the ceiling would work," Kurt offered. "If they have access to that kind of metal."

"They do." Ben nodded. "But this fast, I'm not sure."

Fuck.

"We need to consider that they do," Brayden said, looking fierce. "Remember, they have the serum, so do what you can to remain out of the line of fire. And assassins, we need you on point. Any warriors who go down, we will have a recovery team ready to move them."

"We will not give them the opportunity to capture a single one of us." Craig stood with his legs spread and fists on his hips. "Tonight, we go to battle with humans."

"Human or not, they are the enemy coming into our world to destroy us," Brayden seethed. "Get your teams around the perimeter ready to eliminate them. Make sure nothing, and I mean fucking nothing, gets near the king or my princesses."

Darnell could feel the fury rolling off the enormous Moretti prince, and a shiver ran through him. Brayden was unquestionably the most powerful vampire in their race. When you had that much juice running through you, you rarely needed to up the ante and express it.

But Brayden's family was vulnerable with their young.

As a Moretti warrior, he felt that in his bones. It was what they had trained for all their lives. Their very existence was to protect the royal family.

No warrior in this room, whether vampire, wolf, or assassin, would let harm come to the king and queen or any of the prince and princesses.

They would give their life for them.

*Who was going to protect Amber?*

# CHAPTER THIRTY

$A$mber stirred the sauce, adding more milk, and found her mind once again drifting.

Were they in danger?

"Did you add the flour? The consistency is wrong," Chef Rogers said, glancing over her shoulder.

*Shit.*

"Oh, sorry. My head is in the clouds today." Amber reached for the flour and scooped out a measured spoonful.

"Everything okay?" Chef asked.

"Sure. Yes. I just…" Amber didn't know what to say and knew she couldn't break Darnell's confidence. So she said the only other thing she could think of. "I was just thinking about when this is all over, and I have to go back to working at Max Bar. I love working here."

She normally wouldn't be so bold, but the words had just spilled out.

"Amber, you have far exceeded my expectations," he said. "I'm ready to have the full team back, but if not all of them do, I'll let you know."

Wow.

She hoped he was serious and not simply being kind.

"Thank you." Amber smiled and added more flour, the sauce now thickening up. Then she reached for some herbs and crumbled the leaves, the aromatics hitting her senses.

"You show real talent. Don't give up either way," Chef Rogers said.

Which meant no.

She had heard that kind of speech before.

"Of course, I just… I know it would be a huge step up to work with you for real."

"Amber, I wasn't saying no. But you're right. It would be cooking for the royal family, not the rest of the castle like you are now. I need to respect the other's positions and look at my budget once we regroup," Chef said, sliding his hands into his pockets.

A hint of hope blossomed within her.

Losing Darnell was going to be hard, but if a full-time job became available with Chef, she could focus on that dream, then it might just take the edge off.

Not a lot.

Amber knew she was going to be heartbroken, but she was a survivor. It had been the only way she'd lived, so what difference would this time make?

She'd lost everyone she ever loved.

Heck, she was a pro at it.

"I very much appreciate you considering me," Amber said. "And if you do, I'll work harder than anyone ever. I'll be so grateful. But no pressure. You need to do what's right."

God, she was babbling.

Chef laughed. "No pressure."

Amber shot him a grin.

And realized she had taken her mind off the situation for a minute and was grateful. Perhaps everythin—

BOOM!

The thick, solid walls of the castle shook violently as the explosion hit them.

"Everyone get down!" Chef yelled.

Amber turned the gas stove off and dropped to the ground as yet another explosion struck.

Then another.

*Amber!* Darnell's voice in her head startled her.

*Oh, my God. Are we being bombed?*

*Get to the Great Hall right now.*

*Okay.*

"We have to go. To the Great Hall," she called out to the team and Chef.

"It's safer if we stay here," Chef said.

"Darnell just telepathed. We have to go now," Amber yelled over another explosion, standing, and waving for everyone to follow. "Come on!"

A couple of them moved, but Chef Rogers hesitated.

"Please, Chef. Come on. Remember, they said to go to the Great Hall if it was red alert? Well, we're being bombed," she yelled as she opened the door.

Another explosion went off, and she heard gunfire in the distance.

Shit.

Finally, he ran toward her, and they all took off down the hallway. When they reached the Great Hall, heavily armed warriors were ushering everyone inside.

Amber spotted Madison and Anna and ran over to join them. "What's going on?" she cried.

"We're being attacked," Anna said, wrapping her arms around herself, shaking. "I'm not letting them take me again. I fucking won't."

*What?*

Amber stared at her friend. "Anna, who took you?"

"Bad humans. Really bad," she whimpered as Madison wrapped an arm around her.

"We won't let that happen," Madison said firmly. "I won't."

Ben suddenly appeared, and Anna ran into his arms. He had a machine gun in one hand, and another wrapped across his body. Then she saw knives strapped to his leg and God knows how many other weapons. "I got you, sweetheart."

Behind him, two other heavily armed warriors were standing with their legs apart, awaiting instruction.

"I have two minutes," Ben said, holding her tightly. "Stay here with these males who will protect you. Orders of the king. And me."

"Okay." Anna nodded quietly.

What the hell had happened to her?

Amber's eyes darted from face to face, looking for answers, but no one was sharing.

"Fuck. These assholes are going to die," Ben growled, kissing Anna's forehead.

"Where's Darnell?" Amber asked, even though she felt she had no right. He wasn't really her mate, and yet...

What if he was?

It was a question she kept asking herself privately, barely acknowledging it herself.

What if it turned out they were mates, and neither had known? Stranger things had happened. Or maybe they could, like, stay together anyway.

They were happy.

He looked happy.

"Fighting," Ben said, glancing her way as he released Anna. "I have to go. All of you, stay here."

"Ben!" Sage Moretti cried as she came running over. "You have to take me to the prince. Right now."

Ben turned. "The hell I will. Ari would kill me. You have to stay here."

"You don't understand." She held up a vial, glanced around, and lowered it. "I think this is needed."

"Telepath Ari," Ben grunted.

"He's ignoring me," Sage confessed.

Amber watched Ben blink silently for a moment as he telepathed someone. Likely Ari.

She didn't know what was going on, only that Sage was a scientist and seemed to think she had something that could help.

"He said you have to stay here." Ben shook his head and then another explosion sounded, the ground shaking. They all dropped to their knees as the plaster from the room loosened and crumbled around them. "We're being heavily attacked. Now is not the time even…even if it works."

"Okay, fine," Sage replied, her shoulders slumping.

Ben kissed Anna's forehead. He glanced at them all, nodded at the two warriors, and ran out the door. The two warriors remained positioned in a protective capacity near Anna.

Amber took a step closer and rubbed her arm. She didn't understand her situation, but she cared and could give her comfort.

Brianna ran into the room and bent over to catch her breath when she reached them. "Shit. Shit. Shit."

"Why aren't you with Willow?" Madison gasped.

"I—the—security barriers went up before I could get there," Brianna panted. "Fucking things."

"Does Craig know?" Anna asked, looking as worried as Madison.

She nodded. "Yeah. He's mad. He's sending Casey."

*Great.*

The female warrior obviously wasn't happy about her union with Darnell. Her friendship with Casey had taken a dive. While the other girls were happy for her, Casey had continued with the glares and eye rolls.

She suspected Casey saw right through their lie and didn't trust her.

"Why Casey?" Amber asked.

"She's badass," Brianna answered.

"So is Charlotte."

"Yeah, but Char nearly won the vampire games and could have been an SLC if she hadn't pulled out. So it's likely the commander has pulled her onto the front line," Madison explained.

"She's right," Bri said, shooting a glance at the warriors near Anna. "What's the story?"

"Ben wants Anna protected," Madison said.

"Oh, shit, babe. I'm sorry," Brianna said, pulling her into a hug. "Are you doing okay?"

"Not really. I want to be with Ben." Anna wrapped her arms around Bri's shoulders, and Amber could see the subtle shudder of her body. She was scared.

It was incredible watching these females support one another. They genuinely cared. This was so foreign to her, yet she felt the same way.

She didn't want any of them to be harmed or scared.

"I know, sweetie. Our boys will be okay, right guys?" Brianna asked the two warriors.

"Yes, ma'am," they both said, nodding sharply.

Amber figured Brianna got a lot of respect being the commander's mate, but she noticed that the warriors' gazes did not linger on the beautiful vampire. Craig was an enormous vampire. If Amber were a single male, she wouldn't be eyeing up his mate either.

"God, I hope Willow and Isabella are okay," Bri said, waving across the room as Casey, layered in black fatigues and weapons, walked over.

She did look badass.

The female glanced at Amber momentarily before she acknowledged the warriors. Then glanced around the room. "Let's move the girls over to the corner by that door so we have some protection and an exit if needed." Casey nodded to the far end of the hall.

The males followed her orders, so Amber figured Casey had some seniority over them. She hadn't paid all that much attention to rank or the army structure beyond the

SLC positions. But she knew Casey was a senior lieutenant or LC, which was directly under the likes of Darnell, Ben, and Kurt.

So yeah, she was pretty senior.

Which was impressive.

"You need to stay alive because if you don't, I don't," Casey said to Brianna.

"Then we both have the same goal," Brianna said, pulling over a chair. "But if those barriers go up, I'm heading straight to the royal wing of Willow and Isabella."

"Not without my permission," Casey said firmly.

Amber watched the two women have a staring match, and she had a feeling that while Casey was a badass warrior, Brianna was much more stubborn. Maybe it was the red hair.

Brianna caught her looking and sent her a wink. Amber hid her smile so Casey didn't hate her more, but she appreciated the private joke.

Someone handed out small bottles of water, and they all huddled while the three warriors surrounded them. Across the hall, she spotted Chef Rogers and a few other vampires she'd met over the past weeks, all looking as concerned as she was.

Was Darnell safe?

What if something happened to him?

When this was over, they would need to part ways. All her dreaming and wishing wasn't going to change that. It was time to come to grips with it. This life of hers was a borrowed one.

At least there was a possibility of a job working in the kitchen. So something good would come of it while she was healing her heart.

Yes, her heart.

She let out a sigh and slid down the wall to sit next to Madison. Hopefully, her friends would buy their next lie that they had been *mistaken.*

Because Casey's reaction had begun to sink in. These females weren't dumb—not that she had ever thought they were—and would likely see right through their lies.

What about the prince?

Was she going to lose everything?

Darnell, her friends, her home, and the job of her dreams were dangling right in front of her.

*Shit.*

A cold dread wound through her.

# CHAPTER THIRTY-ONE

"We think they used drones, sir." one of the junior warriors yelled as Darnell directed them toward the castle entrance at a run.

His sleeves were rolled up to his elbows, black soot covering them, and his muscles taut. Smoke billowed around them. The gates twisted from an explosion, and brick crumbled and tumbled over the lawn.

Two sections of the castle had been compromised so far, and flames billowed from two front rooms. At least they were not close to the royal wing.

*Who was protecting Amber?*

The question played like a record in his head. Even in full war mode, she was bouncing around his mind like a little fucking Pacman.

What if she had been harmed, and he was out here playing soldier?

"How many down?" Darnell yelled, his eyes darting around him.

"A dozen so far," the vampire replied and then slapped his hand on his neck as a dart hit him.

*Fuck. Make that thirteen.*

"They're in the trees," Darnell shouted to his team, pointing in that direction. "Get the retrieval team out here!"

"Yes, sir," one of them answered.

Two of his team crouched behind the parked SUV on the drive and pointed their rifles toward the foliage. Darnell dropped behind them.

*Logan, Two o'clock. Oak trees,* Darnell telepathed the assassin.

*Pop. Pop.*

Two bodies fell to the ground.

*Nice work.*

*I'll send you the bill,* Logan replied, and Darnell chuckled.

The prince had been smart to bring Ari Moretti's team on board. They and the wolves had been a huge help over the past hour.

"Wilson, cover Jeremy. I need you to get the mechanism they're using to shoot us. And any of the serum," Darnell instructed. "Check their pockets and any bags. Bring it all back."

"Yes, sir,"

*Logan. My guys are heading over there. Don't shoot them.*

*Risky.*

*Worth it. Try to keep them alive for me.*

*Not sure I'm that good, but I'll try my best,* Logan replied.

*Save the humble bullshit for the ladies, my friend.*

He heard Logan snigger.

Out of the corner of his eye, he saw Tristan and Mack heading around the back of the castle with a dozen vampire warriors. Smoke billowed around them as gunfire continued like they were in a fucking war movie.

They *were* in a war.

How the fuck had this happened? Darnell was almost impressed with the gangster's achievements, but then again, this is what they did. Go in, guns blazing, and kill.

*Might have a shooter with a serum gun,* Darnell reported to Craig.

*Do you have the perimeter secured yet?*

*Not yet. We're inching closer but need more boots on the ground. We're losing them as fast as we add them. Thirteen down.*

*Fucking assholes,* Craig replied.

More shooters were nearby, but even with their vampire vision and the assassins seeking them out, they were having trouble spotting them because of the smoke.

Clever fuckers.

Darnell wanted to reach out to Amber, but he knew he'd lose focus if he did.

Brayden teleported nearby and ran over, dropping down next to him.

"One of the warriors thinks he saw a drone," Kurt said as he joined them.

"Fuck. That's how they're delivering some of the explosives," the prince cursed.

Darnell nodded.

Wilson ran back carrying a type of pistol. "Jeremy's down. But I found this on the human."

"Good man." Brayden grabbed the unit from Wilson. "Kurt, get your team over to the west side, and let's start herding them."

"Got it."

When the warrior teleported away, Brayden handed Darnell the serum gun.

"Get this to Sage in the lab and tell her to lock it up until it's safe. This could be vital to her research," the prince said.

"On it." Darnell nodded.

"Mack!" Brayden yelled.

Seconds later, the hybrid appeared. "Here."

"Take the lead. Work with Logan to clear the mafia snipers from the trees. Get as many of these things as you can." The prince pointed to the gun in Darnell's hand. "Just don't get fucking shot with it."

"Not my goal." Mack smirked.

"And no shifting." Brayden slapped him on the back. "The last thing we need is these assholes knowing about you and the wolves."

"I mean, I could eat them," Mack said deadpan.

Darnell stared at the hybrid.

"Joke, guys. I don't eat people." Mack lifted his weapon and sniggered. "Just the ladies."

Brayden turned to Darnell. "I hope he's joking. Meanwhile, check on the teams inside. We need to ensure our vampires are safe."

"You think they've gotten inside?" Darnell frowned.

"No. But let's not assume anything. If they have drones working, who knows what they've dropped inside some of those blast holes," Brayden said.

*Jesus.*

Darnell took off, teleporting a couple of times, zigzagging across the lawn, and slipping inside one of the side doors. The red glow of the emergency lighting filled the hallways, and he let his mind flick back to Amber.

It was clear none of them were that safe inside the castle, and they were all at risk.

He raced down the hall to the science lab.

"Sage!" he called as he banged through the doors.

It was immediately obvious that no one was there, and a chill ran through him.

Fuck.

*Craig. Sage is missing.*

He didn't have the ability to telepath with Ari, and even if he did, being the one to tell the ancient vampire that his mate was missing wasn't at the top of his bucket list.

Fuck that.

*She's in the Great Hall,* Craig responded.

*Roger that.* And thank fuck.

Darnell took off the way he came, warmth filling him at knowing he'd get to see his girl.

His feelings for Amber had quadrupled since sinking his teeth into her vein. Even trying to walk away from her this morning as he said goodbye at her workplace had been impossible.

She was his heroin.

When he'd slid into bed, and those deep green eyes had held his as she asked, *Do you want me to leave?* Hell. He'd not had to think for a single second before answering, *No. No!*

Amber belonged to him.

Darnell wasn't sure how he moved forward from here. He wasn't ready for her to leave his bed or his home. He certainly wasn't ready to let another male touch her.

Or fuck her.

A roar swelled in his chest, and Darnell pushed it back.

Fucking bond.

His resistance to it was weakening. They might not have spoken about it, but he knew she felt it now. It was in her eyes when she gazed up at him. In the way she snuggled into him in bed. And in the way she mewled as she came, saying his name.

They were mates.

They just hadn't acknowledged it.

Darnell knew he couldn't and never would. Because fate was now catching up with him.

Tonight, when the team meeting had finished, his father had phoned. With only a few seconds to talk, Darnell answered the phone.

"Hey, Dad. I have about one minute. You guys okay?"

"Son. Yes. Your mother and I wanted to ring and say hello," Joseph Miller had said.

"I meant to call after the king had his broadcast. I'm sorry, it's been crazy busy here," he said, ripping his sweatshirt off as he changed into his battle uniform.

The Moretti vest was lined with the thinnest cutting-edge bulletproof material. Then he slipped on the breathable, long-sleeved black top and a puffer-type vest with a million pockets. Then he tugged on black cargo pants and his socks and boots.

"We heard," his mother said as he began to load up on weapons.

When he heard the smile in her voice, Darnell froze.

"Heard what?" he asked, holding the phone to his ear after taking it off speaker. He might have been alone in the changing rooms, but if someone had leaked information, Brayden would be furious.

Everyone was given directions. This was top-level classified information. The civilians in the castle were silenced due to their contracts. And loyalty to the king. The last thing they needed was this getting into the media or circulating on VampNet.

"What did you hear, Mom?" Darnell asked.

"You know what the females are like, son. The talk about you SLCs is like Gossip Girls." His dad laughed.

A chill ran down his spine.

*What?*

"Dad—"

"Ring us back when you have more time to talk. We want to meet her," he said.

*Oh, shit.*

Why had he not thought about this? Whenever one of the SLCs mated, it was hot news on VampNet. A sort of celebrity status came with being a senior warrior in the Moretti army, and the original four members—Kurt, Marcus, Tom, and Lance had quite the fan base.

Many hearts had been broken when they'd mated.

Now, Ben, Alex, Tristan, and Darnell all had their own groupies, so to speak.

One of the remaining citizens in the castle must've posted about it. Something that was not restricted in their contracts. Or obvious loyalty.

*Goddamn it.*

Not that they had done anything wrong, but it hadn't occurred to him that someone would post about it and it would get back to his parents.

Not this fast, anyway.

To be fair, he was a new SLC.

"Oh. Right. Listen. It's not..." Darnell began, then went silent. Because what could he say? He had lied to the royal family and wasn't about to tell his parents that. Nor could he confirm she was his mate.

"Go. I know you have an important job. We just wanted to let you know we are so proud of you, darling."

*Fuck.*

"What your mom said," his dad added, driving the stake home. "Can't wait to meet this amazing female of yours."

Damn.

Darnell felt his heart tighten.

It was the reminder he needed that this couldn't continue. They needed to talk once the castle was secure and the attack was over. Then, he would explain to his parents there had been confusion. That it was just gossip.

To the prince and their friends, he would say they had been mistaken. It happened. Not often, but like humans, vampires could mistake another—human or vamp—as their mate.

Unrequited love wasn't exclusive to humans.

In his haste, he had not thought this through. Not the social media aspect of it, in any case. And it was better to tidy it up as soon as this was over.

Yet, despite his parent's phone call, he'd been worried about Amber all night. It hadn't changed a single thing about how he felt about her.

Now, as Darnell nodded to the guards outside the door and waited for one of them to open it, his heart thundered as he waited to get his eyes on her.

Then he stepped inside.

# CHAPTER THIRTY-TWO

W illow paced her bedroom, gently patting Isabella's back as she tried to calm her. The baby had been crying and, at one point, screaming. Now, the explosions seem to have stopped. Issie seemed to be relaxing.

Or maybe it was because she was.

Which was bullshit. Willow wasn't relaxed at all.

She couldn't communicate with Brayden because the Tungsten barriers had dropped, imprisoning her.

She hated it.

For all she knew, Brayden could be dead. It was unlikely. She knew he was powerful, but it didn't stop her mind from reeling.

How the hell had the humans achieved such an aggressive and sudden attack on them?

The last words she'd heard from her prince were *Willow, sweetheart, we're under attack and putting the family into lockdown.*

*Bray, no. Please,* she'd pleaded telepathically.

*I love you. Kiss Isabella for me.*

Then the barriers had lowered, the slow whirring noise like nails running down a blackboard, as they locked her and Isabella in.

She'd cursed waking Issie, who had begun crying.

Then the first explosion happened, and her frustration turned to real fear.

She might not be human anymore, but Willow was still aware that her strength was nowhere near that of the warriors in the army.

Not even close.

And what if she lost Brayden? This was what she had feared during those hours and days, deciding if this was the life she wanted.

Never had she regretted it until now, listening to the castle shudder and explode around her as she sat holding her screaming baby in their prison.

But could she regret loving Brayden? Having their beautiful baby?

She thought they'd have more time.

God, she was spiraling.

Maybe if she had someone to talk to. Brianna was supposed to be with her—this was the plan they'd agreed on—but she knew Brayden wouldn't wait for anyone or anything to keep them safe.

The only thing keeping her even mildly sane was the escape button on the wall near her bed. Willow had demanded Brayden have it installed in case of a malfunction or emergency when she had to get out.

It had taken months, but he'd finally agreed.

Thank God.

Brayden was the only one except the king who could authorize the royal barriers. Going up or down.

This gave her some power back.

However, she'd promised she wouldn't use it unless there was no other choice. Her growing panic attack was becoming one consideration.

Glancing down at her beautiful baby girl, Willow knew she had to be strong for Issie. If anything happened, she would never forgive herself, and it would destroy her and Brayden.

Hushing and gently bouncing the baby, she continued her circuit of walking down the hall from her bedroom, past three other rooms, into the living room, through the kitchen, and up the stairs to where Brayden had an office and their private theater room. Down she went and circled the dining room, back into the living room, and down the hall.

Finally, she settled in the rocking chair in her bedroom where she nursed Isabella. Willow closed her eyes, blocking out the sounds of war outside. The explosions might have stopped, but she could still hear the gunfire.

God, please let this night end.

*Come home to us, Brayden, my love.*

*Issie needs her daddy.*

*And I need you.*

# CHAPTER THIRTY-THREE

"Sage," Darnell said, shooting Amber a wink before approaching the scientist.

It took every ounce of willpower not to go to her immediately. He had to prioritize this task first.

What was he, thirteen?

But his cock wasn't in charge. His heart was.

Or was it the bond?

Perhaps they were the same thing?

Sage jumped to her feet. "Is that what I think it is?"

"Be careful," Darnell said, handing the strange-looking gun to her. "It appears to be loaded."

"Are there many... affected?" the scientist asked.

Amber looked confused. He hadn't told her about the serum. It was too important, and the risk was too great, given their relationship was temporary.

So she didn't know what they were talking about. If she was smart, she'd realize it was an indication that whatever was real between them didn't matter. He still planned to end this as they'd agreed.

"Yeah, too fucking many. They're dropping like flies." Darnell rubbed his hand over his face. "The team is moving them into the medical center. Dr. Abbot is attending them."

He took in the two warriors standing near Anna and Casey, taking point a few feet from Brianna.

What was Casey doing in here?

The question must have been on his face because she nodded at Brianna. "Craig sent me."

Darnell nodded, wondering why the commander's mate wasn't in the royal wing as planned.

"Don't start," Brianna warned him, crossing her arms.

Obviously, Craig had already given her hell.

So he should.

These females were a massive distraction. Their safety was hugely important to all of them. On that, he closed the distance between him and Amber.

Finally.

She climbed to her feet, and he pulled her into his arms, his entire system relaxing with relief to be holding her. His eyes flickered closed for a moment, taking in her cherry scent.

"How's my baby?" Darnell asked, feeling the tension in her body, and hating that he couldn't stay here with her.

"Scared." Amber shrugged.

"You're safe in here," he said, knowing it wasn't completely true.

A dozen powerful vampires were guarding over two hundred citizens inside and outside this room, but at any point, those explosives could reach this room.

"We need to get this to the lab and see these patients," Sage said, glancing at Anna.

"I know," Anna said, looking at him and Casey. "Is it safe?"

"No," they both replied simultaneously.

"This is important. The live samples, me studying them while it's active, will give me data that takes me months— or if ever—to gather," Sage said firmly.

Shit.

He tucked Amber under his arm and felt her hand press against his chest.

"Give me a minute," he said, then reached out to Brayden. *I need approval to take Sage and Anna to the medical center. It's time-sensitive.*

*No.*

*Bray, man, I think this might be important.*

The prince went silent for a moment, and then Ari Moretti came flying into the Great Hall.

Like fucking Superman on steroids.

It was a sight to behold and almost made him lose his step. But he didn't. He held Amber tighter as Casey let out a small, surprised curse.

"Ari. Stop," Sage said, holding up her hands. "This is important. It can't wait."

"You aren't leaving this room without me." Ari's voice was powerful and firm. He nodded at Darnell. "Thank you for not letting her out."

Darnell barked out a small laugh. "Hey, I'm not suicidal."

Ari took the serum gun from his mate and glanced around, doing a warrior body count. He pointed at the two warriors. "Can I take these two if you stick around? The prince said they're making headway outside."

Darnell took in the situation.

The warriors were there for Anna's protection, so it made sense for them to go with her, Sage, and Ari. Casey was taking point on Brianna, and if it meant he could keep his eyes on Amber for a while longer, he was happy.

"Go ahead." Darnell nodded.

*Lance. I need you to sweep the castle and check on the teams for Bray. I'm taking point in the Great Hall for a minute.*

*Roger.* The vampire telepathed back.

Ari left with Sage, Anna, and the two warriors. Darnell relaxed, taking his time to review everyone around him.

Vampires were milling about nervously, sitting on tables and the floor. A few were dangling their legs off the stage at the front of the room.

"I need to use the bathroom," Casey said, nodding at Brianna. "Don't let her leave."

The commander's mate rolled her eyes.

"What happened?" Darnell asked her.

"I got there as the barriers were hitting the floor." She tugged her legs up to her chest. "Willow is going to be stressed as fuck."

"It's too dangerous," Darnell said. "She's safer being locked up and stressed."

"I know." Bri sighed. "She's my best friend and...I have a bad feeling. Do you think it's nearly over?"

Darnell glanced down at Amber leaning on him.

"She's your friend. You're worried about her. It's normal," Madison said, rubbing Brianna's knee. "We are too."

"This feels different." Brianna's eyes lifted to his.

He wasn't one to ignore instinct, but Madison was right. They were all worried. She was the Moretti princess.

Brianna and Willow had been friends for years before becoming vampires, so knowing she was a target for their enemy and a young mom to boot was likely making the commander's mate very nervous.

"I can't do anything, Bri. Those barriers are only controlled by the prince."

Technically, they were controlled by the system, but no one was opening them without the prince's permission.

"I know. He's right not to open them, but I can't shift this heavy feeling." Brianna shrugged.

He rubbed Amber's lower back mindlessly as a few vampires came over and asked questions. Answering the best he could while Amber stayed tucked under his arm, Darnell waited until Casey returned to take a break. Then he tugged Amber away and got them a fresh bottle of water.

"I'm glad you're here," she said as he dropped his mouth softly on her lips.

"I might have to go at any moment," Darnell said, chugging back more of the refreshing liquid. "You're right to be concerned, but nobody is hurting you, baby. I want you to telepath if anything, and I mean anything, happens. You hear me?"

"Thank you," Amber said, resting her head against his chest.

Darnell wrapped his arms tightly around her and peered over her head.

He spotted a few people watching them and wondered what they looked like. He knew. They looked like real mates. A warrior protecting his female.

Because he was.

Technically.

With every minute he spent with her, he questioned whether he could walk away.

"I want to ask you a question," Darnell suddenly said. A powerful need to truly understand who she was overcame him. No more games. He had to know if she was considering what he thought he might be.

Amber's face lifted. "Sure."

"After your parents died, what happened to you?"

"Nothing good, D. Please don't ask."

*D.* It was her nickname for him, and Darnell liked it. She'd used it a few times, and each time, it had made his heart do stupid little flips.

"Amber, please. The haunted look in your eyes is making my imagination go wild. Did someone hurt you?" he pressed.

"I told you there was no abuse. It's a stupid, sad story. I survived. That's all there is to know," Amber replied, her eyes darting away.

Bullshit.

"Abuse comes in lots of different packages," he said, knowing he was pushing his luck and wondering why he'd chosen this very minute to do it.

Maybe it was because the clock was ticking.

Their agreement was coming to an end, and they both knew it.

"Yes," Amber said sadly. "Yes, it does."

# CHAPTER THIRTY-FOUR

It was funny how Darnell could make her feel so safe in one second and terrified the next.

The moment Amber saw Darnell walk through the doors of the Great Hall, her heart had fluttered awake. But it was her body that had made the most noise.

He looked so...dangerous. Every inch of him was layered with weapons and soot, and there was an edge to him.

God, he was sexy.

Her eyes had slid up his muscular forearms, which held onto a rifle, and finally made their way over his chest to his handsome face.

It hadn't taken him long to pull her into his arms, and despite being stressed, she felt a million times safer now he was there.

But it had been the conversation taking place between him, Ari, Sage, and Anna, which was a reminder that while she was in the inner circle, she wasn't, really. Clearly, Darnell was only telling her the essential things, knowing this was temporary.

Her shoulders slumped as reality kicked in a little more.

He planned to end this as they had planned.

Of course he did.

Amber tried to tell herself she had no right to be upset. This is what they'd agreed to, and time was nearly up.

So why was he pushing for more details about her life?

Why couldn't he let it go?

Amber leaned against Darnell's body as he rested on the wall, his wide cargo pants' clad legs spread so she fit into him like a jigsaw piece.

Safe.

Unearthing her past and seeing her as this unwanted, pathetic little girl was not how she wanted him to know or remember her.

Or share with the others.

Not that Darnell was a gossiper. She knew he wouldn't do that to her. But to fit into her new world, Amber wanted to put her past behind her.

But she also didn't want him thinking she'd been an abused child. As he'd said, abuse was a broad term and could be physical, emotional, or psychological.

In some ways, she'd experienced neither. She'd simply been neglected.

Of love.

Of security.

Of any type of family.

So, to put his mind at rest and shut down this conversation once and for all, Amber opened up for the first time in her life.

Her heart pounded as the words came out, making her incredibly vulnerable.

"After my parents died, I had no one. Cousins of my mom looked after me while they could afford it, and then I went to live with her brother until I was twenty-one."

Darnell pulled back. "You lived with a man on your own who wasn't your family?"

"Yes. I told you, D. No one touched me."

What he didn't understand was *no one* touched her. No one hugged her. No one held her hand, squeezing it in reassurance. No one laid a hand on her shoulder, laughing.

No one touched her.

She was deprived of love, friendship, or any companionship.

"Lucky for him," he growled, and Amber forced a small smile on her lips.

"That was in Philly?"

"Yes. Oak Hill. It's a small town," she said. "Real small. He didn't want me, and I didn't want to be there. But I had a roof over my head, and when I could leave, I headed to New York."

*When he kicked me out.*

"So you went to school and…who brought you up?" Darnell asked, cupping her chin.

Damn him, why wouldn't he just let it go? This was far more than she wanted to share, but typical Darnell, he had to keep pushing.

"Look. I survived," she snapped, trying to tug out of his arms and failing. "It wasn't that bad, and I think I've done okay for myself."

Under the circumstances.

"You tend bar," Darnell said, "That's not exactly thriving."

Shame rushed through her. She felt the insult in her very bones.

Was that what he thought of her?

Visions of her bringing home her food creations to impress him and sharing her dream of being a successful chef came flooding back.

Amber had been right. Darnell saw her as nothing but a bartender. A sexy girl to fuck. How could he be with someone like her when he was a coveted SLC in the king's army?

Answer: he didn't.

She'd been in such denial, and now all she felt was shame. But it came out as anger.

Hot anger heated her face. "Not all of us came from perfect fucking families, D. Just because I don't have a Harvard education and didn't live in a white house with a picket fence doesn't mean I won't make something of myself."

"That's not what I'm saying." He groaned, rubbing his face. "Fuck, let me start again."

"No. Forget it, and please let go of me."

"No,"

"I'll scream."

"I'll kiss you," he growled.

Amber sighed. This male was intolerable, but she had a feeling he was showing her his truth. People did that if you paid enough attention.

And when you'd grown up having to keep one eye open all the time, you learned to pay attention twenty-four-seven.

Somehow, she'd let her guard down and missed this one. Or maybe she'd just wanted to live inside the delicious fictional life they'd created.

But it was now over.

"I need to pee. So take me, or I'll ask one of the warriors."

Darnell sighed, ran his hand down her side, and released her. The absence of his touch made her want to cry. Because she knew it was the start of the space between them. She had to let him go.

"Let's go," he said, waving his hand for her to go ahead. As they walked past the girls, she called out, "Bathroom break."

"Thank God," Brianna said, climbing to her feet.

"I'm in," Madison said.

"I'll take them," Casey said to Darnell.

"Then looks like we're all going," he growled and shot her a dark look.

Amber was a runner.

Now she'd realized there was no hope, she wanted to curl up in a ball alone and grieve.

DARNELL RAN HIS hand down Amber's back as she stepped away from him, following the other females into the restroom. Then he leaned against the wall outside and held his rifle across his chest, alert and ready.

Casey stood a few feet from him, her eyes on the corridor.

"So what was all that about?" she asked.

"None of your business," Darnell said, adjusting his hold on his weapon.

"Come on, Darnell. It's clear she's not your mate. If you wanted a piece of ass in the castle to fuck while we were in evac, I'm sure you could have convinced Craig to let her stay in your room. She's friends with enough of us. We could have pulled strings."

"Stop talking," he growled.

Casey shook her head and turned away from him. "Even Alex thinks it's bullshit."

His head snapped in her direction. "What did you say?"

She turned to face him. "You heard me. And if we do, I'm sure some of the others do, too."

Fury rose from deep within him.

Yes, he was furious after the conversation with Amber. He was angry with himself. The words had come out wrong, and she'd taken them completely the wrong way.

Had she?

*You tend bar. That's not exactly thriving.*

Despite his reasons for not wanting to mate her and hurting his dad, Darnell believed Amber had a bright future. Hell, she was a young vampire with a sharp mind and vibrant personality, and people seemed to like her.

But oh, no. His big fat mouth had opened, and that shit had fallen out.

Still, he meant it on one level.

She'd finally opened up and told him more about her life, and he'd tried to tell her it wasn't okay. Not in judgment but to support her.

Which he'd royally fucked up.

Now he was pissed.

Pissed at himself, the mafia, and Casey for questioning whether Amber was his mate. Now, he learned that Alex also had doubts. Someone he fought beside.

Well, they were wrong. Amber was his fucking mate.

"Why are you riding my ass, Casey?"

She took a few steps toward him. "I told you, dumbass, if the king finds out you've lied, what do you think it would do to your career?"

"He won't," Darnell said firmly.

"So you're admitting it?"

"Just... Fuck, Casey. Keep out of it," he growled.

"Fuck you. I care. You think it's okay to be there for me, but I can't help you?" Casey sneered at him. "You think I liked all of you stepping between my father and me and forcing me to face my fears? I nearly lost... everything. You will never understand. But I do. And what you're doing is too risky."

Darnell blinked.

*You will never understand.* What did she mean?

"What are you not telling me?" he asked.

"Nothing I can ever share with anyone. You are too precious to this army, Darnell. To your friends. I like Amber, I do. But you both need to sort this out before this destroys your lives."

Fuck.

His jaw, which had been clenched, relaxed. Casey was a tough little vampire, but she had a huge heart.

"I hear what you're saying. But I've got a plan." Darnell sighed. Then his phone beeped. Tugging it out of his pocket, he kept talking. "We both agreed that after this is over, we'd—"

He stopped as he read the message from his mom.

*Darling, we know you're busy with your job, so your dad and I are coming to Maine to meet Amber. With the king's announcement coming up, things will get crazy. We can't wait to meet her. See you next week.*

Oh, fuck.

"We'd...so we'd agreed..." He tried to regain his train of thought. "Fuck."

"What is it?" Casey asked, her voice alert, her rifle clicking.

His eyes lifted.

Damn, he hadn't meant to freak her out.

"It's my folks," he said, waving his phone. "They want to meet Amber. But they can't. Obviously."

"You told them?

"Fuck, no. They found out on VampNet."

"You dumb ass." Casey shook her head. "Why did you do this? Help me understand."

He let out a sigh. "Case, you saw her. She's like a lost fucking soul. When I heard we were evacuating, I couldn't let her leave. Amber has no one."

"So you have to come clean or introduce them," Casey said, shifting her weapon to her other arm.

"Hell, no," Darnell said, shaking his head. "I can't. She's a fucking bartender, Case. My father would—"

The door came flying open with a bang, and Darnell spun, coming face to face with the furious red-headed female whose eyes were filling with painful tears.

Fuck.

Fuck, fuck, fuck.

Amber glanced at Casey. "I suppose I should thank you. At least I know what he truly thinks of me now."

"Amber—" Darnell stepped closer, but fury rolled off her. Then he saw Madison and Brianna standing behind her, looking confused.

"Do not come near me," Amber said through gritted teeth. "I've never told anyone my story, but I shared it with you. What a fucking idiot.

"Amber, let me explain," he said, reaching out for her hand.

"No." She flinched away from him. "Thank you for reminding me there isn't a single person in this world I can trust or a single place I belong."

Casey went to speak, but he held up a gloved hand to stop her as a sound caught his attention.

"Babes, you belong—" Madison said as the sound increased.

Fuck.

"Is that a chopper?" Casey asked.

*All units, all units, get your teams to take cover.* Brayden and Craig's voices filled his mind.

Darnell stepped over to Amber. "This isn't over. We need to get back to the Great Hall."

"Bri, Maddy, come with me," Casey yelled as explosions started up again.

Amber refused to move, so Darnell lifted her over his shoulder.

"Let me the fuck down. I can walk. I'm not your problem anymore." She slapped him, but Darnell ignored her as he ran down the hallway.

Then, an explosion that sounded too close stopped him in his tracks.

"Oh, my God," Brianna cried, her hands flying to her face. "Willow!"

Darnell dropped Amber, fighting every instinct inside him despite the fact she hated him right now. But as Brianna knew, that explosion was in the royal wing.

He had to go.

Darnell locked eyes with Casey. "Take them. Get them safe."

With one last look at Amber, her pain painted on her face, he cursed and went to reach for her one more time.

"Darnell, get the fuck out of here!" Casey screamed, and his eyes darted to hers. "Choose. Her or your career. This is the fucking princess we're talking about."

Amber shoved at him. "Go. This is over anyway."

"No, it's fucking not." Darnell gripped her, slammed his mouth down on hers, and ran like the fucking wind to Willow Moretti's royal wing.

# CHAPTER THIRTY-FIVE

*B*<sub>oom!</sub>

Willow dropped to the floor, her entire body covering Isabella.

She screamed.

Plaster, wood, and brick flew everywhere as heat blasted her body. Willow remained on the floor as smoke filled the room and her senses rebalanced.

Isabella was screaming.

Oh, my fucking God.

*Brayden! Where are you?!*

Nothing.

Finally, she lifted her head. Above her, she saw a gaping hole and the sky beyond. The whir of helicopter blades filled the air, and building material crashed around her.

*I have to get out of here.*

*Brayden!*

*Brianna!*

Fuck this. Willow had to leave because if someone got through the roof, she was not staying to find out what would happen. No one was harming her or taking her daughter.

Willow leaped to her feet, punched the emergency button on the wall, and ripped the throw blanket off the end of the bed.

Then ran.

Wrapping the blanket around the screaming baby to protect her from the falling debris, Willow quickly reached the front doors and bounced on her feet as the irritatingly slow barriers opened.

*Hurry up.*

She stood there trembling, holding Issie way too tight as her eyes darted around her.

"Shhh, it's okay, my darling. Shhh," Willow said over and over.

*Wahhh.*

"I know. Thirty more seconds," Willow said, sounding way calmer than she felt.

*Click.*

Finally.

She ripped open the door, which bounced off the wall behind her, but she was already running. Running for her life and the life of her child.

The Moretti princess.

Willow collided with a huge chest and an unfamiliar pair of arms, which lifted her and Isabella and, without a word, began running.

Willow screamed.

# CHAPTER THIRTY-SIX

Amber watched the door close behind her. Casey held her rifle against her chest and glared at her. Madison and Bri returned to where they'd been, but Amber had things she wanted to say.

"You need to let him go," Casey said coldly before she could open her mouth.

Amber lifted a brow.

She was not in the mood to be bullied by this vampire, nor would she put up with it. They may not know where she'd come from and what she'd endured in her life, but she was about to give them a taste.

"You've made a lot of assumptions." Amber slid her hands into her pockets, trying to ignore the rumble from the last of the explosions around them. "So let me clear something up for you so you can pack away all your fucking judgments. This entire thing was Darnell's idea. I can see now that I made a big mistake agreeing to go along with it."

"You think? Lying to the king?" Casey shook her head.

But it didn't feel like a lie.

Or it had started to feel like it was.

What a damn fool she'd been. The vampire had only wanted some fun and sex while he was trapped in the castle. Amber had heard the tail end of their conversation, but it was enough. And his words, on top of what he'd said to her moments before, had struck her right in the middle of her heart.

What was left of it.

And now it was shutting down.

"No one would be any the wiser. We both planned to end it when this was over. It was a harmless lie, and you know it." Amber huffed.

"One that could cost him his career," Casey snapped quietly.

"It was his choice. Darnell is a grown male capable of making his own decisions. Why are you making me out to be the enemy here?" Amber snapped back. "He lied to me."

"He was doing it because he felt sorry for you. Because you're alone," Casey said. "Look, babe. I like you. I do. But if you wreck that male's life, I won't."

There it was.

Loyalty and friendship.

Even if she found a way to apologize to everyone for lying, she would always be someone they never trusted now. And the newbie who came last on the friendship ladder.

Tears prickled her eyes, so she turned away.

"Amber—"

She couldn't hear another word.

Opening her heart to friendships and a male had turned out to be painful. She needed to be alone. The one place that was safe.

Turning back to Casey before she could say another word, Amber took a big step behind her and shook her head.

Then teleported away.

Landing in the kitchen, Amber hurried inside and slid to the floor near the back, tucking herself under the prep table. She pulled her legs up and closed her eyes.

Then she let the tears fall.

*You either have to come clean or introduce Amber to your parents.*

*Hell, no. I can't. She's a fucking bartender, Case. My father would—*

Would what? Amber had never let him finish, but she wished she had. Clearly, Darnell was ashamed of her. Okay, to be fair, she wasn't proud of being a bar girl. But she was fucking proud she wasn't living under a bridge or on the streets.

She was proud she hadn't sold her body every night to pay the bills.

She was proud she had dreams and a goal she was working toward.

And she was fucking proud she had found the strength every day to keep going after the way life had treated her, and not walk out into the sun.

Giving up was easy.

Trying every day was hard.

So yeah, if he couldn't see that and was a shallow asshole, she was happy to see the back of him.

In fact, it was clear he was, so Amber wondered if she should pack up and leave. Find another job and start again. It wouldn't be the first time.

Clearly, she wasn't very good at this relationship thing. With males or girlfriends. After all, Casey was right. They had both lied. To their friends and the king.

But despite all of those things, what she was most ashamed about was Darnell's judgment. He'd never tried to see who she really was.

Not her past.

Not her body.

Just her.

Making him meals, folding his stupid oversized clothes, and tidying his bachelor pad, holding his dumb hand, and opening up to him.

When all he had thought of her was some hot bartender to shag.

Amber dropped her head onto her elbows and sobbed. It had taken so much courage to open her heart up to that male, and all this time, she'd been some female to fuck.

He had no respect for her.

It hadn't even occurred to him that the food she shared with him was cooked by her.

He'd pegged her as a bartender.

Nothing wrong with bartenders—they were important members of society in her opinion, but she was more than that. Amber was working to create opportunities in her life to be more. To be what she might have been, had she had a normal childhood.

To make herself proud.

Soon, all of them would know she had lied about her relationship with Darnell. Madison and Brianna had been there and heard the whole thing.

What if they told the king?

Thankfully, since working for the Moretti's—who paid very well–Amber had saved, so if she had to leave, she would. It was scary, knowing that humans could discover them at any time.

She felt safe in the Moretti castle, despite being bombed at present. At least the warriors were fighting and defending them. Out in the world, she would be alone.

Again.

Would their race have to go underground and live like animals? Shit. Amber knew she was spiraling.

This was what happened when you were alone in life. Your imagination went wild and leaped to the worst-case scenario. She'd read once that it was a survival technique. It was better to be prepared than surprised.

But it also meant that you lived in fight-or-flight mode, even when you weren't aware of it and appeared to be functioning as a happy, normal vampire.

Amber had felt normal when she was with Darnell.

Happy even.

Not to mention wanted and adored. All of which had been a fucking lie.

Amber let out a sigh and rested her chin on her arm. He'd never promised her anything. They'd agreed when this was over, they'd part ways and be all like *oopsie. We were wrong.*

Then, by the lake, everything had changed.

She had felt a connection with Darnell that she had never had before. Not even close. Even now, she could feel him as a part of her.

Almost like she could sense his worry.

Feel him through this cord that existed between them. A lifeline.

What a silly romantic she was.

While Darnell had been enjoying some good pussy.

*I'm so fucking dumb.*

She had no one else to blame. After all, every single person in her life had let her down.

Amber pushed herself deeper into the safe, tight space and let the tears flow. Once this was over, she would pack up and leave. Perhaps she could get Chef to give her a reference and she could get a night job in a kitchen.

Amber knew she'd never have an easy life. That was becoming obvious. One filled with love and family, Christmases, and birthdays.

But she could have a career she was proud of.

One day.

It might take her ten years, but she was determined to make something of herself. If it wasn't here with the Moretti's, she'd do it elsewhere.

She'd slip out and leave the girls a note, apologizing, and not make the same mistake again.

Amber planned to trust her instincts going forward. She'd known from the moment she saw Darnell Miller that he was going to disrupt her life.

And he had.

# CHAPTER THIRTY-SEVEN

Darnell caught Willow in his arms, feeling the baby princess slam between them. Both their screams filled his senses.

He ignored it.

His training dominated all his emotions as he did what he knew he had to do. Protect the royal family at all costs.

And what do you know? Here he was fucking doing it.

To be honest, anyone in this position knew it was a possibility, but the chances were always slim.

When Willow had come running out with Isabella, Darnell hadn't hesitated. He'd grabbed them and teleported.

But that didn't mean he couldn't feel Amber's pain in the back of his mind. The bond was so strong now, it was like a tightrope, and her emotions were leaking along it in waves.

She was hurting.

And shutting down.

That was painful for him in return. His heart aching for her unrequited...love.

Fuck.

Knowing his words had hurt her beyond repair was something he couldn't deal with right now. The princesses were in his arms, and he had a job to do.

But fuck, he had no idea how he would navigate this.

He wanted Amber.

And he didn't want to hurt his father.

Worse, three of the females had overheard it all and unless he bonded with Amber, he could be outed for lying to the king. Darnell couldn't do that. He wouldn't use her to save his job.

But he might lose it all.

He might lose everyone and everything. Including his father's respect.

*Fuck!*

Willow drew in a breath and gasped when she recognized him as they rematerialized. Immediately, she began to tremble in relief and burst into tears. "Don't let me go."

"I won't. I've got you," Darnell replied, hoping like hell Brayden didn't rip open the door of the random room he'd taken them to.

And rip off his head.

Darnell half expected the prince to show up at any second, somehow tracking them, but he hadn't. Yet.

"It's okay. The prince will be here any minute," Darnell said, rubbing her arm.

"He's alive? Is he alive?" Willow whimpered, and damn, he hated hearing this powerful female so vulnerable.

"Yes. You know Brayden. He's like a cockroach." Darnell smiled down at her, trying to calm her. "No one is killing that vampire."

"Your daddy is coming, Issie. He's coming," Willow repeated over and over.

When the little princesses' screams began to quieten, Darnell reached out to the prince and waited to hear back from him.

They were in the middle of a Goddamn battle with humans. The mafia. He knew this was the start of something big. Even if they were—and they would be—successful today.

Dread slid through him as he stared into Isabella Moretti's blue eyes. So like her dad.

And he had this powerful feeling that he had to sort this shit out with Amber.

He loved her.

He didn't want another man holding his mate like he was having to do for Willow and Isabella. It was his job. One he wanted so fucking much.

Their world was changing.

Maybe none of them had much longer.

If he only had a short time left on this earth, he knew he wanted Amber in his arms. But after the life she had lived, getting her to believe him and trust him after letting her down would be tough.

Darnell wasn't sure Amber had the tools or the inclination to accept him as her real mate.

Or if he deserved her.

# CHAPTER THIRTY-EIGHT

"Use all the force necessary!" Brayden hollered. "Craig, with me!"

He and the commander teleported directly outside his royal wing. Brayden nearly lost his fucking mind when he saw the barriers up and the two front doors burst wide open.

"Willow!" He glanced around, screaming her name.

There were so many voices in his head trying to telepath, he'd blocked them out. Except now he tuned in, seeking out his mate.

Craig ran in before him, smoke billowing down the hall from their bedroom. Brayden was right behind him.

"Fuck me," Craig growled, hoisting the rocket launcher up on his shoulder.

The Bratva helicopter roared above them.

"Willow!" Brayden yelled again.

"Give me the green light, Bray," Craig roared. "Then these fuckers are toast."

His eyes shot over to his best friend and commander of the Moretti army. He hesitated for less than a second.

"Do it!" Brayden growled.

"With fucking pleasure," Craig said and leaped straight up into the air, landing on the beams on the torn open roof.

Next minute, the launcher was pointed at the chopper, and he heard the Russians yell in warning.

*Too late, fuckers.*

The blades picked up speed, but Brayden knew Craig was waiting for them to clear the castle.

Then click.

A slight whoosh.

And boom!

"*Sayonara,* motherfuckers." Craig laughed, then yelled. "Callan. Logan. Get down to that wreckage. Lance, get Kurt and your teams and find whatever survivors you can. Put them in the dungeon."

Brayden disappeared, leaving Craig, and ran from room to room, searching for Willow.

"Where the fuck are you?" *Willow!*

*Bray?* Her voice was shaking and weak even in his head.

Thank fuck. *Where are you?*

*Bray, Willow is with me,* Darnell's voice replied.

His shoulders relaxed, knowing one of his trusted warriors was with the princess.

*Where are you?* he asked.

*In the stationery room.*

*Why?*

*Um, it was the first place I thought of.*

If he hadn't been so fucking stressed, he might have smiled.

*Are they okay?*

*Yes. But you need to get here if you can. And don't kill me for touching them. I'm not sure Willow can stand without assistance right now.*

Jesus. Willow was a strong female, so this must have terrified her. Being a new mother on her fucking own with their baby and having to sit this night out was not acceptable.

The Bratva would pay for this.

"Craig. Take over," Brayden yelled as he walked back to the entrance of the bedroom.

"Roger that," the commander boomed, dropping down from the ceiling in a crouch. "Anyone else left to kill?"

"Yeah, plenty. And you can," Brayden said darkly. "They nearly harmed Willow and Isabella. I'm done playing nice."

"Go get your girls," Craig said. "I've got this."

"Maybe keep one or two alive for interrogation and to fuck with Mikhailov."

Then he teleported away.


WHEN HE REFORMED outside the stationery room, he could hear Isabella crying. Brayden ripped open the doors, and every part of his being wanted to tear Darnell to pieces.

But this was the male who likely saved his princesses.

He was getting a medal, not his fist.

In a flash, he took in the scene. Willow was leaning into the warrior's chest, Issie between them, as Darnell wrapped his arm around them.

Willow was trembling.

The warrior's eyes met his and he could see the fear in them. Brayden knew he was a terrifying force to others— well, except his beautiful mate—but right now he just needed him to stop touching her and hand them over.

"Willow." Brayden heard the predatory sound of his voice and hoped he wasn't scaring her.

She lifted her head and the fear he saw made him want to howl.

And kill.

"Go. Now," Brayden said without taking his eyes off his mate.

Darnell vanished.

Brayden vamp sped, closing the gap at the same time, and pulled Willow and Isabella into his arms. "It's okay. I've got you. You're safe now."

"I never wanted to be a fucking vampire. I hate you so much right now," Willow cried, sobbing on his chest.

"I know, sweetheart," he said, rubbing her back, knowing she meant it and also didn't.

Nudging a space between them, he checked on his baby girl who was now crying in spurts. "How's my pretty girl? Daddy's here. You're safe, Issie."

Her cries slowed and she let out a hiccup as she stared back at him.

"Good girl," he said, keeping his tone even, calming them. "I'm here."

"I don't hate you. Bray, I love you." Willow sniffed.

"I know, baby. I fucking love you so much." He peeled Isabella out of her mother's grip and laid her on his upper chest, then pulled Willow under his arm. "I know. It's okay. They are dead. All of them. Dead."

"Can we just stay in here?" Willow asked, her palm on his stomach.

"Yup. Come here." Brayden pulled his mate down to the floor and tucked her between his legs. Issie nestled on her mother's lap, and he wrapped his arms around both of them.

Feeling comfort having his girls where they belonged.

It wasn't in his nature to hide out. But that's not what this was. Brayden was providing them with the protection and sense of safety they needed. He would stay there for as long as was needed.

It was his job as Willow's mate and Isabella's father.

Craig would let him know if anything was needed.

Right now, Willow and Isabella came first.

# CHAPTER THIRTY-NINE

"Demetri," Nikolay answered. "Where are you?"

"I'm inside," Demetri said quietly.

Nikolay grinned and stood, striding over to the glass windows.

This was incredible.

Their plan had worked.

*Fuck you, Vincent Moretti, I'm about to take something very valuable to you.*

"Excellent. You know what to do. The men are on standby, ready for your signal. Let us know when you have the package."

"I only have one dart left," Demetri advised him.

"Then use it wisely," Nikolay said and pressed end. Then he slid the phone into his pocket.

The game was about to get serious.

He glanced up as Elizabeth walked into the room.

"I spoke with Mr. Waltmore," she said, referring to the director of BioZen. "He confirmed the cell the vampire was kept in was reinforced with Tungsten."

"Interesting," he said, walking over and laying his hand on her belly.

A small bump was growing.

"Nikolay, I still have more work to do," she said, frowning at him.

Elizabeth knew him well.

"And I need my cock inside your hot pussy. Go into our room and prepare. I will get Alexi to arrange the Tungsten to contain our guest," he said, sliding his hand between her legs.

"I am no use to you if I have to stop every four hours and be your sex slave," Elizabeth replied.

"On the contrary. That is your sole responsibility." He laughed, turning to her and patting her ass. "Don't forget it."

Elizabeth spun back around. "I won't stand for this when our child arrives."

Nikolay's smile vanished as he grabbed her neck tightly. Her eyes widened as panic filled them.

Good.

"Do not forget who I am, Elizabeth," Nikolay ground out. "I am not a good man. I can be good to you, but I am *not* a good man. Now get your pussy ready for me, and then you can return to your other duties."

When he released her, her hand flew to her neck as she sucked in breath after breath.

She spat out some Italian at him and spun, running from the room.

Fantastic.

She was always a better fuck when she was angry.

# CHAPTER FORTY

Amber jolted awake. Not that she'd really been asleep. More like dozing when she heard footsteps in the kitchen. Overhearing a conversation, she picked up that the battle was over, and the princesses were safe.

Thanks to Darnell, likely.

She was happy for him. And happy that things were now going back to normal for all of them.

Which meant it was time for her to move on.

"There you are!" Chef Rogers said, squatting down in front of her. "Are you all right?"

"Yes, sorry, I just—" She didn't know what to say. Did it matter anyway?

He reached out his hand.

"Thanks," Amber said, taking it and letting him help her out of the space.

"Sounds like your mate is a hero. Word's going around that he saved the princesses," Chef said.

Amber forced a smile. "Oh, yeah? That's great."

"It's his job, of course, but still, if I know the Moretti's, and I do, they will make sure he is rewarded."

Hopefully, he wouldn't lose his job and the fact she had quit and left would mean there was no reminder of this entire mess.

"Cool," she said as sadness filled her chest.

"Amber," the chef said, frowning. "It's none of my business, but I've seen you two together and you're clearly in love. But tonight, I was watching you. Did you fight?"

Clearly in love?

Had they been that convincing?

Not to Casey, that's for sure.

Dusting off her pants, she began formulating a story in her head—something she was great at after living a life of lies and having to fit in. But she was exhausted.

Plus, everyone would know soon.

Amber wanted Chef to hear it from her first. He'd been good to her and given her an opportunity no one else ever had. Not just a job, but free rein to create dishes she'd always imagined in her head.

She understood now that he'd done it, not to be nice, but because he'd been watching her and saw potential in her.

Having someone believe in you was a powerful thing.

Perhaps the past week had been a dream. Waking up with Darnell, cooking during the evenings. Even though it was only temporary, she knew she'd look back and remember it as some of the happiest few days of her life.

Now, it was over.

Now, everyone knew Darnell saw her as a common bartender, and she wasn't his mate. And that they were liars.

He'd be forgiven and heralded as a hero.

She had to leave.

Chef had said there might be a job for her, but Amber knew she couldn't stay now. It could take months or years for that opportunity to arise again, and there was no way she was working as a *shitty bartender* so she could prove how useless she was to Darnell every single day.

And witness his judgment and her friend's rejection.

No thanks.

Amber had decided she would leave as soon as it was safe.

"No," Amber said. "The truth is, we were mistaken, Chef. Darnell isn't my mate. Embarrassing as that is. We got it wrong."

"Are you sure?" Chef asked.

"Very. Irrevocably." She nodded. "So I will be leaving. I want you to know I've loved working with you. This has been a dream. More than you will ever know."

Amber sniffed.

*Don't cry.*

"You know I've loved you being here." The vampire nodded, glancing around thoughtfully.

"Would you mind…"Amber twined her fingers together nervously. This was so important. It could open doors. "Um, would you mind being a reference for me? I know I was only here a short time, but I'm going to head to LA or Chicago. See if I can get a job in a kitchen. Hey, maybe you'll hear about me one day because of my killer cheesecake, as you called it."

She shot him a shy smile, lifting a shoulder.

"Keep cooking like you have been and I have no doubt I will." Chef crossed his arms. "I will be a reference for you, but hear me out first."


AMBER RETURNED TO Darnell's room and began to pack up her things.

It didn't take her long as she didn't own much, which in this instance was good. Not that she had to worry—he would show up as there was still a lot of chaos about the castle, and with daylight fast approaching, all the warriors were still working.

Everyone else had been told to stay in their quarters and lay low until the property was secured.

Still, Amber didn't want to linger in the space she'd shared with Darnell over the past several days, so she made quick work of stuffing all her things into a bag.

She stood in the bathroom, pulling her toothbrush out of their shared holder, and stared in the mirror. Remembering how he'd stand behind her, his sex-filled eyes on hers, smirking as he brushed his teeth, teasing her just by existing.

Her eyes dropped, and she saw the jacket he'd brought her. A Moretti jacket in *tiny girl size*, as he'd called it.

Amber picked it up and folded it, then placed it on the end of the bed. It was her way of saying goodbye.

There was nothing else to say.

Darnell knew she would walk away, so why drag it out? Theirs had been a fake relationship, anyway.

Deep down, she knew what they had was more than sex. The feelings were more intense than just a couple of great orgasms. But if he thought she was an embarrassment because of what she did, then it was irrelevant.

Had she wondered if he was her real mate?

Yes.

The day she'd woken up wrapped in his dark, beautiful arms, the bite mark on her neck throbbing.

But he'd never said anything.

And the part deep inside her that had learned she wasn't worth anything. The little child who had been tossed from home to home and never held, and said *forget him, Amber. He doesn't want you.*

Guess what?

She had been right.

Nobody wanted her.

Maybe Darnell Miller was her mate, and maybe he wasn't. It would be just her luck he—whoever he was—would reject her.

Either way, he had.

Amber wasn't sticking around to be his sex toy anymore. No matter how many times he smirked at her or talked her into more of this sanity.

Amber picked up her bag and walked out the door.

It was time to start her new life.

Amber didn't know if it was going to work out as she planned, but it was worth a shot. That's what life seemed to be about. Taking one shot at a time and hoping like hell it led somewhere.

Maybe somewhere down this road she was walking, she'd land in the right spot with the right people.

# CHAPTER FORTY-ONE

## Two days later

Darnell sat on his bed, staring at the folded Moretti jacket on the chair. He'd moved it off the bed so he could sleep, but you'd think it was made of fucking glass the way he'd carefully lifted it and placed it on the pile of washing.

Now he was staring at it, wondering how he could get the female it belonged to back into his arms.

Amber wouldn't speak to him.

She was working in the king's kitchen, and now things were semi-back to normal, he wasn't allowed in there. His sexy little five-foot-nothing, curly-haired firecracker was still angry. And she had a right to be.

But she was his mate, so sooner or later, she had to.

*No, she doesn't.*

Darnell sighed, knowing Amber thought he would judge her for the job she did now, cleaning dishes and all that shit.

Honestly, he didn't care.

She could scrub the floors, and he'd still love her. Because he did. And these past two days without her in his arms had been painful.

Physically.

Amber had to be feeling it, too. But she was ignoring his telepathy, and she was ignoring his texts.

Because they had been run off their feet day and night getting the castle repaired and secured, Darnell had had little time to pursue her. He decided she could also do with some space. In truth, he wasn't sure how he was going to resolve this, even if he did have a lot of time.

He missed her.

He wanted her naked in his bed with that damn jacket on and her legs spread. And he wanted the world to know Amber Evans was his real fucking mate.

Tonight he had to put on a monkey suit, also known as a tux. A dinner was being held in his honor, which was real nice but not necessary. He'd just been doing his job when he got Willow and Isabella to safety.

But the prince and princess, and the king, had insisted.

He felt like a fraud.

Darnell had yet to tell Brayden that he'd lied. Technically, he hadn't. Amber *was* his mate. So he was still hoping things would play out.

To make matters even more complicated, his parents were joining the dinner.

With the attack on the castle being top secret information, he'd told them they were doing major repairs and delayed their trip. Now, they were in town and a few hours from arriving.

Oh, and Amber was invited.

Of course she was. She was his mate.

*Amber. Please. Just come with me tonight and we can talk after.*

Silence.

More fucking silence.

Darnell sighed and slid down the bed, glancing up at the ceiling. If Amber turned up, he'd be introducing her as a kitchen hand and have to face his father's reaction.

If she didn't show up, he'd be forced to come up with yet another lie.

But she was his mate.

And to Darnell, none of this mattered if he couldn't have her. Maybe the whole mates for life, fated shit was real.

Damn it.


A FEW HOURS later, Darnell walked into the king's private dining room.

Alone.

Well, that wasn't true. His parents were standing next to him.

"What an incredible room," his mother said, glancing around.

As always, his parents had presented immaculately. His mother in a designer dress, and his father in Tom Ford. Everything fit perfectly in the royal wing.

Would Amber have felt comfortable here tonight? He'd buy her any fucking thing she wanted. Chanel? Prada? Gap. He didn't care as long as she was by his side.

Darnell was disappointed she hadn't responded, given the special occasion. But could he blame her? The things he'd said had been hurtful.

She owed him nothing.

"Proud of you, son." His father lay his hand on the middle of his back. "Really proud."

"Here he is. The guest of honor," Vincent Moretti boomed, lifting his drink. "Come in."

"Oh, wow. Look at the king," his mom whispered. "He's tall."

As Vincent made his way over and shook their hands, Darnell smiled and took a moment to savor this moment. At least they got to share this experience with him. He'd made them proud, and whatever happened next, at least he'd have this memory.

"Let's sit," the king said.

Around the table he spotted the prince and princess, Kate Moretti, their queen, Craig, Brianna, and his fellow SLCs with their mates.

Yeah, it was a huge table.

Tristan stood and shook his hand. "Nice work, buddy."

"Tristan, good to see you son." His father greeted the warrior, and they all sat.

Between him and Tris was an empty seat.

Shit.

He still hadn't come up with a good excuse for Amber not being with him this evening and was running out of time. His eyes lifted, and he saw Brianna watching him.

Then she winked.

Huh?

Darnell narrowed his eyes and glanced around at the females. Was it him, or did they all have weird smiles on their faces?

As he was flapping out his fancy white napkin and the wine was being poured, servers began to place their entrees in front of him.

"Darling, where is—" his mom started.

"Here, sorry, hi, I'm here," a voice called out behind him.

Darnell's brows shot up as he slowly turned around.


AMBER HURRIED INTO the king's private dining room, tugging on her shoes, and wiping her hands down her black dress. It had been the quickest change in the history of changing.

Bri had loaned her the dress because there was nothing in her wardrobe that was suitable for dining with the king.

Or Darnell's parents.

The warrior she'd been aching for and crying over for days turned and shot out of his chair. Then stood facing her.

As Amber's heart thundered, she tried to act normally. There was no faking it now. She knew he was her mate.

Darnell Miller was her mate.

Holy heck.

The fact all the females had staged an intervention had blown her mind.

One minute she was waking up, ready to start her new job with Chef Rogers. The next, a knock at the door had her crawling out of bed and stepping back when she opened it to find Madison, Brianna, Anna, Casey, Charlotte, and Ginny standing with their arms loaded.

Then Casey shrugged. "I was wrong."

"What—"

"First," Charlotte said, "we don't have long. Second, Casey is an idiot."

"Hey!" Casey cried. "It's true but say it nicer."

Madison and Anna had giggled while Ginny closed the door behind her.

"I'm making us breakfast while we unbrainwash you," Anna said.

Unbrainwash?

"It's a thing. We all need a lobotomy when we meet our mates. It's like we reject happiness or something," Madison explained.

"Trust me. They're right. I'm a lawyer, and even I needed a sledgehammer to the frontal lobe," Ginny said, pouring champagne and orange juice into a bunch of glasses.

"So a full breakfast fixes it?" Amber frowned, noticing that Anna's claim to make breakfast was more of a *serve up* breakfast as she unpacked boxes of delicious smelling bacon, eggs, and other morsels.

"This is... you guys... I lied to you," Amber confessed, crossing her arms over her thin singlet top.

"Well, technically, you lied to yourself, so you can have a chat after we leave," Anna said, waving her over to the sitting area in her room. The others crowded around. "Eat."

Chat?

To herself.

Yeah, that tracked. But, what?

"Okay, explain," Amber said.

"Darnell is your mate," Brianna said, crossing her legs on the sofa and lifting her plate. "And we are here to make sure true love wins."

"Ooh, that was good," Charlotte said.

"Right?" Bri grinned.

"You guys. This is...I thought you'd hate me." Amber plonked down in the armchair and accepted the Mimosa.

"God no. We've all been absolute idiots when we met our guys," Casey said. "Yes, fine, I'm the worst. No need to spell it out, Char."

Charlotte giggled silently.

"I want to apologize. I nearly messed up my life because of a small—okay, big—error in judgment, and when I figured out you two were lying, which, as it turned out, was only to yourselves I projected my shit onto you," Casey said, leaning her elbows on her knees.

"See? That wasn't hard."

"Pushing it." Casey darted her eyes to Charlotte.

Amber gave them a wobbly smile. "So you don't hate me?"

"Nope," they all said at the same time.,

"But you aren't going to like this next bit. Because you need to forgive the big dumb warrior and let him love you," Brianna said.

Oh.

And yeah, that next part had been hard.

Amber still wasn't sure she was ready. But here she was, standing in front of her warrior with her heart open, and she wanted to cry.

Darnell stared at her.

And stared at her.

His vibrant blue eyes swirling with emotions.

Amber wished he'd do something.

"Hi," she said.

No sooner had that vowel escaped her lips than she was wrapped in his huge warm arms.

*Thank God.*

"You came," he whispered into her hair.

She tried to nod but there was no space. He was holding her so tight.

"You need to let go so I can breathe," she squeaked.

"Fuck," Darnell said, and stepped away. His eyes dipped, rolling over her. "You look… wow… beautiful."

Amber blushed. Then she glanced around and saw everyone watching them. The girls grinning their faces off.

"The entrées," she said. "Let's eat."

Darnell pulled her chair out. As he sat beside her, he reached out and took her hand under the table.

Her heart pounded. They hadn't seen each other in days, and there was still so much unspoken.

"Mom, Dad, this is Amber," Darnell said.

What?

*Oh, fuck.* His parents were here? Brianna had left that little fucking detail out. Holy shit.

Why had he invited her?

This was the piece they still needed to talk about. She was still hurting and had no idea where his mind was. Why hadn't he told her they were coming?

That things had changed for her slightly in her career was beside the point. She had to know Darnell wasn't ashamed of her, or there was no way she was bonding with him.

Now, she was sitting mere feet from the people he'd confessed he never wanted her to meet.

Freaking out, she planted a friendly smile on her face and leaned forward, giving them a little wave.

"Amber, it's a pleasure to meet you," his father said. "I hope we have time afterward to get to know you a little."

*God.*

Her cheeks heated, and she glanced at Darnell.

"Yes. We'll make time. If Amber is able," he said.

Her eyes darted away as her wine glass was filled. A thankful distraction.

Amber wished she'd spoken to him first, but until she'd put the dress on approximately seven minutes ago, she wasn't sure she would find the courage to attend.

But here she was.

*Thank you.*

*You're welcome. I didn't know they were coming tonight. I'm sorry.*

*Babe, no. Don't. We need to talk. If you are willing.*

Amber glanced down at the entrees she had made minutes earlier and nodded. His hand squeezed hers.

"God, this is incredible," Darnell's father said with his mouth full.

Amber smiled to herself.

When she'd found out who his father was, it was a surprise. A famous Michelin Star chef. What were the chances? Knowing Chef Miller was eating her entrée felt a little daunting, on top of everything else, but his compliment made it a whole lot better.

And that familiar feeling of home had returned now she was sitting beside her mate.

She just hoped Darnell could accept who and what she was. Or it would end before it even really got started.

# CHAPTER FORTY-TWO

Darnell couldn't keep his hands off Amber. Or rather, his one hand. It made eating difficult. Which his father pointed out.

"Let the girl be and eat your meal. It's absolutely delicious." Joseph laughed.

It was.

Now, dessert was on the way, and the king was giving a speech.

"Tonight, we are recognizing SLC Miller's heroic act and fast thinking while protecting one of the royal family," Vincent said.

Darnell's eyes slid over to the princess, and she gave him a warm smile. He still thought he had just been doing his job, but he understood the need to show gratitude.

"But it was a team—"

"All of the warriors in this room deserve our gratitude," the king said right on cue. "Including the teams outside this room and around the world. We only rule because of the loyalty of the race. I am aware of that each and every day."

Wow.

Amber's hand slid into his lap, and he took it. Whether she knew she'd done it or not, he didn't care. There was still so much unsaid between them, and thankfully, she'd indicated she was willing with a small nod.

A small but mighty nod.

A toast was made, and Darnell was forced to stand and say a few words. He wasn't a shy male, but this felt different.

Important.

"Honestly, I was just doing my job. Like any of you would've done." Darnell shrugged, and all the SLCs grinned at him. "It was an honor to help Willow. I am and always will be here to serve the Moretti family. While I breathe, I will fight to protect you, my fellow warriors and"—he glanced down at Amber—"my family."

Her mouth parted in surprise.

Darnell had a few choice words to add about the mafia, but because there were a few non-informed people in the room, he kept them to himself.

"Now, the important part. Dessert," he said.

The king gave him a nod and his chest swelled with pride. But what he really wanted, even though he had no idea how it was going to go down, was…

Darnell turned, held Amber's eyes briefly, and leaned in to press his lips to hers. Her fingers reached and pressed his cheek as the mating bond flared to life so powerfully he nearly ripped her out of the seat and teleported them home.

Straightening, he saw a beautiful mix of love and arousal in her eyes, which he was pretty sure mirrored his. Then annoying servers began placing plates in front of them, forcing him to let her go.

"What do you do, Amber?" his mother asked a little while later as the plates were cleared away. She leaned forward with her wineglass in her hand so she could see his mate.

*Fuck.*

At the same time, his father moaned, "Jesus, I need to meet this chef. Ask him to come out so we can pay our compliments, will you?"

Darnell wasn't sure who he was speaking to because his eyes were locked on Amber's. The worry lining her face made him ache. He never wanted her to feel this way again. But a life of wanting to make his family proud and making sure his father never felt less than, had him fighting internally about what to do.

Yet his mate was crumbling in front of him.

*You don't have to answer. It doesn't matter,* he said.

*I don't know what to say.* Amber's eyes dipped.

No.

Fucking no way was this happening.

He loved this woman. She was... his priority.

"Oh, have I asked the wrong question?" his mom queried before he could say a word. "I'm sorry."

"No," Amber said. "It's okay. I don't have a fancy job like your son."

*Fuck this.*

He couldn't let her down.

"My mate works in the kitchen, Mom," Darnell said, taking Amber's hand.

He glanced down at the cake in front of him and narrowed his eyes. Was this the same cake they'd had by the lake? The night his fangs had slid into her vein, and he'd truly tasted Amber for the first time.

Amber eyes were moist, full of emotion.

He felt like he was missing something.

"She does?" his father asked. "That's great. Keep it in the family, boy."

What?

That was all his father had to say?

*I can't believe you just said that,* Amber whispered telepathically.

*I love you, Amber. I don't care if you scrub floors. You are mine.*

Darnell reached up and touched her cheek. He was so close to giving their apologies and taking her out of here so he could say all the things he wanted to say. And do all the things he desperately wanted to do.

Make love to her.

Bond with her.

Make her his so she could never leave him.

"Chef Rogers," his father exclaimed loudly and pushed his chair back to greet him. "Chef Miller, nice to meet you."

"I know who you are, sir. It's a great pleasure to meet you," the royal chef said, nodding his respect.

"This meal was outstanding. If I'd known you were this good, I might have stolen you years ago." His father laughed loudly."

Beside him, Amber let out a little noise, and Darnell glanced down. Her cheeks were pink, and she was shaking her head.

At the chef.

When he glanced up, Chef Rogers was grinning.

"Ah, well. I will take the compliment, but not completely," the chef said. "You see, the menu was designed and partly cooked by your daughter-in-law."

The entire room went quiet.

*Holy fucking shit.*

Darnell's head snapped back around, and Amber's face was as bright as her hair.

"No. I—" She cleared her throat and waved at the plates awkwardly. "Just made the entrée and dessert."

"Just?" his father asked. "Amber, they were divine. Son, you never told us your mate was a fine chef."

No.

Because he didn't fucking know.

Her eyes lifted to his, and Darnell shook his head. "There is a lot about this beautiful female I still have to learn. Luckily, we have forever."

Across the room, Brianna began clapping in glee.

# CHAPTER FORTY-THREE

Logan stretched out his denim-clad legs. "Fuck, what a week."

Oliver nodded slowly and lifted his beer to his lips. While he was loving being with the Moretti warriors, it was nice to have a quiet beer with his team.

Elijah, Jason, and Oli, who were now back in Maine, along with Ben, who was now an SLC, had worked together for a long time. They traveled around the world frequently, but now, more often than not, their focus was on this growing war with humans.

The mafia, more specifically.

Which was ironic as they'd had their eyes on the gangsters for decades in their role as assassins in Ari Moretti's organization. The Institute was a private security company which…well, they took out the bad guys.

Logan had been an assassin for over fifty years and had racked up a decent body count.

Fuck, humans were shitty. Which was why… yeah, no. He couldn't sleep with them.

Gross.

"So what was it like?" Oliver asked.

"Shit. What do you think?" Logan laughed. "It knocked me the fuck out."

He'd been shot with one of the serum darts during the attack. Fortunately, when he woke, he was in the medical room with a pretty nurse leaning over him, so that was nice.

At first.

For those seconds, as he was falling on his ass, his life had flashed before his eyes.

Frankly, it was terrifying.

They were surrounded by gangsters with choppers going overhead, bullets flying and bombs exploding. Not exactly a day at the park.

Ari shot him a look. "Sage said you were banned from the ward."

Logan groaned into his beer.

"Jesus, what did you do?" Elijah laughed.

"One pinch." Logan shrugged.

"Of salt?" Oliver teased.

"He pinched one of the nurse's asses," Ari said, waving his hand for their bill.

The server jumped to attention, nodding, and heading over.

Brooklyn.

That was her name. A human. What the hell was a human doing in the castle?

"And?" Jason asked, whipping out his wallet.

"I've got this," Ari said, handing the server his black card.

"Exactly. And? If she can't handle playing with the big, fanged boys, she should go home," Logan said, "Someone please tell me why there are humans working in there."

"Because Brooklyn is both a nurse and a scientist, and Sage needs her help to get this antidote created. Very few have both qualifications, so we took the risk of talking to her, and she was excited to help. Hence her being here in Maine," Ari explained. "Under my protection."

Ugh.

But it made sense. Logan knew, firsthand now, the serum was their greatest threat.

But why did she have to be so...hot?

And human.

"I don't plan to get shot with that crap again, so you can tell Sage and *Brooklyn the Human* she will not have to deal with me again."

Ari barked out a laugh. "She'll be pleased. You scared her."

"Bullshit," Logan replied. Brooklyn hadn't looked at all scared when she went all nurse psycho on him.

To be fair, he'd just woken up from the serum coma and had been presented with a raven-haired (evil) goddess leaning over him, presenting two beautiful globes.

Any male would reach out and grab them.

When she screamed and yelped, slapping at him, his head began pounding.

"Jesus, what have you done to me?" he groaned, glaring at her.

"Me? You just assaulted me," Brooklyn accused.

Logan snorted and laughed.

A lot.

While she glared at him.

"You find that funny? Grabbing my tits?" Brooklyn said, crossing her arms.

He did and as Logan took in her tiny frame and the extra insulation on her body, he realized she was human.

*What the hell?*

"It was hardly assault," he said. "If I wanted to assault you, I would flip you onto this bed and rip open your jacket to get a better look."

And taste.

Again, apparently not the right thing to say. Her face paled, and she called out to Dr. Abbot.

Logan rolled his eyes as the doctor came running.

"What is it?" Dr. Abbot asked.

"This patient is behaving inappropriately with me," Brooklyn said. "You can see to him."

The doctor faced him.

"Probably a good idea," Logan smirked. "See ya, sunshine."

Brooklyn shot him a dark look as she left the room, but Ari was right. He'd seen fear in her eyes. And…Goddamn, interestingly, it had made his cock sit to attention. Thankfully, he was still wearing his loose fatigues.

The doc probably noticed, but whatever.

Logan got a lecture from Dr. Abbot about protocol in medical areas, and he nodded and murmured in all the right places.

He didn't know why he'd done it.

But then again, he'd never been good at following stupid rules. Or letting a woman make him hard and walking away.

So when he walked through the medical center and Brooklyn was standing at the front desk with her back to him, Logan had teleported the short space between them and pinched her ass.

A nice, soft, plump ass.

"See ya, sunshine. Sleep with one eye open, okay?" Logan had said as she screamed.

Damn, he wanted that mouth around his cock. He figured she was probably on her way to Australia or somewhere to hide from him by now.

But apparently not.

"Don't scare the humans, Logan." Oliver, their head assassin, told him. "That team is important."

"Dude, I know," he replied. "But you know how much I hate their species."

He'd seen enough over the past four hundred years to be disgusted by the lot of them. But Brooklyn the Human had him hard as a rock with her scared little eyes, and he hated her for it.

And wanted to fuck her screams right out of her.

"She's fundamental in creating an antidote for our race, so be nice," Ari said, standing.

The ancient vampire didn't need to say anymore. When Ari spoke, they all obeyed.

They all stood, following his lead, sliding phones and wallets into their pockets.

Then made their way back to the Moretti castle.

# CHAPTER FORTY-FOUR

Darnell waved as his parents climbed into the car while his other hand rested on Amber's hip. As they drove away, Darnell hesitated, waiting for her reaction.

They both turned to each other at the same time.

"Oh, my god, you told them." She shook her head.

"You're a chef?" he exclaimed.

"Darnell, you told them I was a kitchen girl," Amber pressed.

"Can we focus on the fact I've mated one of the royal chefs and will spend the rest of my days eating like a king?" He tugged her against his chest, grinning.

Amber let out a little laugh, but then her eyes dimmed. "You know we need to talk. Plus, I'm just the Pastry Chef right now."

"I'm happy for you, baby."

"Thank you." She smiled. "I've dreamed of this for years."

"I missed you," Darnell said, cupping her face. "So fucking much."

"Me too." Amber leaned into his touch.

"Let me take you somewhere," he said. "Will you trust me?"

She nodded, so he wrapped his arms around her and teleported them down to the lake.

It felt like their spot.

Amber glanced around and lifted her eyes to his. He took her hand and led her down to the water. The ripples reminding him that with every action there was a reaction.

He hoped he could say the right words and get this right.

"I never believed in fated mates," Darnell said as they stared out at the water. "I thought, like humans, there were many. But I was wrong."

"Maybe you're not," she said softly.

Darnell turned. "Perhaps. But I don't care. I love you. *You*, Amber. I love *you*."

Her lips parted, but he wasn't done.

"I've completely messed this all up, and I wouldn't blame you for never trusting me. Not after what you've been through in your life."

"I haven't told you everything," she whispered.

"Oh, I know," Darnell said, tugging her closer, her hip in his hand. "But I think I know enough to understand you find it hard to forgive, and almost impossible to trust again once hurt."

"Yes." Her voice was almost silent.

"You weren't abused, but you were neglected, baby." He needed her to know he wasn't going to expect this to go perfectly, and that she had his understanding and patience.

"I know. I lived it." Her voice had an edge.

"But I'm your mate. I won't do that. Ever."

"You did hurt me, Darnell. You might again," Amber said, her eyes full of fear.

"If I hurt you, it will hurt me. I'll spend eternity showing you how important you are. How loved you are. How adored you are," he said, running his thumb over her dark pink lips.

A little sob escaped her, a tear building in her eyes.

"Do you think you can trust me, baby? Do you think you can love me?"

The tear fell, and she nodded.

"I do. I do love you. I'm not sure I can live without you. But I'm scared," Amber cried softly. "Really scared."

"Then we'll take it one step at a time," he said, dropping his mouth to hers.

They lapped at each other gently until their hands began to roam and clothes started disappearing. Darnell lowered Amber to the soft ground and, resting an elbow beside her head, tugged up her pretty black dress.

"You looked so beautiful tonight. I swear I could barely breathe," he rasped as his fingers pushed her panties to the side.

"I need you inside me, D."

"You will. I'm going to… oh, God, you're already wet,"

Amber pulled his mouth down to hers.

"I'm going to fuck your sweet pussy, and then I'm going to claim you, baby," he growled as the material of her panties snapped. "That I won't wait for. We can work out the rest."

Amber unzipped his black pants and his cock swelled in her warm, eager hand.

"Put me inside you," he ordered, lifting her hips.

"Will it hurt?"

"My cock?" Darnell asked.

"No, bonding?" Amber asked.

"I don't know," he groaned, sliding inside her. "But living without you will, so let's make this an orgasm and bonding to remember."

"Do it. Make me yours, Darnell," Amber moaned as he thrust in deeply. "Make me yours."

Fuck waiting any longer. His mouth navigated to the throbbing vein in her neck, and he growled as his fangs released.

"Mate," he hissed as he clamped down on her flesh. "Mine."

Amber arched as the bond roared between them, pleasure plowing through them.

Fuck.

Fire sliced down his spine, tightening his balls and spreading through his cock as he filled her with his come and vampire essence.

"Now, Amber," Darnell said, releasing his mouth for a second. "Bite me."

Amber took his arm and her own smaller incisors bit down on his inner forearm as she groaned.

"Mine," she cried.

Her pussy clenched around his cock, her orgasm making her shudder as he continued thrusting into her.

But it was the rush of energy blasting through them that took his breath away as the bond clicked into place. Darnell thought he'd been able to feel and connect with Amber before, but this was a whole other level.

She belonged to him.

She was now a part of him. As he was her.

His to protect.

Darnell pleaded to the heavens in this moment that he got to love this female until his last dying breath.

# CHAPTER FORTY-FIVE

Amber writhed as Darnell licked at the swollen flesh between her legs. God, he was one talented vampire.

And hers forever.

Perhaps she'd felt something akin to this as a child when she was in the arms of her mother at birth, but she doubted it. All this time, she'd been looking for a place to belong, but it was never a physical location. It was with her mate.

When the bond had linked them, Amber had surrendered herself, letting Darnell into her heart and soul. And it *was* a soul connection. There was no other word for it. The essence of who they were seemed to be conversing on another plane while they enjoyed the physical benefits.

At least that's how she translated it.

Knowing that she would always be a *we* not just a *me* in life now, was such a blessing. All her doubts and fears vanished when their mating bond had triggered like magic.

"Come on my face, baby," Darnell purred. "One more time."

"I don't think I can," Amber cried, having lost count. Everything was so much more erotic now, but he'd sated her appetite plenty.

"You underestimate me, mate," he said, sliding his finger over her puckered hole.

Amber jolted as pleasure roared through her lower region.

"Jesus," she groaned, as her pussy shuddered out number five. Or was it six?

Darnell's head lifted after a few more long, delicious licks. "Atta girl."

He flopped beside her, and they stared up at the stars. The sky was still black, but hints of the morning were starting to show.

"We should head back," he said, "I need some sleep. It's been impossible without you in our bed."

*Our.*

Amber smiled and accepted his hand as he stood, pulling her up. They dressed and wandered back to the castle, hand in hand of course, now mated vampires.

*Wow.*

Who would've thought applying for that job at Max Bar would lead her to her mate, a group of wild, beautiful friends, and her dream job?

But most importantly, she thought, hugging his arm and smiling up at the sexy vampire, this male.

DARNELL KISSED AMBER'S forehead as they walked along the path toward the castle. He knew she loved those butterfly—

*Chop, chop, chop.*

"Stop," he ordered her quietly, and they stilled.

Instinctively, he pushed Amber behind him, which made no sense as the helicopter was above them.

In quiet stealth mode.

Which was stupid because they were vampires.

*Brayden.*

*Craig.*

He reeled off all the warrior names as fast as he could, telepathing them all.

*What's up?* Craig answered first.

*Chopper flying overhead, in stealth, and fuck its...FUCK.*

*Where are you?*

*Front lawn. Get out here now!*

"What's going on?" Amber asked as he tugged her into a crouch.

"Stay here, baby. Stay in the trees. Please don't move." Darnell pushed her behind a thick trunk and glanced at her one last time before quickly moving to the tree line.

The helicopter was almost landing.

At a guess, it was the Russians again. Were they fucking insane?

Everything happened at speed. A male ran from the side of the castle carrying something.

*Was that—?*

Brayden, Craig, and Kurt landed on the lawn surrounding the helicopter.

"Stop—" the prince began to scream, then *pop, pop, pop,* the three enormous vampires went down like dominoes.

*Shit. Team, get the fuck out here!* Darnell telepathed everyone.

His brain fizzed as he quickly assessed the situation. If he ran out and exposed himself, he'd get shot and go down.

The helicopter twisted and turned as it lowered, moving closer to the man running with...

*Fuck.*

He lost sight of the package, but it didn't matter. Darnell knew what they had.

Or rather, who.

They had Willow Moretti.

Darnell let out a roar and ran like the fucking wind as Marcus and Logan appeared to his left.

"They have the princess," he screamed over the helicopter blade. "Stop them!"

"Fuck!" Logan yelled and leaped for the chopper, which was already in the air. Marcus did the same, and the two of them hung from the landing gear.

*Pop, pop.*

Darnell watched from underneath the chopper as they scrambled to get inside, both gripping their legs.

Fuck.

They'd been shot, and the bird was high in the sky.

He patted his pants, searching for weapons he didn't have as Amber screamed in the distance.

Ben teleported beside him with a massive gun.

"Shoot it down. Now. They have the princess!" he yelled as Ben it up toward the chopper.

Then the former assassin froze.

"What?" Ben yelled as Logan and Marcus fell to the earth. "Fuck."

"Shoot—" he repeated, and then he clicked.

"I can't shoot it with the princess in there. It could explode."

*Motherfucker.*

Ari appeared beside them.

"What—" He took in the scene, cursing as their most powerful warriors lay on the grass before them.

"They have Willow Moretti!" Darnell yelled at him over the noise of the blades. "Ari, they have Willow."

The helicopter began to pick up speed as it turned and lifted higher.

"Fuck." Ari let out a roar and leaped at the chopper.

# THE END

To read **The Vampire's Storm** with Logan and Brooklyn visit **www.juliettebanks.com**

**Turn the page** to read The Vampire's Storm blurb.

Also, if you love dark mafia romances, check out my NEW series, **The Dark Kings of NYC.** To read chapter one **turn the page.**

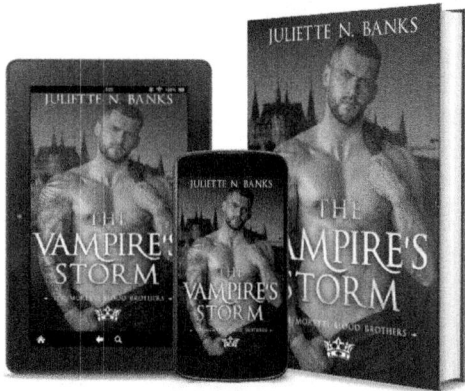

# THE VAMPIRE'S STORM

Vampire assassin, Logan Mathieson has joined the king's fight against their human enemies. He's spent decades as a sniper eliminating the evil living among the inferior race and has a healthy distaste for all of them. That includes sexy Brooklyn Wade, a scientist working for the vampire king, tasked with producing an antidote to protect them in the war.

Even if he can't help antagonizing her or control his body's reaction to her lustrous angry blue eyes and dangerous curves.

But when he discovers Brooklyn's reason for joining the science team and the ethical boundary she's crossed, Logan has a decision to make. Now they're connected in ways that can't be undone. At least while she lives.
He can help her… or he can destroy her.
And he has the power to do both.

Visit **www.juliettebanks.com** to get **THE VAMPIRE'S STORM** now and keep reading the Moretti Blood Brother series!

# HAVE YOU SEEN MY NEW MILITARY ROMANCE SERIES LAUNCHING IN 2024?

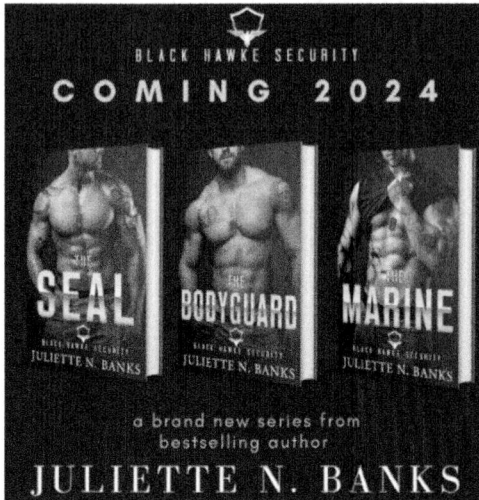

**BLACK HAWKE SECURITY**

**COMING 2024**

THE SEAL

THE BODYGUARD

THE MARINE

JULIETTE N. BANKS

a brand new series from bestselling author

**JULIETTE N. BANKS**

**He's sworn to protect, and never love again, but will she be the one to breach his walls?**

My name is Josh Black, decorated SEAL, and founder of Black Hawke Security. Some might call me arrogant. Women call me cold. Those who truly know me call me dangerous.

I'm all those things.

My priority is my elite team of former special ops who fulfill our contracts with governments and some of the most powerful people in the world.

When a famous rockstar hires us to protect his daughter, it's just another job. Until I meet Cassy Cartwright, and her intense green eyes send a bolt of chemistry through me.

She's as infuriated as I am by it.

The last thing I want is private security intruding on my quiet, hard-fought-for life. Even if he is six foot four and the most gorgeous man I've ever seen.

Not interested.

Josh is going to distract all the clients in my hair salon and… protect me from the stalker who is out of prison and looking for me again thanks to my rock star father's comeback hit.

But that's all I want from him.

*Black Hawke Security is a steamy private security romance with spice and tons of suspense and action. If you love former military and special ops alphas who fall for sassy heroines, you'll love this series. Each book can be read as a standalone and has a happy ever after.*

Visit **www.juliettebanks.com** to get **THE SEAL**

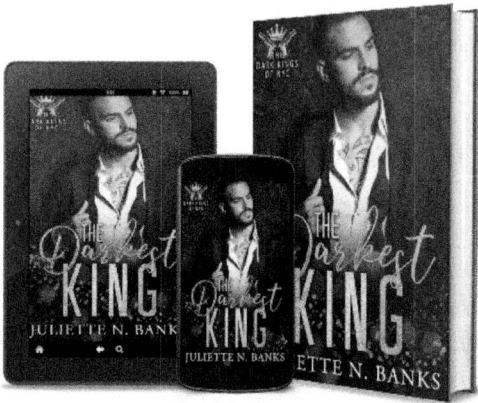

## 1

_____

### CONNOR

Here we fucking go again.

Another gala event. Another speech. Another night spent with strangers who schmooze me for my money and power.

*It's all part of the charade I'm playing*, I remind myself, tugging on the sleeve of my Armani jacket and adjusting my cufflinks before leaning back into the soft leather seats of my limousine. Nothing to prepare. My finance manager arranged the transfer of funds this afternoon, and my scriptwriter emailed me the same cut-and-paste version of the speech I've already given at least five times this year.

Only the name changes, with a modified reason why the cause is so important to Barrett Enterprises.

Except this one *is* important to me…personally.

The We Are Family Foundation is committed to the care of orphans in the US and around the world—a cause I deem important. No one should be alone because they don't have parents or a family.

There are eight fucking billion people on the planet. Few of them with the sort of money I have to contribute, to make a difference. Still, I'd rather have sent a check and sat at home, sipping on my Macallan Gold, watching porn, and jacking off.

Or rather, ordering in.

I don't mean Chinese food.

Truth is, I don't watch porn. I have no need for it. If I want a woman spread before me, I can have one at any time.

I'm Connor Barrett, one of the wealthiest and most powerful men in New York City.

Yet, I'm not who I say I am.

I'm both a ghost and, ironically, one of the most visible men in America. Why hide in the shadows when you can hide out in the open? The opposite of what they trained me to do in the marines.

Even more ironic—I have skilled security protecting me, which even they know is unnecessary. I'm six foot four, broad and muscular. And I've been trained to kill.

I *have* killed.

Still, I can't look over my shoulder while running a billion-dollar empire, doing deals with politicians and untrustworthy businessmen who would love nothing more than to see me fail.

That happens when people owe you favors. They know I'll come knocking, and when I do, they won't say no.

*No one* says no.

I'm the founder and CEO of Barrett Enterprises. Entrepreneur, philanthropist, investor, and prolific businessman.

Men want to destroy me.

Women want to fuck me.

I reach for the crystal cut glass filled with whisky in the console beside me and bring it to my lips, remembering the last woman who slid down my black silk sheets and wrapped her red-stained mouth around my cock.

God, I could do with round two.

It's been weeks since I've had a good release without using my fist. I should've booked someone for this evening, but I didn't think ahead.

Booked? Yes. They're not prostitutes—I'm paying for their discretion. I'm paying for control.

Something I never give away.

But I'm careful about the women I fuck. By the time they enter my penthouse, they've accepted payment and signed a confidentiality agreement—one no lawyer would ever let their client sign—which demands their silence and agreement to the terms of our time together.

One, should they break, that would destroy their lives.

So, not prostitutes, but they *are* escorts.

They're instructed to undress and blindfold themselves in my private elevator. I'm not fucking Batman—everyone in NYC knows my address—but it just sets the scene. One which makes it clear why they are here, and that intimacy is not welcome.

I'm not looking for a wife.

I need to stay a ghost.

If my enemies knew I was alive, I would be hunted.

The last words my father said to me...*Never tell anyone who you are, son. Run!*

The familiar grinding of my teeth, the pain slicing up the back of my neck from my fury, brings me back to the present, and I blink. I stretch one of my legs and check that the knife strapped just above my sock remains invisible. Just as all the other weapons on my body are.

I don't leave home without them.

"We're going to be a few minutes late, sir," Benson, my driver, says. I pulled him out of the military a few years ago. He knows how to scan for bombs, drive if we're attacked, and protect both of us if shit goes down. "The traffic was built up near Madison Square Gardens."

I'm silent, my body tensing, and my eyes slide over to Mack.

As if on cue, Mack Turner, my head of security, turns from the passenger seat and gives me a reassuring look. "It's an accident, Mr. Barrett. Turn up here, Benson. Then take 27th Street."

My body relaxes.

Mack is one of three men I trust with my life. He's by my side ninety percent of the time.

Not when I fuck.

That's not my kink.

While the We Are Family Foundation is important to me, I don't give a damn about being on time—I'm the VIP guest, and they'll wait for me. However, when you're hiding in broad daylight from the mafia—that's correct, *all* the mobsters and cartels—and are as powerful as I am, it would only take two minutes to go from being the *hunter* to the *hunted*.

Because I *am* hunting them.

They just don't fucking know it.

Glancing at my Rolex, I note I'm ten minutes late. I run my hand over my solid jaw, rubbing my dark scruff. I need to fuck. I've been agitated and impatient recently. As a dominant and controlling lover, the act helps me release built-up energy.

I nearly snort at the word *love*. There's no love in my life.

"Keep the car close when we arrive, Benson," I say darkly. "I'm only staying an hour."

"Yes, sir."

When the limo pulls up outside the Convention Center, I wait for Mack to open the door, then I climb out and stand, running my hands over my Armani tux and glancing around.

The red carpet is empty. Everyone inside is waiting for me.

In and out. That's the plan.

"Give Billy the night off tomorrow," I say to Mack without looking his way. When I take a few steps and he hasn't responded, I turn.

My dark eyes connect with his.

"You need a new location. It's not safe, Connor," Mack replies.

I nod.

He's not disagreeing with me. No one would. He'll have his reasons, and I trust him.

"Arrange it," I say, then step into the hotel lobby. The sign for the event points to the large conference rooms in the back.

To be honest, I'm surprised someone from the company organizing the event is not greeting me. I was told they would. But it's one less annoying person on this planet to deal with, so I couldn't care less.

I make my way through the space and find the room and the main door. As I reach for it, it flings open.

*Ommph.*

"Oh, shit!" the small body who just slammed into me whisper-yells, and the door closes behind her with a click.

Then I feel it...

Wet, cold, and seeping through the front of my tuxedo.

As I grip the petite brunette's arms and remove her from my chest, her eyes fly open wide, and I can't ignore the magnetic pull from the crystal blue globes.

*Jesus, she's fucking gorgeous.*

My cock wakes up and begins to swell. I imagine gripping all that long dark hair and wrapping it around my fist. Then, as panic fills her eyes, I'm tempted to smirk. But I never smile, and my hands, which have released her, want to touch her again, and that bothers me.

Who is this young woman?

"Connor Barrett," she gasps quietly, knowing who I am. Her eyes drift down over the dark liquid on my shirt, and she bites her lip, letting out a soft curse. Then those lids dip further down my body.

*Don't look any lower, sweetheart, or…*

Too late.

Her eyes shoot back to mine, and I say in a dark, thick voice, "You shouldn't have done that."

As she swallows, my lips curl up at the corners.

Tonight just got a whole lot more interesting.

**DOWNLOAD THE DARKEST KING FREE NOW!**

**Visit www.juliettebanks.com to get your copy!**

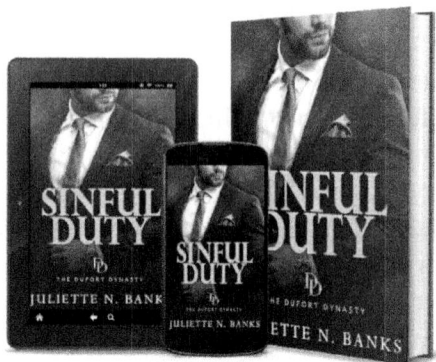

**1**

---

Daniel Dufort lifted his whisky to his lips and nodded at the blonde who was regaling him with an apparently *hilarious* story of her father at their recent New Year's party.

Daniel knew who the man was. The fact he'd actually spent time with his wife and family was a small Christmas miracle. He'd heard rumors—and his source was pretty reliable—that her father, Senator Johnson, had two girlfriends. Neither of which knew about the other. With Valentine's Day approaching, it would be an expensive one for the politician.

Three women. *Ugh.*

Daniel shivered at the thought. He preferred his women in and out in an evening, not sticking around for breakfast or a ring on their fingers.

He glanced around *Bar Hugo*, one of Manhattan's most exclusive bars, and saw most of his key connections had now left. The only reason he was still nursing his Macallan was, to put it bluntly, his cock. The blonde, who wouldn't stop talking, was going to have her mouth around it within the next hour.

*Beep, beep.*

**Daniel, we need to speak. Meet me in your office in an hour.**

After reading his father's message, he mentally rearranged his plans. Dropping his crystal glass onto the polished wooden bar, he replied to confirm he'd see him there, and then took the petite blonde's arm. "Shall we go?"

Her face lit up.

"Your place or mine?" she purred.

"I have a meeting in my office tonight, so let's head there," he replied, leading her to the private exit. The last thing he wanted was to be photographed with her and more gossip spread about his relationship status.

When would the media give up? He was never getting married.

She hesitated slightly as his offer sank in. There would be no breakfast in bed. Daniel held her gaze. The decision was hers—she could take it or leave it.

He knew she'd take it.

They all did.

A billionaire in a suit was an aphrodisiac to these types of women.

Like his brothers, he had inherited their father's good looks. At six-foot-three with a muscular frame—which he worked hard to maintain in his gym—and a square jaw, Daniel was confident and powerful.

Some of it learned. Some of it was natural.

In the United States, and other places around the world, Daniel Dufort was frequently quoted in business and economic media, and unfortunately in less respected publications for the women he took to events. Rarely, if ever, was it the same women, and yet they insisted on discussing his marital status.

The gossip columns had a few cringe-worthy nicknames for him. Try as he may, Daniel struggled to keep his sex life private. He only had a few rules.

No promises.

Nothing overnight.

No, do-overs.

Okay, fine—he occasionally slept with the same woman twice, but not in the same quarter or it gave the wrong impression.

Daniel Dufort wasn't interested in a relationship. Of any kind. He didn't believe in true love, nor was he going to settle for something vanilla. However, he did enjoy female company, and the activities at the end of the evening, so he took dates to the events he had to attend, or to meet some social obligation.

And he wasn't lacking in options.

But a relationship was not for him.

Settling down with a *best friend* and having missionary-style sex three times a week? No thanks.

As predicted, she'd walked through the door, so they head to Dufort Towers. Daniel hung his dark gray Tom Ford jacket on the hanger and turned.

Miss Johnson—*fuck, he'd forgotten her name*—lingered, taking in the valuable 57th Avenue view that overlooked Central Park. It was one of the best along Billionaire Row.

"Stunning," she said, stepping up to the full-length glass.

Daniel removed his cufflinks, and they pinged as he dropped them on his custom-made oak wood desk. He rolled his shirt sleeves to his elbows and checked the time on his Piguet watch.

They had thirty-five minutes.

Daniel moved to stand beside Miss Johnson and dug his hands in his pockets. "I'm going to assume you give head."

She turned, her mouth opening.

A good start.

Daniel leaned in and ran his finger through her hair. "Or I can bend you over my desk and fuck you. You decide."

Her mouth closed and acceptance settled over her features. She was too proud to storm out, and he knew she was wet for him.

She reached for his fly and slid to her knees. "Both." Her eyes lifted to his as she gripped his cock.

Daniel didn't answer. He simply watched her tongue swirl around his swollen head and take him deeper, inch by inch.

Daniel let out a low moan. He gripped her hair and pressed in further while she moved skillfully over and around him. It wasn't long before he was fucking her throat as she milked him dry. He groaned out his orgasm while she swallowed.

That was a bonus—he thought she'd be a spitter.

She sat back on her Manolo Blahnik heels and licked her lips. She was a beautiful woman, more natural than many in this town, but like all those before her, Daniel suddenly lost interest.

Most of them were here for his last name. They often had trust funds or money of their own, but he had power and they falsely believed by marrying him, they would also have power.

They were wrong. Power was something one either had or didn't have. It came from within, as much as a bank balance.

Dufort Hotels, which made up most of the Dufort Dynasty, had properties all over the world. It had been built by his father and went public five years ago. Two years ago, his father had stepped away—though remained the majority shareholder—and Daniel had taken on the position he'd been groomed for all his life.

CEO of Dufort Hotels.

"Thank you for being my date tonight," he said, zipping his pants. God, why could he not remember her name? Megan. Shit. "Give your father my regards, Megan."

She stood and smiled at him, all sultry. "I think you've forgotten about part two."

No.

He hadn't.

Fortunately, his father was always early, and at any moment he'd be interrupted if things got tense. Occasionally, claws came out when they felt rejected.

"Looks like we are out of time. I need to prepare for my meeting," he replied with no pretense of disappointment, then stepped away. "Please make use of the facilities before you leave if you need to."

Daniel stepped behind his large desk and lifted his laptop open.

Megan cleared her throat and picked up her purse. "No, thank you. I will gargle the sperm from my throat with a glass of *Cristal* champagne when I get home," she replied, then spun and walked out of the office with her head held high.

Despite himself, Daniel smiled.

Good for her.

A moment later, his father stepped into his office, thumbing his finger over his shoulder. "Was that Senator Johnson's daughter I saw leaving?"

"Yes. She accompanied me to the *Glass Towers* rebrand launch this evening," Daniel said.

*Glass Towers* were a friendly competitor in New York City, but a competitor, nevertheless. He'd chosen the senator's daughter as a political statement because of some government lobbying he was doing regarding the water system in Manhattan. The CEO, David Glass, disagreed with Dufort, which could cost *Glass Towers* a small fortune if it went ahead. But it was the right thing to do, and they both knew it.

Daniel smiled. He loved the game, and he was good at it.

Johnathan Dufort walked over to the same spot Megan had *performed* in and rocked on his feet. It wasn't unusual for them to meet in the evenings, but Daniel knew what this was about. It had been a hot topic for weeks and was his least favorite subject right now.

"I don't have good news, son," he said. "The agreement is still missing and now Senator Mackenzie is trying to extort us."

He looked up.

"With what?" Daniel asked loudly. "He's already doing that by claiming we owe him more interest on the initial loan than was originally agreed to."

Nearly two decades ago his father had entered into an agreement with his then-friend, Bill Mackenzie. The amount had been substantial—in the high six figures—and was paramount in Dufort Hotels growing into what it was today. The loan was to be repaid in twenty years with three percent interest.

It was no secret. Their finance team had been putting the money aside over the years and were preparing to pay it out in this financial year.

A few weeks ago, they'd received a letter from the *now* senator requesting payment for a much larger sum. Attached was a copy of the agreement.

Except it wasn't the original—it had been doctored.

The three percent interest had ballooned to *fifteen* percent. A rate no one in their right mind would agree to.

Very few people were aware of the situation, outside of his father and his brothers, Fletcher and Hunter, their financial advisor and lawyer. The latter had advised them to hunt down a copy of the agreement before going to the authorities.

Johnathan Dufort had thought he had a copy at home in his own files, along with the one kept in the vault at Dufort Dynasty.

Apparently not.

His father ran a hand over his face.

*Shit.*

"Father. Tell me."

Johnathan slammed his fist down onto the arm of the sofa next to him.

"He has said we have thirty days to pay, or he wants his daughter married into the Dufort family. The prenup cannot exclude her from the Dynasty shares."

"You have got to be fucking kidding me," Daniel growled.

He knew what was coming next.

"She has asked for you."

**Visit www.juliettebanks.com for a FREE download or get a paperback copy.**

**Each book in the Dufort Dynasty can be read as a standalone.**

# ALSO BY JULIETTE N. BANKS

## THE MORETTI BLOOD BROTHERS
*Steamy paranormal romance*
The Vampire Prince - **FREE**
The Vampire Protector
The Vampire Spy
The Vampire's Christmas
The Vampire Assassin
The Vampire Awoken
The Vampire Lover
The Vampire Wolf
The Vampire Warrior
The Vampire's Oath
The Vampire's Fate
The Vampire's Obsession
The Vampire's Storm

Related books in the Moretti universe
The Vampire King
The Claimed Wolf - **FREE**
The Alpha Wolf

## THE DARK KINGS OF NYC — NEW
*Steamy dark mafia romance*
The Darkest King - **FREE**
The Ruthless King
The Savage King
The Avenged King

## THE DUFORT DYNASTY
*Steamy billionaire romance*
Sinful Duty - **FREE**

Forbidden Touch
Total Possession
Desire Unbound
Dark Surrender
Ruthless Temptation
Naughty Festivities
Wicked Praise
Beautiful Ruin


**BLACK HAWKE SECURITY**
The SEAL
The BODYGUARD
The MARINE


**REALM OF THE IMMORTALS**
*Steamy paranormal fantasy romance*
The Archangels Battle - **FREE**
The Archangel's Heart
The Archangel's Star

# LET'S STAY IN TOUCH

**JOIN MY PRIVATE READERS GROUP!**
www.facebook.com/groups/authorjuliettebanksreaders

**Official Juliette N. Banks website:**
www.juliettebanks.com

**Instagram:**
www.instagram.com/juliettebanksauthor

**Facebook:**
www.facebook.com/juliettenbanks

**TikTok:**
@juliettebanksauthor

Printed in Great Britain
by Amazon

43193085R00192